The Last Time We Saw Marion

Tracey Scott-Townsend

Inspired Quill Publishing

Published by Inspired Quill: April 2014

First Edition

The Last Time We Saw Marion © 2014 by Tracey Scott-Townsend
Contact the author through their website:
http://traceyscotttownsend.com/

Chief Editor: Sara-Jayne Slack
Cover design by: Venetia Jackson

Paperback ISBN: 978-1-908600-26-4
eBook ISBN: 978-1-908600-27-1
Print Edition
Printed in the United Kingdom
1 2 3 4 5 6 7 8 9 10

Inspired Quill Publishing, UK
Business Reg. No. 7592847
http://www.inspired-quill.com

Dedication

For Felix, Ruben, Zakary and Faye
And in memory of the gone-baby, Alice.
Fruits of my womb.

*　　*　　*

The Last Time We Saw Marion is set in the fictional landscape of Pottersea. This is based on the real village of Kilnsea and the landscape around Spurn Point and the Humber Estuary in East Yorkshire.

I spent one life-changing year living there between 1984 and 1985, in a house called Blackmore House which no longer exists. In my mind, Cal and Sarah's home Blackberry House is situated on the same spot.

Acknowledgements

Firstly, I want to express an extra-special thank you to Philip Scott-Townsend for your unflagging support; and for stepping out of your comfort zone to join me in mine.

Thanks to Ali Edgley, who read the very early drafts of *The Last Time We Saw Marion* and gave me helpful comments and enthusiasm.

Also to fellow members of the Lit-Fic group on Authonomy for my invigorating weeks in the spotlight when I received invaluable comments and critique, such as "Who exactly is your protagonist?" from Frances Kay, which really made me think. Thanks especially to Andrew Stevens who helped me revise the first two chapters again and again until I felt I'd got them right.

Thanks for that intimate writerly year with Rena Rossner, Judith Williamson, Gordon Hall and Robert Heath. We set out on our imaginary 'Yellow Brick Road' to agent-dom and publication together. Rena, particularly, gave us so much help and support.

Members of YouWriteOn gave me my first ever crits of the manuscript and opened my mind to the craft of writing.

Thank you as well to the agents and small presses who gave me useful feedback over the past two years.

It's been enriching and improving to receive insightful edits from Matt Shoard of Fleeting Books, and Sara-Jayne Slack and Fiona Campbell of Inspired Quill Publishing.

A note of appreciation to Kevin and Yvette Clarke of Strawbs Bar in Leeds, where Cal and Sarah in the book first take Marianne. Phil and I visited the bar, along with the old Broadcasting House building on Woodhouse Lane, and were delighted to find it hadn't changed hands since 1989 when the story is set. Yvette described to me the décor and atmosphere in the bar at the time and it really brought the physical setting of the story alive to me.

Last but never least, thank you to my children: having me for a mother must have been difficult at times, and I'm very proud of you all for what you're doing with your lives.

The Last Time
We Saw Marion

Chapter 1

Leeds, May 1989

Sarah

MARION HAD BEEN dead seventeen years when I saw her again. Cal had seen her too; the microphone on his shirt registered his sharp intake of breath and his "Fuck!" rang out into the packed auditorium. I'd half-risen out of my chair, and at his exclamation felt myself drop back like a stone. I was thinking of the night they had taken her body away. Now that image was juxtaposed with the white-lit girl sitting a mere couple of metres away from me in the audience.

———◆———

Marianne

"YOU'RE LOOKING EVEN more unwell than usual," her mother's voice jangled in Marianne's head. The grimace on Geraldine's face was unmistakable as she tested her daughter's forehead with the back of her hand; so was her involuntary wiping movement on the leg of her slacks after withdrawing it. "Maybe you should stay away from college."

Impossible, thought Marianne. Geraldine didn't know this was the day of the TV recording, the only chance Marianne would have to see the author Callum Wilde. "I'm fine."

She went, inured to the physical discomforts of illness, pain or hunger. She sat through her lessons, not taking in a thing, and stayed on to eat the apple that passed as her evening meal in the canteen.

"Are you getting the bus to Broadcasting House?"

The lights in the refectory seemed to intensify as Nicola from her history group slid into a seat at the table with her. Marianne fought the urge to cover her mouth with her hand. She could not speak until she'd methodically chewed her bite of apple. "No, I'm just gonna walk."

"It's free, you know."

Marianne avoided travelling in crowds. People always stared at her, even fellow students. She set off early, reached Woodhouse Lane before the college bus got there; climbed the grey stone stairs to the entrance of Broadcasting House alone. She flicked glances around the large atrium inside the glass doors, but couldn't see the one she was searching for.

"Are you here for the Artists of the North recording?" A young woman scribbling notes on a clipboard hurried over to Marianne. Stopping just short of her, she paused to push her glasses up the bridge of her nose.

"Yes." Marianne had to force the word from her throat.

"You want to go round the back. You're not allowed in to the auditorium through these doors. You'll see a sign with an arrow pointing the way."

In the dust-hung space of the auditorium Marianne seated herself within view of the stage, moving several times before she could settle. She picked at the fluff on her white cotton dress, suddenly aware of her fingers' extreme boniness. They seemed alien, belonging to someone else, not hers at all.

The auditorium filled up with people. Her coat and bag were on the seat next to her but she had to move them so that someone could sit down, a large girl whose flesh spread over the armrests, sweat mixing with cloying perfume. Marianne prodded her own arms, took short breaths. She hunched herself into the centre of her seat.

Music began; a man wearing headphones stood at the front of the stage. He encouraged the audience to break into applause as the tanned presenter entered. Another man walked in from a far corner. The air buzzed, rippling, cracking open Marianne's internal silence. The two men lowered themselves into leather chairs and exchanged a private joke. The audience applauded louder; the sound hurt her ears. The man on the right wore a white loose-sleeved shirt with designer jeans. It was him, the author. He looked much as he did in the picture Marianne had seen, but was heavier now around the face and shoulders. His eyes in the lights appeared golden. She glanced from side to side, shifting in her seat, wondering if anyone could feel the heat off her skin. She recognised him so strongly, it was frightening. The recognition of him sparked awareness of another version of herself, a foreign presence within her which she feared she would disappear into. She snatched a breath and looked around in confusion, but the large girl only gave her a grin, and offered her a mint from a ragged paper tube.

Marianne couldn't take in what the interviewer said, or the responses of the author. He had once been the boy from the back of a book, but was now a vibrant physical presence. Thick, coppery hair fell across half of his face; he looked young still, but real now, not a shadowy figure from her dreams. *Small steps, Marianne. This must have happened for a reason.*

Her awareness of the spotlight's movement, the sway of the audience following the microphone on its fish pole; questions from around the auditorium, camera crew sometimes blocking her view of the author, all were secondary to the gravel voice of Callum Wilde. It rumbled through her like a pounding bass from amplified speakers. The spotlight settled on her, the microphone hovering just above her head. Time to ask her question. Her thighs pressed into the seat beneath her, but at the same time her mind and body felt disconnected from each other. She knew her lips worked, and felt air escaping as she spoke, but she couldn't hear her own voice.

A single sharp response rang from somewhere, a rolling wave through the audience. She saw the author's mouth moving and tried to make eye contact with him through the white light.

The girl in the next seat nudged her, still grinning. As she moved, scents of perfume, sweat and cigarettes broke away from her and hung in the air. Marianne held her breath. The girl offered another mint. "Get you, you made him swear!"

❦

Sarah

I SENSED RATHER than heard the audience's collective gasp after Cal swore. I fished for my inhaler among the debris in my bag, tried to convey thoughts of calm to my brother. Cal's twin sister, apparently sitting in the audience only a few metres away from us, looked the same age as when she died. It was impossible, but she was there. The white light on her face made her look like a ghost.

Sitting slightly behind and to the left of Cal, out of the stage lights, I saw his jaws moving. The Marion girl had asked him what made him write the brutal story of *The Shell* and he seemed to struggle for an answer. A few coughs came out of the audience and eventually the lengthening pause registered with Cal. He flexed his shoulders and straightened his spine. His shirt jutted out from the back of his neck and then settled uneasily against his skin again as he folded his arms. I noticed that my fingernails were digging into my palms and let them out slowly.

Part of me wanted to push my way into the audience and shake her shoulders. I was right back in our teenage years, when everything Marion did was calculated for greatest effect, most of all her prolonged death. Cal glanced at me, then slid down in his seat. The air in the studio felt unbreathable and hot. My mind was pulled between the present and the past, and I saw again Cal's hands clenching and unclenching the day he told Marion about the book.

"It was a long time ago; I was young," managed Cal, finally finding his voice deep in his chest. "I wouldn't have written it like that today." *The Shell* was the story of a deaf, mute girl who was raped. "I would not have had Maria murder her rapist."

After speaking about it, he barely held his composure. The muscles in his neck tightened and his hands clenched in his lap. He sat up straight again, jiggled his long legs. I calmed myself by counting my breaths.

The spotlight in the second row had dimmed. Stage lights between me and the audience meant I could no longer see them. I craved another glimpse of Marion then. And I was sorry. *So sorry Marion, that in those few moments I was angry with you.* It was ironic that I always associated Marion with hunger: mine – to have done something different.

The presenter, Rick Dibley, had worked with Cal before. I could see him monitoring Cal's erratic movements, the restlessness of his long limbs, taking care to speak for him as the conversation tripped and waned. Cal cleared his throat a lot and had frequent sips of water. I was sure the interview would fall apart if I took my eyes off Cal. The fabric of my dress trembled. The final section of the programme was a discussion of Cal's current book.

"I've asked you a similar question before" Rick said, "but bear with me on this occasion. For the benefit of our young audience, can you tell me why your books always feature a female protagonist?" When Cal didn't answer immediately Rick said, "I'm just trying to remember whether the main characters of any of your novels are male, and I can't think of any."

Cal took another sip of water, lowered the glass carefully to the table. "I was brought up in a mainly female household. I guess my earliest influences just stuck with me." Rick was sensitive enough not to mention Marion. He paused while a screen behind the stage lit up. "We're going to finish by having a look at some footage of you at a recent awards ceremony." He looked up at the audience. "This is Callum Wilde, ladies and gentlemen, receiving the Johnson-Davies prize for *When Angels Came,* voted best psychological thriller of

1988. Please put your hands together and join me in thanking Cal for his time this evening."

Now I could stop watching Cal. I got out of my seat with as little fuss as possible and left the auditorium. Away from the stuffy studio, a cool breeze reached where I stood in the foyer, blowing through my dress. I slipped on my jacket, irritated by its weight on my arm. I needed freedom to move quickly, determined to catch a glimpse of the Marion girl before she had a chance to leave and then...I didn't know what. I just had to see her. Maybe I suspected that if she was real I would discover reassuring differences between her and our dead sister.

I could just hear the programme's closing music through the seal of the doors behind me. The girl behind the reception desk looked as if she wanted to ask me something. It would be about Cal. She opened her mouth and blurted, "I remember you, Miss."

"I beg your pardon?"

"You taught me in Art about two years ago. You've changed your hair, Miss. It used to be longer but it's nice like that."

I was flattered for a brief moment. I tried to make conversation with her and it helped me to stay calm until the doors at the end of a corridor were wedged open. The cramped space quickly filled up with people. I pushed into the crowd against the forward flow, scanned as many faces as I could. The noise of mingled voices was confusing. I was in a dream. I couldn't see her, even when the crowd had thinned right out. I must have missed her. Relief, warm as bathwater, trickled through me. At least if Cal asked I'd be able to say I tried to find her. We would go home and in the morning we'd remember seeing a girl whose hair was the same colour as Marion's, who had the same eyes and the same skeletal face. But the memory would fade.

—◆●◆—

Marianne

THE LIGHTS CAME up in the auditorium as the recording finished. Marianne's compunction to raid a vending machine she'd spotted on the way in was powerful. She badly needed to challenge her strength of will, confront the source of her greatest fear and desire. Food. She pictured herself eating, saw how the food would blur her edges, swamp her outline until she would disappear inside the blubber. She waited until there were only a few people left, not wanting to meet anyone she knew from college. She wrapped her arms tightly around herself to control the quaking which threatened eruption. Her shell would finally break open, expose her real self. A relief, perhaps.

She thought she was alone in the passageway, but as she moved towards the brighter lights of the foyer she saw the figure leaning against the wall. The small woman, face turned away, had blonde hair cut into a kind of cap that curled around her face. Marianne knew without being able to see that the woman's eyes were blue. She was certain of it. But as she drew level with the preoccupied figure she saw that they were covered by her eyelids. Oh, surely they would fly open in a moment! She must try and slip past unnoticed.

—◆●◆—

Sarah

I REACHED FOR my inhaler again, bending forward as I leaned against the wall and took a deep breath. Held it in. Spots floated in front of my eyes. I closed them and steadied myself. When I straightened up my bag slipped off my shoulder and dropped onto the floor.

I hadn't heard her approach; the two feet almost tripped over my bag. Instinctively my hand went out to catch the girl's elbow, a sharp bone in my palm. I met her eyes, oh so familiar, felt her exhale at the same moment as I did: *You.*

Her breath was warm, bitter – an olfactory recall for me. I recoiled. *The last time I saw you, Marion, you were dead.*

She *was* dead. I'd touched her cold skin afterwards. A feeling prickled at the back of my neck: pine needles caught in my clothes. The drumming in my ears was the irregular beat of this young woman's heart. I saw it, her near skeletal hand trembling to its rhythm over her fragile ribs. She jerked her chin up and I saw her carved cheeks were furred like the skin of a peach, holding a haze of light.

"Excuse me…" I made my voice low, unthreatening.

She stared at me, light on her face making her hair seem to hover.

"I'm really sorry, I don't know how to…" *Get a grip on yourself Sarah – you're going to lose her.*

"You look like…are you?"

She slipped past me with the smooth movement of a dancer. I suddenly heard my sister's violin music in my head.

"Marion!" It broke out.

A pause. She turned to face me, the foyer lights preventing me from seeing her expression. But if I could I think she would have been looking at me in that hard way she had. Marion had. "My name is Mar*ianne*."

The light outlined her hair from behind now, throwing shadows across her face. "Marianne?" I blinked, reminded myself to breathe. Her gaze raised hairs on my arms. Her frame jerked as if she had just snapped back into herself. She raised her palms, white and empty. "Marianne Fairchild."

She wore an old-fashioned white dress with a green woollen coat: a heroine in an Emily Brontë novel. Her fingers trailed the insides of her wrists, thin as branches. She plunged one hand into a deep pocket on her coat, and moved a strand of hair off her face with the other. *She could leave now, I'm not stopping her, but she's just standing here. She seems to expect something from me. I'm not ready for this. I hoped when I saw her it would be obvious she wasn't Marion. But it's not obvious enough. I don't know what to say.*

"I'm Sarah Wilde. You look just like my sister, her name was Marion... My, err – my brother is Callum Wilde, the author. Would you be interested in meeting him? I'm sure he'd be pleased to meet you..."

She was taller than me. Her hand came out of her coat pocket with a tube of lip balm, which she applied first to her bottom lip and then the top. "You look like someone as well, but I can't think who."

I forced myself to breathe in and out. The moment stretched; my impulsion to keep looking at her apparently matched by hers to stare at me.

"I'll meet your brother, if you like." Her hand shook as she replaced it in her pocket. I had the strongest sense that she had planned our meeting.

"There are some seats over there, if you don't mind waiting; I'll go and get him."

I half hoped she'd be gone when I got back.

———●●———

I WAITED FOR Cal outside the Green Room, wondering if I'd done the right thing. What good could it do – bringing Marion back into our lives now? When the door opened he barged past me. He ignored the huddle of students waiting for autographs. I hurried after him but a cough built in my chest and I had to slow down.

He stopped. "You should have dealt with them, Sarah. Why haven't you been handing out those precious bookmarks of yours? I signed enough."

He set off again. I'd forgotten all about the bookmarks. I got my breath. "You'd better stop a minute. There's a girl… I asked her to wait in the foyer."

He slowed down and then stopped. He had a wardrobe of faces for different occasions but I couldn't make out the one he turned on me then. "Is it that girl, that one…?"

"She said she would meet you. Don't be aggressive with her. Or too charming. She's just a girl."

I could feel sweat under my arms. Cal was highly-strung enough as it was on a good day. As for her, I couldn't work it out. Physically she seemed brittle, but there was a steely dimension when she'd looked at me.

There she stood at the vending machine in the corner of the foyer. When she heard us, she furtively shovelled some things into her knitted bag – chocolate bars. The combination of the gaunt girl and the chocolate was jarring. She raised her chin and gave me a half-smile, flicked her eyes over me. I knew her, and she compounded it with that artful look.

Her stark face was framed by a fringe, wings of dark reddish hair like Cal's. Almond eyes that in the foyer appeared green but memory told me would reflect amber in other lights – large and deep-set. She had a narrow nose and a deep indent above her upper lip. She pushed her lower lip out slightly at our approach, a defiant look. I told my brother her name. He took no notice of what I was saying. "Marion?" he said – "Sweet Jesus!" She didn't move or speak at first. Did she recognise him? She seemed nonchalant. Her glance slid over mine and alighted on white-faced Cal.

"Good to meet you." A clear, cool voice. I hardly remembered Marion's. Someone began to turn off the lights but we remained in the foyer. Marianne fiddled with the shoulder strap of her bag. She shaved at a straying thread with her thumbnail. We seemed to have synchronised our breathing. I had that 'three of us' feeling I had grown up with. Could a ghost be so physical?

The words came fast. "Would you like to come for a coffee at Strawberry Fields with us? It's just across the road." I could feel the blush spread across my face. My heart thumped. Marianne looked impassively from my face to Cal's. She always did well in a game of 'cheat', Marion did. She hooked her hair back behind her – 'pixie ears', we used to call Marion's. She had the shutters in her eyes down, but she changed everything with her response.

"I'll come, just for a while."

Chapter 2

Hull, May 1972

Jane

EVEN IN THE last few days before Marion died, Jane couldn't believe her daughter would really go through with it. *It was only seventeen years ago that I pushed the twins down The Avenues in their big Silver Cross pram, Sarah perched on top. There was always blossom on the trees and it seemed nothing bad would ever happen. How happy George and I were in those days.*

Jane had to take a break. She untied her apron and hurried out the front door of her tall, red-brick house on Westbourne Avenue, crossing the wide road diagonally to the fountain at the intersection with the narrower Salisbury Street. The four carved mermaids at the base of the fountain had their heads thrown back as usual, everlastingly blowing into their conch shells. Above them four life-sized herons tucked their beaks in against their chests, keeping guard. George was sitting with Marion upstairs in the house, hollows under his eyes. Eyes that never left his daughter's face.

Some blossom was still on the trees and Jane remembered coming here as a bride, this very month in 1953. They were so proud of their incongruously large home, bought with

George's hard-saved deposit and a small inheritance from Jane's grandmother. Chasing Jane up the three staircases to the tiny attic room at the top George had vowed they would fill the house with children. The couple were given special permission to hold an outdoor wedding reception around the fountain. She caught water in her hand, letting it pour through her fingers.

I was a neglectful mother after my baby died. The twins were only five then.

She was convinced her detachment was the reason Marion had become anorexic by the age of fourteen. She'd taken her remaining children for granted, let Marion slip away. A comforting hymn ran through her head: *God of Mercy and Compassion look with Pity upon me.*

When Jane returned to her daughter's flowery-wallpapered bedroom on the third floor of their house, Marion smiled in her sleep.

Marion

SOMETIMES I DIDN'T go to school at all. I walked as far as Princes Avenue with Cal and Sarah and then I shook my head at them. Cal just laughed, shaking his head back at me, and went to meet his friend on the corner of Marlborough. Sarah worried and tried to persuade me to go with her but eventually she would give up and get the bus without me. I walked all the way into town and then took a different bus out to the coast. When I got to Hornsea or Withernsea or Bridlington I stood on a cliff-

top and held my hands out to the wind. It rustled through the tiny hairs on the backs of my fingers and all the way up my arms and down my spine. While I stood there, arms open, the rushing air seemed to penetrate right through my skin to the empty space in my stomach. I wanted to break apart, scatter into the wind; be a particle carried out across the sea. I was too heavy, too much of an entity. I didn't want to be this ugly thing; it wasn't really me. I wanted to be a part of the synergetic forces that made the grass grow and waves crash onto the beach. I didn't want to be physical and solid.

Let me go.

JANE SAT BESIDE her daughter's bed and held her hand. Her child slept open-mouthed, the occasional gargle catching in her throat. Jane pictured her as an infant, only truly relaxed in sleep, the pink-bow lips and sweet baby breath she had then. Now her breath smelled faintly of decay. She frowned and groaned in her sleep. Jane hunched over, felt the ache of her imminent loss.

But once Marion opened her eyes and saw her mother, her face opened into a smile. Before her extreme illness she'd always worn a closed expression. But now she had a look of innocence. Jane truly believed Marion could begin again. *Father let me call Thee Father, 'tis Thy child, returned to Thee.*

"You'll come back to me." Jane flicked back her hair, leaned forward to whisper to Marion. She wet her daughter's cracked lips with a cotton bud. Marion's tongue poked out minutely, receiving moisture like Communion. "I've always known it."

This was some sort of cleansing process and before long her daughter would 'snap out of it'. She enjoyed thrill-seeking, getting close to the edge. Marion had never had a proper sense of danger. Jane recollected a neighbour ringing her doorbell one day when the twins were about six, to inform Jane that the little girl had climbed out of the attic window onto the roof. Callum was desperately trying to call his sister back inside.

Marion's bed was by the open dormer window, which had a view down through branches onto the long green lawn. There was a huge old apple tree outside and a particular blackbird that liked to sing on a branch right next to the windowsill. She used to leave crumbs there for it when she was well enough.

When she fell asleep Jane sang to her. *Goodbye Ruby Tuesday* was one of Marion's favourites, but Jane hadn't realised how heartbreakingly the lyrics applied until she sang them. That's when she realised this would really happen, she would lose another daughter. "Don't do it, Marion." She found her voice getting harsher. She had to stop the game. "George!" Jane yelled for her husband, "Tell Marion…Tell her she's got to stop this, now."

George hurried up the staircases. He massaged his wife's shoulders. "You have to do something, this time," Jane complained. He tried to lead her out of the room but she insisted on hanging onto him in the doorway, to watch Callum replace her at Marion's bedside. Marion opened her eyes and looked at her twin brother. She hadn't spoken for a long time.

Cal voiced a lengthy apology. Jane had urged her son to express contrition for whatever sins he held himself responsible, but for the past two years the twins had eschewed Saturday Confession along with Sunday Mass. "I don't know why I did it without you", she heard him babble to his sister, "It wasn't meant to be about you, honestly." The character in his novel resembled Marion. His sister had taken the story personally.

<hr />

Marion

WHEN I WAS a child I wanted to fly away. It confused me when Mum's baby died because I should have been leaving, not her. I was angry that Caitlin had been able to let go but my body kept holding on to me. It pinned me inside. I couldn't stand it when Mum tried to take me on her knee or Dad tried to carry me, even though I could hardly walk by myself. My skin felt so sensitive I couldn't bear to be touched. All I wanted was to grow up and get away, be my real self but my body was trying to stop me from being that. At school the other children teased me. They said I would have to have an operation on my face so it would be able to smile, like theirs. I tried to hide away so far inside myself that I would become small enough to evaporate. Maybe my body would carry on without me and nobody else would notice. They couldn't understand that the person shouldn't be defined by the mechanical thing that carried them around. I suspected that Cal understood, but he'd turned his back on the truth and decided to let his body rule his real self, pretending that was the way he wanted to be.

When Cal wrote The Shell he betrayed me more utterly than the fact he had gone behind my back to get his book published. He had stripped off my defences, exposed the curled-up core of me in his story. I flapped around like a frightened bird but eventually I made myself go as quiet as my put-away voice. And now it's nearly time. Everything has settled.

Let me go.

JANE HAD TO accept the truth eventually. She refused to come into the room anymore. If she resisted acknowledging it, it still mightn't happen. She shook her head when George encouraged her to visit her daughter. "I can't be a part of it, George. I sat and held my baby girl in my arms when she died. I just can't do it again." To her, twelve years seemed like no time at all.

Sarah was eighteen. Inexplicably, Jane picked on her. "You're Marion's older sister. You ought to have been able to get her to listen to you! You could have taken some of the responsibility from Callum."

Sarah was the easier child to blame. Callum would have got aggressive with her; he would have fought back, but Sarah only wilted. Jane was emotionally comfortable with her son. Better to keep Sarah at a distance. It was only daughters who died.

She couldn't watch when George took his healthy daughter in his arms and comforted her.

On the night Marion died Jane still wouldn't come into the room. George, Callum and Sarah were up there and she was in the kitchen. *Jesus Lord, I ask for Mercy, let me not implore in vain.* She tried to listen to a play on the radio; she knew it would happen that night – Marion would die, but she pretended it wouldn't. *All my sins, I now detest them, never will I sin again.* Until the point of no return she still had three children left.

The hymn didn't work. In her mind another rhyme circulated: 'Chickadee, Chickadee, who's been at my cherry tree? Four small robbers wearing wings, very small but greedy things.'

Her mind was jumbled. Marion's friend Lisa rang, a good and loyal girl who had supported Jane's ailing daughter and comforted Callum over the previous months. Lisa asked if she could come and spend some time with Marion but Jane refused. She replaced the receiver very carefully, sorry about being cruel to Lisa, but it couldn't be helped.

She felt a familiar cold wave envelop her when she heard the others coming down the stairs. The cold ran through her like water, right down into her toes. She was going to be sick. *Can I go back? Is it possible to go back a couple of hours – a few minutes even, and take my daughter in my arms to say goodbye? I'm sorry, Marion. I love you, whoever you are.* But by the time the others had got all the way downstairs and down the hall and through the vestibule; by the time they'd walked through the living room and into the kitchen where Jane was sitting, the look of implacability, similar to Marion's, was back on Jane's face. It made her seem as if she didn't care.

❦

Marion

ONE OF THE most lucid and beautiful moments in my life was when I was five years old. Our teacher Mrs Hobbs had made us take off our school shirts as well as our skirts or trousers. I had been frightened and confused, standing in my vest and PE shorts. I felt my face tightening with shame. She said we were going to have our first session of Musical Movement. She made us curl up into a ball on the floor and she told us she wanted us to grow like a tree. Then she put the music on and my awkward girl's body began to unfold like a flower. The music was Edvard Grieg's 'Morning' and the way it filled my body and mind made more sense to me than anything had ever done in my life before. As if looking down from the ceiling, I could see the small shape that everybody thought of as me, whirling its arms. It had an alien expression on its face which I realised was a smile.

'Morning' is the music I can hear all around me now, as I leave, dipping to touch my violin in the corner; as I sweep over the heads of Cal, Sarah and my father. In the kitchen, I hover for an infinitesimal moment over my mother. Let me go.

And then I am gone.

Chapter 3

Sarah

IT IRRITATED ME to see Marianne's bag, with its odd corners, bumping against her hip as she walked. It must have been uncomfortable. But she never adjusted its position or even seemed to notice. I saw that I was rubbing at my own hip, wanting it to stop. Marianne and Cal stared ahead and didn't speak; their footsteps almost in rhythm. I had a flashback of them – Marion and Cal I mean, not Marianne – walking ahead of me in similar rhythm down Marlborough Avenue in Hull. We'd all been going to the cemetery to put flowers on Caitlin's grave, Mum and Dad completing our procession.

Crossing Woodhouse Lane in Leeds I kept my head down, put one foot in front of the other, wondering what the hell had happened. I didn't know how we had managed to get across the busy road safely, traffic whizzing by on either side, but we were suddenly outside Strawberry Fields.

Strawbs' compact frontage led into a narrow interior. Curved stairs rose up on the left of the entranceway, and a bar was tucked under the stairs inside. Cal and I had been here before, popular as it was with staff and guests at Broadcasting House. There was a brown cord carpet on the floor, church pews arranged around the cream walls. An assortment of tables and chairs in the middle were all painted brown to match the other woodwork.

A group of girls wearing brightly coloured string vests tumbled out of the lobby as we went in. We stood back to let them past. Cigarette smoke drifted downstairs from the upper bar. Conversation and laughter rolled over a Stevie Nicks song on the sound system. The three of us stood there awkwardly, our eyes roving the crowded space until we found the table they had just vacated. Marianne squeezed around the side onto a pew, opposite Cal and me who each took a chair. But I couldn't sit still yet. I sprang up again, asked what they wanted to drink, weaved through other customers to the bar under the stairs. I counted the upturned bottles at the back until my heartbeat slowed. Then I summoned up names for the colours of liqueurs glowing through the bottles of curved glass: viridian, amber, alizarin, burnt umber.

"Would you like to order any food?" For some reason the question threw me. I turned back to Cal, catching his eye through the diners and drinkers.

"Are you hungry?" I mouthed, miming the use of cutlery and lifting invisible food to my lips.

He shook his head, flicked his eyes towards Marianne. There was a thump in my chest. The memory of awkward mealtimes.

"Just the drinks, please."

I was served with Cal's whisky, my coffee and Marianne's water. I wished our encounter was already over. It couldn't be right, any of it. I wanted the recollection but not the tedious detail. How could it now be anything but anti-climax? Marianne could not be Marion; the excitement of meeting her was already over. But not the hunger.

Suzanne Vega sang 'Marlene watches from the wall'. I fitted my chair back into the space next to Cal's. His leg jiggled under the table. My jacket slipped off the back of my chair and I leaned sideways to pick it up. I spread it over my knees, hooked my finger through the handle of my cup; took a sip of coffee, kept my eyes down. Swallowed the hot liquid. Invisible threads reconnected the three of us that had snapped the day Marion left. A cobweb of fear was spun. *She isn't just a girl that looks like Marion. I'm sure of it.* But also not sure. How could she be anything else?

Cal spoke, "I saw you in the audience…"

"I asked you a question." She coughed into her hand.

"But then I *saw* you." Perhaps Cal thought she would own up.

She said nothing.

"I… have we… met before…?" Cal was still trying to capture her gaze with his. I watched Marianne's eyes turn from green to amber.

"I've never seen you before, except on the back cover of your book. And you've got a lot older since then."

I almost heard a cock crowing. *Surely she must remember?*

"Books, plural."

"I've only read one of them."

Her knuckles whitened where she gripped the glass. I was afraid it would splinter in her hand.

"*The Shell?*"

"Yes."

That was the one everyone knew.

"You wrote it before I was even born."

"When was that?"

He edged his clenching and unclenching hands across the table. Marianne glanced down, hesitated.

"Pardon?"

"How old are you?"

"I'm seventeen."

He looked at me out the corner of his eye. Marianne became engrossed in the contents of her glass. She picked it up again, taking a sip. She kept her teeth on its edge and then released it. She wiped water off her chin with the back of her hand. Noise buzzed all around us but the three of us may as well have been alone in there. I watched the slice of lemon floating around in Marianne's tap water. She put her drink down and picked at the skin near her fingernails. *Marianne, Marion, Marianne.* Pulling the petals off a flower: is she Marion, or is she not?

There were dark hollows around her eyes. She chewed off a scrap of skin and stroked it onto the table edge. I saw it float to the floor, this fragment of her. The moment was surreal. She was nothing like a ghost, or someone resurrected. I wanted her to be Marion, back again, and yet of course I didn't, because that would have negated the previous seventeen years. How would we have unshaped our grief and reformed the disarranged grouping of our family? If somehow she was Marion, she was trapped in time, while Cal and I had both grown older. None of us knew what to say. Cal's chin jerked up and he suddenly excused himself, pressing past me, knocking over a stool.

I pictured home. I wanted to hear the sea. This room was too noisy, too close. My eyes stung and my chest felt tight with even the whiff of cigarette smoke from upstairs. And Cal had left me alone with this echo.

I needed to set her into context, separate from us, establish that she had another existence entirely. "Have you got any brothers and sisters?"

She came to as if roused from sleep. "I have two sisters, Charissa and Justine," she mumbled into her glass, "Charissa's fifteen and Justine's ten."

I gave her an encouraging nod. "Charissa works as a model. Mum takes her to casting auditions in London sometimes."

Cal came back carrying another drink, his face blotchy.

"Do you two want another?" We both declined. I turned my cup around on its saucer.

"You said your sister's name *was* Marion." Marianne gave me that steely look again, then switched it to Cal, who had his head down, his hands together as if in prayer. Her expression softened, twisted, set hard again.

I hesitated. "Marion died, seventeen years ago."

Again I noticed that skittering of muscle activity on the downy surface of her hard cheek but her gaze returned to the water in her glass. *Drowning Man* came through the speakers. Eleven years after Marion died I'd just completed an MA and got a job working as a technician at the further education college in Hull. So I had to stay at home for a bit. I was driven mad night after night by Cal playing that song over and over again in his bedroom in what I still thought of as my parents' new house on Beverley Road. I couldn't wait to get away again but Cal was stuck in time, had never left home.

His betrayal in keeping his first novel a secret was not just that he'd gone to publication without Marion – his story was like a rape. He took the essence of her character, forced her into his book. And now she had returned: a variation on the heroine of every novel he'd written since *The Shell*. Now she was Marianne. She sat before us in her shapeless white dress like an accusation or a second chance. She said nothing but emotion vibrated off her, feelings I couldn't tune in to.

Last orders were called at the bar. Marianne got up, dragged on her coat. As she moved the light from an overhead lamp hit her face and I clearly saw the shape of her skeleton beneath the skin. She reached down behind her seat for the bag that bulged with chocolate bars, threw Cal a pleading glance. He didn't look up.

"I've got to go now."

"Cal," I prompted.

He had a deep frown line on his forehead. Swinging his head to look at me the hunk of hair that would never stay back fell across his eyes. He couldn't seem to focus. "Sarah." He raised a hand to my shoulder, gripped hard, indenting me with his fingers. My brother's face loomed into mine and I knew every line of it. I loved it and hated it, feared I would never escape from it. I steered his gaze into focus with my own.

"You're hurting me."

"I know," Cal laughed. His eyes flashed with the madness I sometimes spotted in them. I had the sense that something threatening hovered around him. The sudden awareness made me pull back. He loosened his fingers, removed his hand. Then he downed his drink and suddenly rose to his feet, towering over Marianne.

"We'll take you home."

"No," said Marianne, "it's not far."

"I insist," Cal's voice was rough. "Sarah, car keys?" He bent towards the bag at my feet. I moved my leg in front of it.

"I can't possibly give you the keys. You've had far too much to drink." I took a breath. "I'm driving. And Marianne doesn't want a lift."

She looked at me, a struggle playing across her features. She made a dance of little gestures, a slight shake of her head, a raising and outward turning of her hands, and then let them drop.

"Thanks for the drink." She lifted her shoulders, turned to go. But Cal blocked her way. He offered his hand, palm up. It shook as he held it in front of him. Marianne hesitated before placing hers in it. It lay there like a broken bird. She was such a young girl, and yet she didn't come across that way. Cal's fingers closed slowly. His skin looked brown and textured around hers. The sleeve of her unusual coat fell back, exposing her wrist, so thin it looked snappable. I saw it all with the graininess of film. Marion's eyes – I mean Marianne's, had partly closed and her bottom lip trembled. Cal breathed harder than normal, making the smoke drifting through the open door from upstairs spiral into the coloured lights overhead.

He lifted her hand just short of his lips. Marianne swallowed hard. "You know when I read that book, *The Shell*…" But a couple of people on their way out bumped into the two of them and they were separated by laughing, apologising revellers who were wearing paper party hats. In slow motion, Cal lost his balance and stumbled to the floor with a chair-leg screech on wood. He rose in stages, pulling himself up first to stool height then table. Finally he was upright, looking more bewildered than angry.

"Shit!" Marianne's bag had been knocked from her shoulder, its contents spilled out. She scrabbled furiously about under the table; grabbing chocolate bars and jamming them quickly back into the bag. She pushed away my attempts to assist.

"I've really got to go now." She manoeuvred her way quickly through the thinning groups of people finishing up drinks and pulling on jackets.

"Marianne." Cal was frantic. "Sarah, grab everything!"

He took off after her, surprisingly nimble, and left me to collect our jackets and my bag, struggling to catch up.

✦

WOODHOUSE LANE WAS busy. On the pavement, people coming out of Strawbs and the Fenton Hotel next door milled closely around Marianne and Cal. They stood still as a pair of street artists. Then he placed his hands loosely on her shoulders. She craned her neck to meet his eyes. Their breath mingled in the street lights.

A young man with what looked like a silver coin dangling from his left ear stopped in front of me, asking if I had a light. His studded leather jacket hung open and brushed my arm as he moved away and I caught a glimpse of a brightly patterned shirt. The Bangles belted out 'Eternal Flame' from a jukebox. There was me, a spare part as usual. *Break the spell.*

"Marianne!"

She turned. As if following directions in a play, Cal dropped his quivering hands, reached for his jacket. I helped him slide his arms into it and he went to lean against the wall next to the pub doorway. I sorted through my purse.

"Take this." I offered her my card with our phone number on it. "If you want to call us, you can, whenever you want.

No pressure. OK?" I wasn't even sure why we should continue to stay in touch. She was a girl who looked like our dead sister. Who was exactly like our dead sister, alive again and causing me to feel the same emotions I'd had in the final months of her life: sorrow for her emaciated state, guilt because I hadn't fulfilled my mother's hope that I could influence her to change her mind. The card was leaving my fingers, Marianne repeating that little gesture with her head and hands. Suddenly she seemed like the kind of student I'd taught many times, another young girl with an eating disorder.

"Come on," I said, "let's get you home. Shall we walk with you?"

"No, thank you, I'm alright."

It took me by surprise when she gave me an awkward hug, bones brushing against me. Marion would never have done that. A laugh bubbled in the back of my throat; I tightened my arms for just a second, afraid of her outward fragility.

Chapter 4

MARIANNE MINGLED WITH the crowd coming out of the pub next door. She turned right onto Fenton Street. *Don't look back.* She was cold but she prided herself on her apparent imperviousness to deprivation. She heard echoes in her head of the conversations she'd just had. The strange thing was they were voices she was once familiar with. The cold was more than on the outside of her skin, she felt it everywhere, deep inside. She was hollow but now with an expectancy of being filled. Her physical senses were distorted. Things around her blurred, visually: traffic lights, road signs, cars, lorries and buses, taxis with their orange lights on, hurrying or dawdling human figures, single or in groups, a dog that trotted purposefully by on its own. Sounds: car horns, the babble of voices, music coming out of a corner pub when the doors opened and closed – ebbed and flowed, all jumbled together. It made a cacophonic soundtrack to the muddle in her mind.

She walked fast. At the entrance to Willow Terrace Road the shadows of street lamps loomed in front of her. She smelt grass, dampening in the chill. She was unaware that a couple of people she knew from college passed her.

She felt his skin on her fingertips still, she rubbed finger and thumb together, tasting him through her pores. Cal. He'd held out his hand, trusting she would place hers in it. The way his hair fell over his face, it stirred a tenderness she had never felt. His eyes were utterly familiar. There was an unacknowledged truth in her mind and she gasped at it, pulling internal shutters down in a practised way. She concentrated instead on the physical. To be sensate now made sense. To see and touch and smell, to have had the warmth of his skin reflecting back onto hers, it must be the reason for her being in the physical body she had fought so long. She hunched herself up against her eternal internal resident, but it merely shifted in its sleep, turned over, rested again.

Two weeks previously…

MARIANNE ARRANGED A rag-rug on the bare wooden floor. There was just enough space for a single bed, a small desk and chair, and a huge, inherited chest of drawers. Her dresses and skirts hung from a row of pegs her father had screwed into the door. The shelves he'd put up were filled with paperback novels and her many hard-backed notebooks. She scribbled constantly: ideas for characters and dialogue; settings and scenarios for plays and short stories. Charissa was supposed to be helping with the unpacking. After all, she was getting their old room to herself now. Marianne tutted. "Can't you keep away from the mirror for once?"

Her younger sister patted her dark brown hair, carefully styled to look messy, and pouted her red lips, adjusting the huge bow on top of her head. Marianne looked over her shoulder into the mirror. *My face looks like a ghost behind you.* Charissa dabbed at a speck of mascara on her cheek. "Do you remember that game, 'Writers', we used to play when we were little?"

Marianne focused on the view of old red brick houses and a strip of grass. Looking through the square window she was a baby again, viewing the world from beneath the hood of a great big pram. The pram was a recurrent memory but her mother had said she'd never had one like that.

"You used to make me pretend to be your brother," Charissa said. "You used to say 'you're my sister now, but I had another sister before you. And I had a brother as well. Mum got cross with you for telling lies. Remember?"

No, no. Marianne pulled her dry lips into her mouth, bit down; let them out with a breath. "Here, if you've got to hang around, at least help me unpack."

Charissa staggered on her high heels when Marianne dumped the box in her arms. She delved into it, handing Marianne assorted objects. Mostly they went straight into the bin bag hooked over the spindly chair.

"What?" Marianne noticed Charissa staring at her.

"Why did you take those pills?"

It still shocked Marianne that Geraldine had referred to it as a 'suicide attempt.' "I don't know. I don't really want to talk about it. It's stupid." She would never tell anyone about the voice. They would think she was crazy.

"What do you mean, what is?"

"That book, *The Shell*. I felt sick when I saw it. Worse than sick, like I was going to die. I can't explain."

She wished she hadn't said anything at all, the way Charissa was staring at her. Her sister abandoned the cardboard box. She sat down on the bed, pinching at the pattern of looped threads on the bedspread, catching Marianne's eye. "Something weird happened... I was scared to tell you."

Prepare yourself, Marianne.

"You went... into some kind of fit. I don't know. You went rigid. You just kind of – froze in position, with the book held in front of you. I didn't know what to do."

Tingling in my fingers and jaw. Awareness of the room coming back slowly.

"You'd dropped the book on the floor. Afterwards you just bent down and picked it up as if nothing had happened."

Then I read the book; it told me the story was about me, the voice did. I just wanted to escape.

Charissa pulled a face. "I'll never forget waking up and seeing that book covered in sick!" She stood up and waved a glittery-nailed hand as if wafting away a persistent insect, hitched up her pink Ra-Ra skirt at the waist. She bent down, pulling a soft toy out of the box, one eyebrow lifted.

Marianne breathed deeply, considered. "Give it to Justine. She's always wanted it."

Charissa placed the bear out on the landing for their younger sister.

⬩◆◆⬩

MARIANNE'S FEET STOPPED at the bridge that spanned the inner ring road. She looked down at the blur of traffic beneath. The night had darkened and was quieter now. Her body, strung so tight, relaxed slightly. She felt now that she could walk forever, when before, she'd been so tired. Turning up Willow Terrace Road, it occurred to her to take the long way home so she could keep walking for a while longer. Her bag, containing its angles and corners, bumped sharply against her hip – this discomfort another self-imposed test of her endurance. She considered the pull of familiarity she had when she looked in Sarah's blue eyes. A comforting kind of feeling she would have liked to get from her mother, but it was too late with Geraldine.

She passed by the empty car park of the dental hospital and searched for her key with her hand in the deep pocket of her coat, holding it between finger and thumb, suddenly vulnerable. Crossing through Springfield Mount to Clarendon Road she kept her chin pointing forwards but her eyes maintained a watchful scanning of the shadows on either side.

At the top of the steps to the front door on Hyde Terrace she inserted her key in the lock, entered the tiled internal porch. There was a lamp on in the living room. Joseph, her father, sat in an armchair. He smiled. "Alright, Love?" He must have been waiting up for her.

"Yeah, fine."

She hadn't told him where she was going. He only knew she was going to a college thing, she guessed he hoped she'd had a fun night out with friends. She made her way up the stairs to her tiny room, folding her arm protectively around her bag, which contained the assessors of her willpower. With the door closed, she tucked the chocolate away in a box under her bed.

Chapter 5

1955 – 1960

Jane

HER AWARENESS OF *him grew as the space they shared became more cramped. At first she was irritated not to be able to move without always feeling his actions mirroring her own, but soon their synchronicity became second nature. When her eyes opened for the first time, she watched his opening a second later. They each gazed in amazement at the dim outline of their twin. Soon they were squashed up so close they could not really see each other at all, or distinguish that they were separate.*

Communication, mute, buzzed between them in the swish of their mother's heartbeat. Her thoughts were always a jump ahead.

'We don't have to go from here, we could just stay.'

Able to flit in and out of her tiny form, she saw no reason ever to physically leave her mother's womb. But her brother was afraid to travel; he sat tight in the flesh he'd been allotted.

'No, we have to go. Something's telling me it's time to go.'

'Then I'm going first. I just want you to know it's under duress. And if I don't like where we're going, I'm not going to stay there.'

<hr>

JANE WAS SURPRISED, and just a tiny bit disappointed to get pregnant again when Sarah was only nine months old. She'd wanted to enjoy the exclusivity of one baby for longer. She'd only just got over the fatigue of her first pregnancy.

But God was sending her the blessings of twins, and she would cope. Marion and Callum were born three weeks early, and suddenly Jane had three children under eighteen months. *Lord, give me the serenity to accept the things I cannot change…*

It could have been because Marion and Callum were twins that they seemed to develop so quickly; or maybe because she had her hands full so she tended to throw paper and crayons at them and let them get on with it, but by the time all the children were toddlers the twins seemed to have accelerated past Sarah. By the age of three Jane's twins could read, while Sarah struggled to make a tower with alphabet blocks. The twins became avid writers of stories. Sarah tried to join in but she always gave up before the end of the story.

With Sarah now six and the twins four and a half, Jane longed for the birth of the new baby she was expecting.

Caitlin was born at home. Jane allowed Sarah into the room immediately afterwards. The baby looked just like her eldest sister: yellow-blonde hair and blue eyes.

Sarah loved blowing raspberries on her tummy, making her squeal. She and her mother loved Caitlin's chubby body in her massive nappy. It brought Jane and Sarah closer, while the twins became more self-contained than ever.

In the middle of Caitlin's Christening, Jane's stomach plunged to hear Marion asking when the baby was 'going to fly back to its proper home'. The priest paused in the service to admonish Marion that little girls should be seen and not heard.

That summer, Jane took her four children to Pearson Park most Sundays after Mass, leaving George peeling potatoes and basting a chicken. The twins wore matching playsuits and sunhats. They disgorged the contents of their satchels so they could continue writing stories. Sarah, in a ruffled dress sewn by her mother, pushed the baby in her Silver Cross carriage on meandering paths between the flowerbeds while Jane sunbathed. Later, Jane helped Sarah to lift Caitlin out of her pram and the baby crawled like a fat little spider or crab, using one foot and one knee and two pudgy hands, propelling herself across the grass with a look of determination. On she charged, panting like a puppy, scattering the twins' crayons and scrunching up paper in her wake as she sped towards the sand pit. Cal got upset at the destruction she caused but Marion just fixed her baby sister with a baleful stare.

"Pat-a-cake, pat-a-cake, baker's man", Sarah pressed her six-year-old palms to Caitlin's nine-month-old ones.

❦

IN SEPTEMBER THE Wildes' suffered a severe bout of sickness and diarrhoea. Caitlin's cot was brought into the living room so her parents could tend to the whole family together. Towards evening Jane got up to lift Caitlin out and change her nappy. She left her lying on the folded towel while she dealt with the badly soiled nappy. Then she came back, pinned a clean nappy on and buttoned her into a fresh nightdress.

She opened the front of her sweater to offer Caitlin a feed. But the baby first doubled up and then flung herself backwards; uttering a piercing scream.

"Oh my God…what's happening to her? GEORGE!"

George came to bend over the baby screaming in Jane's arms. Caitlin's face had turned the colour and consistency of candle wax.

"Mammmmy!" The twins whined.

"Mummy, what's the matter with her?" Jane felt Sarah pulling the bottom of her sweater, trying to be heard over the cacophony.

By the time Dr Corcoran arrived Caitlin had gone quiet and limp. The doctor examined her and insisted on taking all their temperatures. He asked them how many times they'd been sick. Caitlin was suffering the effects of her tummy-bug, he said, and told them to drink plenty of fluids.

Everything that was poured into Caitlin's mouth came back again. It couldn't even be described as vomiting. For the first time ever, the baby rejected her mother's milk. She lay unmoving wherever she was placed.

"What's the matter with her, Mummy?" Sarah fretted. "She doesn't look like Caitlin anymore."

"Mammmmy!" The twins had never been whiny before.

That night, with Sarah asleep on the sofa, Jane tried to relax in the armchair by the range. A dull red glowed behind the glass door, warmed her legs. She had a woollen rug around her shoulders. There was a spreading sense of dread – a layer of unreality between her instinctive knowledge that there was something terribly wrong with Caitlin and the heavy warmth of the baby in her arms. She still felt and smelled like Caitlin. Jane found it less terrifying to accept the doctor's platitudes and make herself believe that everything was going to be fine.

❧❧

THE NEXT MORNING she was dimly aware of Sarah coming over to the armchair.

"Caitlin…" Sarah whispered. Jane woke up properly to see Caitlin's eyeballs, underneath closed lids, moving rapidly.

"Caitlin!" Sarah whispered it again. Caitlin shuddered and let out a small gasp. She opened her eyes slowly and saw her big sister making a funny face. Caitlin tried to smile and Sarah tickled her cheek. Jane started to relax; everything was going to be alright.

"Chickadee, Chickadee," said Sarah, "who's been at my cherry tree?"

Then Caitlin opened her mouth, and out came a brownish dribble. Caitlin gave a little hiccupping cry. Sarah gasped.

"Mummy! Look what Caitlin did."

Dr Corcoran took Caitlin's temperature again and promised the baby would be better in a day or two. "Give me a call tomorrow if you're still worried then, Mrs Wilde."

Jane was quieter than ever, unable to find a way to express her concerns over Caitlin's condition. That afternoon, waiting at the school gate for the twins and Sarah, she tried to pretend nothing was wrong.

She waited on the outskirts of the group of mothers until her best friend Brenda came over.

"Aren't you coming into the playground?"

Jane slowly shook her head. Brenda took a look at her face and dipped her head under the hood of the pram. When she straightened up she met Jane's eyes with shock.

"What on earth's the matter with her?"

Jane pulled her lips together tightly, struggling for composure. The children came running out of the school doors. Callum charged towards his mother like a bullet from a gun;

she found herself clinging tightly to the pram handle for fear of becoming separated from it.

She could not force her lips to smile but Callum didn't notice, hauling off his school cap and hurling it with his satchel onto the wire tray beneath the pram. He chattered ten-to-the-dozen over his shoulder to Marion. His twin followed slowly behind, a hand covering her mouth as she whispered something to Brenda's daughter, Lisa. Sarah came out last. She was holding hands with Helen, Brenda's other daughter. They came over to the pram and Sarah peeped inside. "Why isn't Caitlin smiling at me Mummy?"

That evening, while George was putting the older children to bed, Jane lowered Caitlin into a warm bath in front of the range. A strange grunt came out of her, stopping Jane's breath. She rinsed the soap off with the utmost tenderness, lifted her out and enfolded her in a towel, warm from the range door. When George returned downstairs, Jane was dressing the baby in a clean nighty. She told her husband very calmly, "I need you to telephone for an ambulance."

◆●◆

1 A.M. DIM LIGHTS and muted voices, closed curtains around beds. Jane came to on a hard chair in a hospital cubicle, realising she'd dozed off with Caitlin on her lap. A drip had been inserted into Caitlin's arm. A doctor would come soon to offer a second opinion. On the other side of the curtain rubber-soled footsteps hurried in both directions. An occasional sharp sound of metal against metal jarred the quiet. Jane tilted her arm and lifted Caitlin into a more upright position. She unbuttoned her blouse and encouraged Caitlin

to feed, but her head only flopped away to one side, eyes staring glassily at nothing. For the previous two days, Jane had had the uncanny feeling that Caitlin wanted everyone to leave her alone.

At 2 a.m. a nurse with hair escaping from her cap arrived. "Mrs…" she consulted her clipboard. "Mrs Wilde. I'm very sorry but Mr Gordon has been called into theatre and won't be able to see you until morning. But don't worry. The drip will help your baby to become rehydrated." She fiddled for a moment with the tube going into Caitlin's arm, her breath hot on Jane's cheek, and then bustled away.

That feeling of helplessness swept over Jane again, forcing her to play a part in a story that she was unable to influence. She slept for a short while. She wondered whether George's dreams were fitful or whether he was sleeping peacefully. She worried about Sarah and the twins. Just after it got light she sensed Caitlin awakening in the cot beside her chair. She reached over and placed her hand gently on Caitlin's stomach so she would know straight away her mother was there. Caitlin turned her face towards Jane and fixed her with a blue gaze, focused and clearer than Jane had seen it for the previous few days. It went straight into Jane's heart.

"Hello Chickadee!" Jane whispered, "Chickadee, Chicka-dee…" Her voice broke and she couldn't continue. Caitlin's blonde curls were plastered to her scalp. Jane lifted her up, taking care not to dislodge the drip in her arm. There was a spreading brown stain on the sheet where Caitlin's face had been.

Calmly, Jane went to the curtain and opened it. "Can I speak to somebody, please?"

"I'll get somebody to come as quickly as I can." The passing nurse looked apologetic.

Jane didn't want to upset her baby by making a fuss. So she sat back down on the hard chair. Leaving the curtain open she watched the ward, which had never really slept. She sat there for a further half hour, holding Caitlin very close and whispering loving things from time to time.

GEORGE HAD ATTEMPTED to ring the hospital that morning but the line was busy and so was he, struggling with the unaccustomed task of preparing the children's breakfasts and getting them off to school. The children seemed hyperactive now they'd got their energy back. Sarah asked too many questions about when her mother was coming home with the baby, huge tears welling at the bottom of her eyes. Cal buzzed around manically with his toy car. But Marion intrigued George. He found her staring into Caitlin's empty cot. She tipped her face up to his. "Why did Caitlin get to fly away and not me, Daddy?"

George started explaining that Caitlin would be on her way home shortly with her mother but his daughter had already turned away, looking disappointed.

At school, on the request of the twins' classroom teacher, he had to stay behind to have a chat. They had only started school that term. There was a problem with Marion's communication abilities, apparently. Had George noticed anything unusual? Not that he could think of. When the teacher finished with him, George did some grocery shopping, brought it home and put it all away to the best of his ability.

Jane was still not back but he felt she would be extremely pleased with him for saving her a job. He went to the main reception at the hospital because he didn't know what ward Jane and Caitlin were on. There seemed to be some difficulty finding out. "I'm sorry," said the receptionist, shifting through papers, looking puzzled, "there is a record of them coming in but I don't know what…?"

There was a pause while she chewed the top of her pen. "Ah, I'm sorry," she repeated. "I do believe they have tried several times to contact you. Could you just wait a moment, please? Someone will be down to talk to you as soon as possible." With a sidelong glance at George, the receptionist picked up the telephone. And even then, George suspected nothing. How could he have? But he felt heavy, his earlier positivity popped like a bubble.

"I'll just be over there." He pointed to some benches by the wooden news stand at the entrance. George got himself a magazine and sat down. After hurrying around all morning, he was relieved to take the weight off his feet.

Engrossed in his angling magazine, it took George a while to notice a pair of highly-polished shoes that had come to a stop right in front of him. He looked up. A young chap with an oiled moustache stood there – slightly foreign looking, wearing a white coat. And a name badge, but George couldn't pronounce what was written on it.

"Hello," George said.

"Hello, sir…" the young man couldn't seem to meet George's eyes. "I'm sorry, sir."

George felt uncomfortable. "No need. No need at all."

The doctor gave him a puzzled look. "My name is Dr Sureshi."

"Ah, pleased to meet you," George shook the doctor's hand.

"It's your wife, sir…"

"My wife, what about my wife? Could you please take me to her now?"

"Yes I'll do that right now sir," said the young doctor. "This is why I've come down to meet you."

"Well thank goodness for that." George let out a small laugh. "I was wondering where she'd got to!" He was led over to an elevator.

"It's on the second floor." Dr Sureshi turned partly away from him.

George's insides tightened. The elevator ride seemed to take forever. Panic started to swamp him; he couldn't seem to hear what the doctor was saying. The lift doors opened and he felt a slight lessening of tension as he stepped out into the corridor. "It's just in here." said Dr Sureshi.

There was a sign placed outside the room they were about to enter, it said 'No Entry'. 'In here' was the hospital chapel. George followed the doctor inside the room with feet made of lead. The inside of his head screeched violently. He looked across what seemed a chasm of distance in the dark, warm chapel. There was Jane, sitting in a throne-like wooden chair, with Caitlin pressed against her breast. A candle burned behind her head. She looked like a Madonna, only all wrong. It should have been a happy scene.

"Ah," murmured an older man with silver hair and a pressed, grey suit. He was crouching beside Jane's chair. He now straightened and walked forward to meet George, offering his hand. George found himself responding although his hand was shaking badly.

"Mr Wilde, I presume?"

George nodded.

"My name is Mr Gordon; I'm the paediatric consultant on this case. We have a problem here, I'm afraid. I'm very sorry, but we may need your help." He ran the hand that had just shaken George's through his hair. "You see, we can't get your wife to let go of the baby."

George looked at his wife. She let Caitlin down from her chest and the baby flopped back over her arm, yellow curls dangling. The screeching noise, George realised, was coming out of Jane's mouth.

THEY GAVE ALL of Caitlin's clothes and toys to the Catholic Children's Society. Jane began to spend her empty days in the city library. She spent many hours researching the condition Caitlin had died from: undiagnosed intussusception. Each evening on George's return from work she hurried up to the Catholic Church on Cottingham Road, hitherto only visited on Sundays and Holy Days of Obligation. Her feet slid on wet leaves and she pulled her buttonless coat together in the middle with one gloved hand. She had forgotten the mending again. Callum had holes in his socks. George wore a shirt with a frayed collar to work.

She lit a candle for Caitlin and prayed to the Virgin Mary. But she felt no connection. The Madonna's Son had exercised a choice in his own fate, unlike her own baby. Before she left the church she attended Confession, portioning out the hard seeds of her bitterness. But she was too angry to believe the penance would do any good. *Lord, give me the serenity to accept the things I cannot change...*

She wanted so badly to be able to get back in touch with reality, to plough a way out of the fog in her head. But no rosary twisted around her hands, no amount of penance could make up for the guilt of sitting on a busy hospital ward with her dying child in her arms.

George, she knew, would have to spend a long time trying to fill the holes in their family left by his wife's emotional absences. He would persist in trying to iron out her rage. Sarah would obviously grow into a nervous child, always anxious to please, worrying constantly about everybody's well-being. Jane expected that the twins would just become more insular. Marion had a powerful personality, directing Cal in most of their decisions. Soon after the baby's death, Jane found her now-youngest daughter standing on the spot in her parents' bedroom where Caitlin's carrycot used to be. Marion was humming in her toneless voice. She stared intently at nothing her mother could see. Jane's blood chilled. She felt helpless as to how to deal with the child.

Marion looked up at her mother. "Caitlin's flown away to the place I wanted to go, Mammy."

Jane knew she ought not to be afraid of her own daughter.

Chapter 6

Sarah

THE DRIVE HOME took an hour and a half. Before we'd even got out of Leeds, Cal had drunk most of a half-bottle of whisky. I followed the signs for Hull and Pontefract. By the time I was cruising along the M62 the empty bottle had fallen into Cal's lap and his head had lolled onto his shoulder. His snoring formed a comforting backdrop to my thoughts. I'd always found driving at night a soothing experience: the wavering light on the road in front of me, the rumble of tires on tarmac. I was glad Cal was asleep.

The A63 led me under the Humber Bridge into Hull, a massive expanse of river on my right. Our village was right at the end of it. I drove down Hessle Road, which by day was a market-like hubbub of activity, and eventually reached the eerily-lit Hedon Road, presided over by Hull Prison. Salt End, a massive chemical works, looked like a space station in the dark. The final stretch of unlit road wound like a ribbon through blackness for twenty-seven miles. There was a series of villages and I recited the names like an incantation, ticking off each one on my mental list. At nearly one o'clock we arrived home in Pottersea. Cal woke up, managed to make it into the house. He collapsed on the kitchen couch. I threw a blanket over him.

"You stay with him, Jude." The dog seemed to know when Cal needed to pee. He'd woken him lots of times since the night he'd tried to use the fridge as a toilet.

I drank some water and filled another glass for Cal, placed it on the carved table next to his snoring face, watched by Jude. Leaving my dog on guard I went up the uncarpeted kitchen staircase to my room. I washed my face and cleaned my teeth at the built-in vanity cubicle, opened the window next to my bed and slid into a long t-shirt. With a sigh I sank under the quilt. I wasn't yet ready to review the events of the evening. Bobbing gently in and out of sleep, lulled by the rhythmic voices of the distant sea and the river close by on the other side, images drifted through my mind like feathers. I was barely aware of them until a face appeared; one I hadn't seen for two years. I hardly ever let myself think about Mark, my last chance of a normal relationship. I wiped my eyes on the edge of my pillowcase.

◆◆◆

I MET MARK at a traditional Irish music festival in County Leitrim, a week-long summer-school bonanza of fiddle, flute, pipe and mandolin, bodhran, harp, whistle and song. The streets of the village were crammed with people, the doors of the pubs open, spilling out the sounds of bands accompanied by hand-clapping and foot-stamping. And the weather was hot, the atmosphere electric. I went there with my Mum. She developed an interest in Irish music after Marion died, listening to the tapes her daughter had played along to on her violin. Mum missed the sound of Marion's music and she encouraged me to take up violin just before I went to university. I only had a go to make her happy but I continued with my efforts once I was settled in York. Still, I wasn't really a musician. I only played for a couple of years but I agreed to drag out my dusty instrument from Mum and Dad's house for the festival. Going with her was Mum's fiftieth birthday present.

My class was fiddle, run by Mark O'Toole from an Irish band called The Shanbos. I'd heard of the band because Mum had their new CD. She developed a crush on the fiddle player as soon as she met him. "I'm sorry I decided to attend the penny-whistle class instead now," she said. I pressed my lips together, glad she had. I wouldn't have wanted her in the fiddle class with me, for two reasons. One was that I was rubbish at the Irish tunes we played. I know I slowed down the rest of the group but I was carried along by pure adrenalin and we all had a fantastic week. The other reason was that by the second evening of the course, the attraction between Mark and me was like a punch in the stomach every time we got close to each other. That happened often because I needed more help than the other students. He picked Mum and me up from our B&B that night and drove us up a winding road to a place called the Mountain Tavern. There was a music session in the bar, beginning just as it got dark. The wood-stove-lit room was filled with the sound of fiddles, mandolins, flutes and penny whistles. I found it mind-blowing, coming from my semi-reclusive life with Cal. I was encouraged to bring out my violin and have a go but I couldn't keep up. Then Mum surprised me by shaking her penny whistle out of its cotton case and picking up a tune half-way through.

I put down my violin and watched Mum play. She looked like a stranger to me at that moment, more like a young girl than someone's mother. Her cheeks were flushed and her light brown hair flickered with red-golden highlights from the stove. It curled prettily behind her ears. Her fingers flew up and down the holes of the penny whistle. Light from the fire and the candles on the table danced in her eyes.

I watched this woman who'd suffered the deaths of two daughters, and wondered how she'd managed to go on. I'd spent so much of my life worrying about her feelings but never managing to get close to her. I'd always thought this must have been due to some kind of lack in me. But now I perceived that I'd always tried too hard. That instead of constantly watching out for what might upset her I could have simply tried enjoying the things she enjoyed. I realised I'd probably been as hard work for her as she was for me.

On our third night in Ireland, Mark took me out alone. On the way to a restaurant in Sligo he drove the car around the side of a loch and found a secluded place to park. It had been a year since my previous relationship had fallen apart, immediately before I took up Cal's offer of moving into his new home. I also took up the job he offered me, as his personal assistant. I proofread his manuscripts, answered the telephone, organised his life. Going to Ireland with Mum opened me to the possibility of changes. An unaccustomed time spent with my mother – a new country – fresh and washed clean by recent rain, golden with sunshine by the time Mum and I got there.

That night, the mountains and the loch were quiet when Mark turned the engine off. Moonlight shone on the water and he told me it turned my blonde hair silver. Mountains loomed over us. Mark took hold of my chin and tipped my face up so I had to look right in his eyes. His voice was a low growl. He told me he would like to fuck my pants off, but that he wasn't going to. His voice sounded broken and put back together again. The lines of his face looked melted and his eyes were like blackberry stains.

I whispered, "Why?" He must have changed his mind, decided I wasn't good enough.

"Ah, Sarah." Mark took a shuddering breath. "Me little Sarah, fair play to you… I want it more than anythin'. But not like this; I'd be disrespectin' you, and your muther. She trusts me to treat you properly." He managed a rueful smile and chucked me under the chin like a child. "There'll be other, more appropriate times, I promise you." He was laughing as he spoke but I sensed the seriousness in his words. I could feel his heart under my palm.

"Mark," I pointed out, "I'm thirty-one!"

But I could see his point. I wasn't keen on these circumstances either. I didn't know where else we could go; I was sharing a room with my mother at the Bed and Breakfast and Mark was staying in a caravan on a friend's land with Frank, The Shanbos' mandolin player. I was secretly thrilled that he seemed to care for me enough to want to make an 'appropriate' situation for us to come together properly. And most of all that he was promising me we would.

Chapter 7

AH. MARK'S FACE was close to mine – the heat of his breath on my cheek. A mixture of gratitude and grief for our two lost years flooded me. But when I managed to force my eyes open I saw that Cal loomed over me, not Mark. His hot breath gusted onto my face. I nearly choked on the whisky fumes. In the dark his form seemed monstrous. "Whaaaa…?" I struggled to sit up, fingers scrabbling on the sheet. I tried to place myself, fumbled for my inhaler on the bedside cabinet. Cal reached over and switched on the bedside lamp. He sank into the wicker armchair beside the bed and I blinked uncontrollably as he jammed his feet under the quilt. He let out a lengthy sigh.

"Finally, you're awake!"

I edged myself away from his icy feet. *Be careful, Sarah.* Jude slithered onto the bed next to me and lay on top of the quilt, fixing me with a love-filled gaze. I stroked him absently, watching Cal. I couldn't shake off the feeling that I didn't know him. "What do you want?"

He repeated his exaggerated sigh. "She was – in the house – Marion, I'm sure she was." He fiddled with a button on his shirt. He must have had a bad dream but he'd brought the essence of it into my bedroom. "It's not that I haven't felt her presence before," he said, "but this time I was really disturbed by it. She was angry with me. You know what she was like, Sarah."

I pictured Marion with her look of stony disapproval, wondering what she would think of this Marianne business. How confusing it all was. If Marion had come back again, would she necessarily have had a choice in the matter, or could it have happened by mistake? And now we had discovered Marianne, would 'Marion', if she had in some way retained a separate consciousness, be angry with us for wanting to get involved with her? It didn't make sense to be afraid of my dead sister. My wired-up brother, on the other hand, was likely to go off at any minute. Jude snuffled at my fingers, contributing two flicks of his warm tongue. I risked meeting Cal's eyes. "I don't know what to think."

Cal tugged a blanket off the back of his chair and shook it out, pulling it round his shoulders. He still wore the jeans and shirt he'd gone to sleep in and the sharp tang of sweat hovered around him. His drumming fingers beat a horror-film rhythm onto the arm of the chair. "Tell me your gut feeling." It was a test. He drew his knees up and hugged himself, watched my face.

"My gut feeling, if you really want to know, but I don't think you're gonna like it, so don't get mad at me, OK?" I took a deep breath, blinked a few too many times, frozen in his glare. Sometimes he had Marion's exact expression, contemptuous but also puzzled. Like he couldn't understand how I was so stupid. He ran a hand through his hair, stuck up all over. When he'd shrugged the blanket off his shoulders, he half-stood, leaned forward. He gave me a hateful look. He pulled his lips back.

"You're such a coward, Sarah, why do you never say what you think? You're always so… fucking careful!"

Now it was happening. He straightened up. "You don't want to offend anybody – you can't bear to be the one who rocks the boat! Far be it from you to express an opinion of your own – or don't you have any?"

Flecks of spit flew out of his mouth. He paced around the floor. Jude trembled, or it might have been me. I hugged the dog tightly.

"Jesus! You sit there bloody blinking – you've always been the same! You should hear what people say about you. You have no idea, do you? You're so fucking – inadequate, you have no ambition of your own at all, do you? Following me round like a dog – why the fuck don't you get a life of your own?" He stopped pacing, pinned me under his gaze, sneering. I made a humming sound but it didn't blank out the gnawing admission that everything he said was true.

"I didn't really want you living here, you know. Dad asked me. He was worried about you, about your poor little nerves. You'd had yet *another* failed relationship and he didn't think you could manage on your own; his precious little Sarah."

My mind snapped into focus.

"And you were always his favourite," Cal added. "Jesus, Sarah, the rest of us never got a look-in with him: why d'you think Marion turned out the way she did?"

Jude licked my face.

"Marion couldn't compete with you. Good Sarah, always doing the right thing. She was worth twenty of you." Cal shoved the chair into the side of the bed, gripping it with white knuckles. Jude sprang forward with a guttural bark.

Cal's outbursts usually made me cry myself to sleep, interrogate my faults, but this time I was calm. I could see the boy in him that Marion had always led. But he was on his own now. He'd never really hurt me, I told myself, and I wasn't going to let him now. "You're a bully, Cal," I said. "Fuck off out of my room and let me get some sleep."

He stared at me a moment, his lips opening and closing like a goldfish. I'd never spoken back to him like that. Then he turned and stomped away. I patted the bed beside me for the dog. Jude yawned widely, settling down with a human-sounding sigh. I was still trembling. "Oh and Cal –" I hurled my parting shot after his retreating footsteps, "– make sure you don't piss yourself; if you do *I'm* not cleaning it up this time!" It wasn't in my job description.

Chapter 8

Sarah, May 1972

WE WENT BACK into the room after the doctor left, just Cal and me.

Those last hours, watching you breathe, wondering if once let out, your breath would ever be drawn in again. Your brother and I should never have had to go through that. You have imprinted those interminable moments between breaths on us forever, Marion. How can we go on with such a stark understanding of mortality?

Our triangle had broken. Cal and I were left struggling to understand the disappeared edge that had been Marion.

Dad had stayed downstairs in the kitchen with Mum. I saw the tensed bones of her hands, clutching a framed photo of Caitlin. Her mouth was a hard line. She must have been crying inside. How could Mum survive going through this again? Possibly the only way was to do what she was doing: refuse to acknowledge the death of a daughter for a second time. She'd slammed down the photograph, her voice bitter and hard.

"This one had no choice!"

I was the only surviving daughter of the three that she'd had. And I didn't think she'd take any more comfort from me now than she had in the past.

MARION LAY ON her back. Well, of course – she wasn't going to be sitting up or anything; was she?

Oh my God, she is *dead. She's really dead.*

When we left the room she was only just past being alive, but on return I could see how irrevocably she had gone. I was trembling all over – more than trembling, I was being shaken in the jaws of a giant dog. Everything inside me tingled – from the blood in my veins to the nerves in my fingertips. There was an icy claw in my chest. I couldn't take in the reality of my departed – and I could see in the sculpted form before me how appropriate that word was – sister. I couldn't stop gazing at her. *Don't take her away.* I didn't think I could face my mother when they did.

The doctor had folded my dead sister's arms across her chest. Her violinist's fingers were very long, like an Egon Shiele painting. Her face was a wax carving. Her closed-eyes expression was inscrutable, though her mouth looked satisfied. Her hair spread out on the pillow. Did the doctor brush it? She was a nice lady who'd known Marion since she was about twelve. Some dried blossom had blown in the window, crunched on the floor under my feet. My face twitched, I had no control over it at all; I imagined my whole body was leaping and jerking about like that –I was a marionette being puppeteered. Retching sobs spewed out of me. My nose poured, my hanky disintegrated in my hand.

But Marion lay oblivious, a carving on a cathedral tomb.

Cal was silent. I think he was content enough at that moment that she was still there. Her silence was nothing unusual – Marion hadn't spoken for a long time anyway. He pulled a chair as close as he could to the bed. He placed his hands over hers and laid his head on top of them. I think he went to sleep. After a while, I went and put my hands on his shoulders. I leant forward and kissed the top of his head, and then I left him to keep her company until the undertaker arrived.

⚫

MUM WAS IN shock. Her skin had the texture of dough. I worried she was going to have a heart attack.

"Call the doctor back, Dad?"

"Try to stay calm, Sarah love, your mum's just upset." He had his arms around her. "D'you want to go up and see Marion now, love?"

"I just want my baby!" Mum responded through chattering teeth. "George," she continued in a keening voice, "George, I want my baby, I just want my baby."

"I know, love, I know."

My father's forbearance was heartbreaking. I went out into the garden. Dried blossom from the apple tree crisped under my feet. My skin welcomed the cool air. I wondered where Marion had gone and if she was feeling a spiritual, bodiless kind of happiness. In my head Samuel Barber's *Adagio for Strings* played, a piece that would be played at her funeral. I couldn't feel myself crying but my shirtsleeve was sodden from wiping my face and every now and then I'd startle myself by almost choking. So many memories were evoked by this garden.

I pictured Caitlin's pram with the fringed canopy parked under the tree. I was only just tall enough to be able to peep inside and see her, even standing on tiptoes. I played 'peek-a-boo' with her and made her giggle. Marion had always been a strange child, she'd never responded to rhymes and games the way Caitlin or Cal did. I could remember trying to play 'row the boat' with her; holding both her hands and rocking her backwards and forwards. It made Cal laugh out loud and try to sing the words when I did it with him, but Marion only stared at me with that puzzled face of hers. Later though I saw her attempting to play it with a doll, or maybe it was a teddy, I can't remember. She had taken its hands or paws and rocked it, singing tonelessly and with the same puzzled expression, as if trying to work it out. I think she spent her whole life trying to work things out. She didn't seem to have the same programming as other people.

And once, I watched Marion go into a trance. She had some kind of illness but she threatened violence if Mum tried to force her to see a doctor. I don't think she ever actually hit anyone, at least not once she had gone through puberty, but she could be frightening. She had already stopped speaking by then, she was about fifteen. I'd been out on a date with my first boyfriend. Mum and Dad didn't know, they thought I'd gone to the pictures with my friend Helen. I was too excited to sleep. So I stood at my bedroom window looking out at the moon, imagining my boyfriend looking up at it too. Then I noticed Marion at the bottom of the garden in her pyjamas, immobile, her arms slightly away from her sides. It seemed a long, long time that she stood there. I wanted to call out, wake up Mum and Dad and tell them. I should have done but I had frozen up as well. Her hair looked silver, a Pre-Raphaelite painting. I almost expected a dove to fly up out of her hands. When she came to, she seemed to shudder, rubbing her arms.

She must have been so cold. I hid behind the curtain in case she saw me.

On the landing outside my room, I heard her crying. Waves of shock reverberated through me. Marion never cried. But she was crying that night, and I wish I'd offered her comfort. I opened my bedroom door a tiny crack and peeped out. There was a votive lamp on a painted table at the end of the hall – Mum had switched it on every night since Caitlin died. Marion looked small and vulnerable. An alone girl with hunched-up, bird-like shoulders, walking as though her feet hurt.

"Marion," I whispered, but not loud enough for her to hear. "Marion." My voice was hoarse, as though I'd been out in the cold. But her sobs overrode it. If she had heard, if she'd turned at the sound of my voice, I'd have seen that closed-up face of hers, shiny as it must have been with the tears that made her hiccup and snort with unfamiliar sensations. I could have opened my arms and she might, because she was so unaccustomed to being overwhelmed by her emotions, have allowed me to enfold her in them. But she didn't. I didn't. I closed my bedroom door after that one feeble attempt. I let it go.

EVENTUALLY I HAD to get up from the base of the apple tree where I'd been sitting. I brushed petals and cut grass from the bum of my jeans. The flared hems had soaked up the dew. I retied my cheesecloth shirt at the waist, stood under the tree a moment. I wanted to howl at the moon. Nothing would ever bring Marion back. Bangles clattered on my wrists as I let my arms fall to my sides. I was dreading going back inside, seeing my mother's grief replayed. I didn't think I could stand it.

I just didn't want to have to do this again. I was only eighteen, I was about to finish my A Levels, I was supposed to be going to university in September. How could I be expected to embark on this journey of bereavement, to suffer the loss of a sister for the second time? My head was full of images of Marion, alive and dead; of violin music and funerals, of sad faces and words. I went back inside and the dark was prevented from going in with me by the bright lights of the kitchen.

Chapter 9

A Postscript: Marion

SAMUEL BARBER'S ADAGIO for Strings was always my
favourite piece of music – I love the way it soars into the
sky and beyond, reminding me of when I journeyed out
of my body. When I was still alive.

It started with a rattle and a hum. My whole body
shook. Then off I went. I flew without wings. Sometimes
I seemed to fly right up into the universe. Oddly, I had
the sensation of air on my skin even though I had no
skin, and once I got past the sky there was no air. Mostly
I hovered around wild places like moors, mountains,
craggy cliffs by the sea. A pure essence of me with the
remembered sensation of wind singing past.

That was how the music affected me in the church. I
wanted it at my funeral so they could all feel it the way I
had. I could spend my last bit of time with them: no
words, no body, nothing that could be misinterpreted. I
would finally just be me.

I was sorry that they took it so bad. I'd tried to prepare them for it – make them understand that this was
the right thing to do. But I didn't seem to have succeed-

ed. I suppose I'd never really thought about their perception of it.

Mum was still angry at the time of my funeral. Her face was pinched and white. There were grandparents, aunts and uncles, family friends there, who'd been present at the funeral of her youngest daughter. She was probably embarrassed – to lose one daughter is unfortunate, etc...

Dad always tried to be patient and understanding but he looked broken that day. Enough said.

Sarah was anxious for my mother and pouring out her own grief at the same time. Poor, insecure Sarah.

There was my best friend Lisa, she'd stuck by me when any other friends I'd had left me alone because I was too weird. I'd tried really hard to explain everything to her before I left, but she looked lonely and devastated now.

And finally there was Cal. What can I say about how the loss of me was going to affect him? He was my other half, incomplete now I was gone, re-shaped by my death. It just couldn't be helped.

So the Adagio for Strings filled the church and the hearts which were lifted by it united with me briefly. The rush of love and joy was worth a lifetime's wait and I hoped they realised it, dancing with me in the hull of that roof-space. Then I had to let them go.

I liked it so much, this flying-dancing-freedom of finally having no body, no face and no voice, that I stayed around too long. After the grave had been covered and after they'd all left the cemetery, I was still around. There was no time anymore, no cold or warm, not even any light or dark though to me it felt as if there was. I should be leaving but I was like the infant Peter Pan in Kensington gardens: he enjoyed flying so much that by the time he decided to go back to his mother it was too late; the window was barred, there was another child in his place.

There was somewhere I was supposed to go. But I missed my exit— I ignored the gentle calling, the seducing lights and music, all in what used to be my mind. The tool for reminding me of the direction I was expected to take. But like a canary released from its cage, I wanted to keep flying and singing because I loved the freedom of being what I had always perceived I could be. And so without meaning to, I had to go back into the vortex from which I would be squeezed into another warm and red-dark place.

Here, things were defined and bounded again. I was forced back into the kind of solid form I'd struggled so hard to escape from. I kicked and fought against the containment of my new body at first but eventually I had to succumb to it, with devastating resignation.

Presently, I was pushed through another tunnel and then there was bright and noise. Night and day came back, ordered time and physical expectations confined me. I was no longer Marion and I was no longer free. I'd been re-formed. I was renamed. I had been reproduced, an unwilling entrant into and out of the womb of an unwilling mother. In turn I became an unwilling baby, never at ease in the body that was allotted to me. I refused to accept the new identity.

Chapter 10

Sarah

JUDE BOUNCED DOWNSTAIRS ahead of me. I kicked the rug Cal had left in a heap on the floor by the sofa, picked it up, folded it, put the kettle on. Pushed open the back door, held myself in the beam of sunlight streaming across the paved yard. It soaked into my skin and hair. The warmth calmed my racing brain. I took my tea outside, strolled down the garden past my brick studio; leaned on the wall which separated our land from a low grass slope that bordered the river. The mud flats mirrored sky in their wet, rippled surface. The smell of saltwater, the vivid light flooding the wide-open landscape moved me to raise my arms as if flying. Light reflected off the slick mud and dazzled my eyes. I contemplated the potential for a charcoal drawing of repetitive shapes and contrasting tones, a meditative study: it would be just the thing for ironing out the creases in my mind. The meeting with the Marion-lookalike felt like a dream, but I couldn't cope with trying to work it out in the morning sunshine. I went back into the house to retrieve the key to my studio and unlocked the door, breathed in the scent of turpentine and oil paint as others might inhale the aroma of flowers. This was me.

On the curved, stony river-beach at the bottom of the grassy bank behind our garden I settled my board on a flat rock and placed chunky sticks of grey and black pastel and a putty rubber around the edge of it. I smoothed a thick sheet of paper onto the centre of the board and taped it in place. Then I sat back on my heels for a moment, watching Jude pick his way gingerly over seaweedy rocks in search of tasty rotting things. I kept an eye on him. "Just don't roll in anything revolting; you're not coming back in the house if you do." The dog mistook my call for an invitation to dine on drawing materials, adopted a hopeful expression, took up a sentry position; fixed his eyes on my every movement. I growled. "Go and play Jude, there's a good boy."

With a disappointed whine he flopped down on the sand. On my hands and knees I used the side of a pastel stick to lay down a grey ground. I put my whole body into it, pushing pastel grains into the paper in mellifluous forms.

"Move, Jude." I nudged the dog's sun-warmed bulk off the edge of the paper. Keeping my eyes as much on the shining reflections in front of me as on my work, I began to take out patches of colour with the putty rubber, exposing the white of paper beneath, making an impression of highlighted ripples on the surface of mud. I worked vigorously until I was out of breath, then I sat back on my heels again. My mind buzzed as if it had just woken up. What had I let myself believe last night? Whatever it was it had to be over now.

My hands were covered in pastel dust and my once-white t-shirt was now a filthy grey but I didn't care. A faint breeze stroked through the roots of my hair, creeping over my neck and arms. I felt like me again. Seagulls screeched over the vast mud landscape. I used my fingers and the heels of my hand to put in contrast with black pastel, manipulated the picture plane into an effect of texture and perspective. The surface of paper looked like mud you would be able to walk on, that you would feel your heels getting sucked into, perfection you wouldn't want to disturb. I'd got what I wanted: a feeling of control and direction.

The light had changed by the time Jude barked twice and stared at me intently, wagging his tail. "I'll take you for a walk later. Help me get this back to the studio." He carried the tube of spare paper. I tipped my pastels into a cotton drawstring bag then sprayed my work with fixative, the stinging smell lost in the tang of salt. I carried it home still clipped to the board. Sun warmed the back of my neck. In the studio I washed my hands and took the drawing off the board, taping it to the wall. I was happy to have made a piece of work for myself, and not just for teaching purposes. I resolved to develop a whole series of pastel drawings on the mud theme. *If I stay here,* said a voice in my mind. *Uh-huh, where did that come from?*

I walked back to the house, dreading bumping into Cal. *Shit.* Dad's birthday was the next day and Cal and I were going to his party. The potential repercussions of our meeting with that girl arrested me. I realised how impossible it would be to continue a relationship with her. Resurrecting Marion could only harm Mum and Dad. It would kill Mum. I fumbled my way into the kitchen, watched the kettle, heart hammering, tapped my fingers on the counter. The rumble of the boiler and the dog's snores were the only things disturbing the quiet. I contemplated a jar of wildflowers I'd placed on the table the day before. The previous night's massive row with Cal brought home how completely I'd subjugated my needs to his. I would never be able to extricate myself from the tragedy of the past while I remained with him. Much as I loved Blackberry House, this estuary landscape, I would have to break away.

———◆◆———

THE TELEPHONE RANG in the office. I was going to answer, but Cal had somehow managed to get to it before me. Had he been sleeping in there? I busied myself putting the previous day's pots away and washing up the ones I'd just used for breakfast, already thinking about the evening meal. I swept the kitchen floor and wiped down all the surfaces. After ten minutes or so, Cal emerged from the office and walked as far as the stretchy telephone cord allowed, holding the receiver out to me. "She wants to have a word with you." He avoided my eyes. I assumed my mum was the caller and prepared to reassure her that we'd be arriving in plenty of time for our dad's birthday party tomorrow.

"Hi Mum." I put on the bright voice of all my conversations with her, my involuntary blinking starting up. Cal gave me a scathing look but its meaning didn't hit me until, after a pause, a very quiet voice said, "Its Marianne."

I had given her my card. She had found us. Shit. *Breathe, Sarah.*

"Marianne!"

I threw a panicked look at Cal, took the phone into the office. It stank of whisky and cigarette smoke. I closed the door and opened the window, fighting claustrophobia. My voice, breathy, asked "How are you?" *Why have you rung?*

"Oh, I'm fine." Her voice was high and light. "It's a gorgeous day. I was wondering if you'd mind me visiting. Cal said I could. Would you mind, Sarah?"

Yes. But my voice said otherwise. When I put the phone down I dropped to my knees and dug in the bottom drawer of the old desk that occupied half of one wall. Jude tried to catch my eyes but failed, flopping down next to me. He pointed his nose at the door and whined. I could hear the water pipes gurgling from the bath that Cal must be taking upstairs. Apart from when he handed me the telephone, we hadn't spoken at all. Jude scrabbled at the doorframe.

"Stop it!" He looked at me with mournful eyes but I avoided them. "Just leave me alone for a minute." I sank back on the carpet of the wood-panelled room. I wanted to cry but my eyes felt hot and dry. The dust from the photograph album I pulled out made me wheeze. Pain blossomed in my chest as a hand-tinted picture of Caitlin fell out from the middle of the book. Thirty years after she died I could still remember her gummy smile. There were Cal, Marion and I on the front lawn of our house on Westbourne Avenue with three other children: Peter, who was our next door neighbour and Helen and Lisa Butler, friends we'd known since we were born. We were all wearing shorts or swimming costumes and there was a paddling pool in the background of the picture. As usual Marion was the only child not smiling, but I did remember that day, and Marion was happy. She and Lisa and Cal had put on a puppet show for the entertainment of our parents.

I stared at another photograph of Marion aged almost seventeen. The only difference I could pinpoint between her and my memory of Marianne last night was the look in

Marion's eyes. From being a very young child – perhaps even from birth, Marion wore a perpetual scowl. Marianne had not had that look. I think Marion had difficulty expressing emotions. She once asked our mother if she could have a 'face operation' so that she would be able to smile the way other children did. In the photograph she was playing the violin. I replaced the album in the drawer and looked at my watch: eleven o'clock. I had to take the dog for a walk and be ready to leave in time to pick Marianne up from the station at one, as promised.

CHUNKS OF CONCRETE were half-buried in sand. The red clay shelves of the East Coast were crumbling at an alarming rate – a redefinition of the coastline had occurred even in the five years I'd lived there. As the cliffs receded, the once-hidden war defences broke free and spilled themselves out onto the beach. I took Jude to the place beyond the caravan site, a stretch of coast between Pottersea and Restingham. The sand was dotted with smooth black natural rocks preceding by hundreds of years those crumbs of human effort only recently ejected from the cliffs. The dog and I returned along a cliff path that would be chewed off by the sea in the space of a decade. Sand between my toes created pleasant abrasiveness. Sunlight glinted from the roofs of the caravan park to my right. I saw her, Marianne, coming towards me through the late May heat haze. I didn't register her as actual at first. She looked different from the previous evening, hair parted in the middle, hanging in two plaits over her shoulders, heavy fringe pushed off to one side. Her bulging knitted bag bounced

against her hip and she stumbled slightly on the uneven path. I wondered if she was carrying chocolate again, considered the ramifications of chocolate against the bald evidence of her emaciated frame. It occurred to me that she must be boiling under all her layers of clothes.

Through a haze of heat, Marianne got close enough that I could see the sheen of perspiration on her face. She waved uncertainly, and I wiggled my fingers back with a small, frozen smile. A tiny breeze lifted tendrils of hair off the slightly damp back of my neck, replaced them one at a time.

Chapter 11

Marianne

MARIANNE HAD GIVEN up all pretence of sleep. Dawn painted the rooftops of Hyde Terrace a pale gold, the shadows beneath the guttering of each house in sharp contrast. Pigeons cooed above her window. She had that impression of looking out through the hood of a pram again. She'd had a familiar dream in which Charissa was her brother. The dream came from a game they used to play when they were small. "Your imaginary brother," Charissa used to call herself, after their mother remarked that Marianne had a lot of imaginary friends. *Even an imaginary self, for heaven's sake!* Geraldine said it made a relationship with her daughter difficult.

"I never feel good enough for her," was the excuse Marianne had heard her giving Joseph for her lack of interaction with her eldest child. Marianne wondered what Geraldine's excuse was for her indifference to her youngest, Justine, a neglected daughter if ever there was one. Geraldine seemed to have no problem relating to Charissa, the one who shared her interest in beauty and fashion, the one she could most easily manipulate.

Marianne donned a vintage dress that came to just below her knees. She admired her own thin legs emerging from it.

She was cold, and added a thick lilac cardigan that had belonged to her grandmother. Marianne liked old things, to Geraldine's disgust and Charissa's bafflement. Marianne was still cold, so she wrapped a pink cotton scarf around her shoulders and knotted it at the front. She brushed her hair, distressed to see the amount of it that came out in the hairbrush. Next she plaited it. Looking in the mirror, her almond shaped eyes told her what she was going to do this day before she'd even decided. As if the mirror-image instructed her.

"I *have* eaten breakfast," is what she would say to Joseph later when he asked why she wasn't partaking of the food she prepared for the family. For Justine especially, since nobody else seemed to take much notice of the child. Marianne needed to supervise her nutrition and she must have a good breakfast before school.

To this end Marianne took money from the housekeeping jug on her grandfather's dresser in the kitchen. How Geraldine hated those old pieces of furniture that were dotted around their house. But Joseph remained firm on the matter, pointing out Geraldine could decorate her inherited London flat "as modern as you like" That was her territory, this was his. Many of the pieces had been brought over from the farm Geraldine persuaded him to leave.

Marianne walked to the small supermarket on the main road, her feet slapping on pavement in their flat sandals. Sun dappled down through the overhanging branches. She filled her basket with wholemeal bread, butter, milk and farm eggs. At the greengrocery section she added apples and bananas. She'd give Justine instructions what to eat later that afternoon.

Marianne averted conscious thoughts of Cal, but she realised she had always known about him. In no way she could explain. Everything strange that had happened to her was connected to him. She had been suffering what Charissa described as her 'fits', ever since she'd picked up that book Cal wrote. Later Charissa had spotted her standing stock-still in the garden one night, wearing her pyjamas. Marianne couldn't remember. She worked out that it must have been when she'd just learned about her college class going to the TV recording. She remembered the way she felt when she heard Cal's name. Stripped from the inside out. Then that whisper in her ear had begun as well.

Terry Wogan was on the radio. It reminded Marianne of her grandmother, who had prided herself on being a 'T.O.G'. After the news bulletin Marianne's mind briefly connected with the 'pause for thought' speaker who was referencing the help that the Hillsborough disaster victims had given each other. But she couldn't feel anything because of her great desire to see Cal. The rest of the world no longer seemed to matter. Forcing concentration, she prepared breakfast and left it on the table. Artfully, she tore sections out of a piece of toast and placed it on one side as if it had been half eaten. For her breakfast, she licked the butter off her fingers and sipped hot water. Then she encouraged Justine, who was a heavy sleeper, to get out of bed.

"I won't be here tonight," she said, "but don't worry about anything. I'll see you again tomorrow."

She saw Justine off on the school bus. Geraldine had not yet risen from bed and Charissa was performing some elaborate make-up routine. Joseph had left an hour before for an appointment in Harrogate. Then Marianne made the telephone call. As soon as Cal answered, her insides turned to treacle. "I…" was all she could get out. But Cal knew who she was straight away.

"You called!" His reaction, immediate, flooded her with relief. This thing that was happening was meant to be; she was certain of it. Her inner voice confirmed it.

She caught an earlier train than she'd told them; she wanted to get all the way out to Pottersea by herself and not have to be picked up in Hull. The day was more like July than May, the air thick with heat. The train drew into Hull's Victorian station and Marianne got out. Although the hair that had escaped from her plaits was sticky on her neck, she still felt cold and pulled her pink scarf more tightly around her shoulders. In the bus station which was right next door to its railway counterpart, Marianne was told she could catch the bus to Pottersea from a stand in the centre of town. She bought herself a sandwich she was unlikely to eat. Then she crossed a busy road and took a shortcut into the town centre. She bought some thin tipped pens, which she liked to use for writing in her notebooks, at a shop called Hull Drawing.

Marianne ignored the stares of other passengers on the coach. The landscape she saw from the windows was flat, dominated by the huge dome of sky. Metal buildings stood close to the road, separated from it by walls. Rows of brick houses were fronted by low banks of grass. She looked down at stone cottages tucked into tight corner gardens. The coach seemed to careen around bends, stopping beside farms and pulling into village streets and then flying out into open countryside again. A straight stretch of road carried her to her destination. To Marianne it seemed like a road in a dream, fields burgeoning with growth on either side of the narrow carriageway, fecund hedges bordering them; birds and butterflies dipping and flitting between. A scattering of houses appeared here and there on either side. The bus stopped next to some of them but Marianne stayed in her seat, the last person on it. To her right she gazed out at the widest expanse of sky and river she had ever seen. On the horizon, the far bank of the river, outlines of Grimsby's industrial apparatus were faintly sketched in the heat-haze. When the bus started up again the road took a sharp right-angle to the river. On Marianne's right now were more houses and farms, and beyond them marshes and water as far as she could see. Fields stretched away to the left, under a massive arc of sky.

"This is it, love," the driver turned his head and called when the coach rumbled to a stop. They had reached the final bus stop on the route, by the entrance of a caravan park. This was Pottersea. She was excited to see that the last stretch of road led directly to a beach. The sea, wide and blue, spread in front of her. A path to her left beyond the caravan site meandered along the cliff edge overlooking the beach. Happily, she adjusted the bag on her shoulder and stretched out her arms. Blue sky touched the ground in all directions. The sea's hollow voice carolled a multitude of harmonies. Here was space and light, proper room to breathe. Instinctively she turned left and began walking the rough cliff path, not even sure where she was going but not caring. She felt so free, at one with nature: her habitual opponent with which she longed for reconciliation.

When she spotted Sarah, approaching with a boisterous black and white dog, her own face broke into a smile. Sarah seemed so familiar, utterly unthreatening. Marianne saw her put one hand up to the back of her short blonde hair. "How did you get here this soon?" Sarah asked.

Chapter 12

Sarah

I COULDN'T STOP blinking. The astoundingly Marion-like entity stopped in front of me, laughing. She bent to stroke Jude. He rolled onto his back in ecstasy. I almost did the same. Marianne was alive, colourful; corporeal. *Oh, Marion.* If I chose to, I could let myself believe the years of death had been thwarted. I stood with numb lips as she poured out a stream of words, about the landscape, the loveliness of the day, the good fortune of her trip to the seaside. Straightening up, she offered me a wide smile. I could see then that she could not be my sister at all. She was too different, with her laughing and her verbosity. I was enjoying her too much, and yet I also had a sense of dread. I wanted, but at the same time didn't want, for her to have resumed Marion where she left off.

"I was so excited; I couldn't wait for the twelve o'clock train! So I caught the ten o'clock one instead and then got a bus out here. I hope you don't mind? I didn't mean to inconvenience you… but I couldn't wait… Oh, look at that sky – I was admiring the sun on the river just before the bus went round that corner onto the sea road, I was surprised you were next to the river and right near the sea too! It's so beautiful here, isn't it?"

I almost warded her off with my hands, but she didn't seem to notice. We left the cliff path and started down the L-shaped road away from the sea. Fields bounded both sides of it. The air was thick with the buzzing of insects and the distant mooing of a herd of black-and-white cows.

Cal and I had avoided each other all morning. I was concerned Marianne would pick up on this. If she felt uncomfortable with us both, she might stop talking. I couldn't stand the thought of a silence filled with this unlikely spectre of Marion. Jude scurried on ahead, snuffling in the hedgerows, retracing his steps repeatedly to check we were still there. As we neared home the dog looked at me questioningly and barked once. "Go on then, boy!"

Blackberry House was constructed of white-painted stone, only two storeys visible from the front but with an added level above, evidenced by the roof windows. You could see part of our back garden and the crumbling red-brick wall at the end. Beyond this the estuary gleamed, its carpet of mud obscured now by a returned surface of river. Marianne smiled at me and my feeling of tension loosened. Sweat cooled on my skin in a breeze from the river. I watched as the girl bounded towards the house like the Border Collie waiting for us on the path, panting with his tongue lolling out.

She let out another flow of words in admiration of the house. She loved the stone porch with its original wooden door, the old glass in the two small windows at the front. She said she loved old things much more than new ones.

I couldn't work her out; she was a totally different girl from last night, unnervingly assertive. Jude pushed through the front door wagging his body. Cal stood at the foot of the stairs, facing us. He snapped at Jude, pushed him away with his foot. The dog let out a whine then slunk past to his lair under the staircase, regarding Cal with sad eyes. Marianne stopped chattering. She looked at me, seemed to seek reassurance. I gave her a sketch of a smile but I did not want to meet Cal's eyes.

Chapter 13

1960

Jane

AT THE END of the twins' first term at school, Jane received a letter requesting that Mr and Mrs Wilde attend a meeting with Marion's classroom teacher Mrs Hobbs, along with the school's headmistress, Miss Carmichael. Jane hadn't been anywhere near the school since Caitlin died. She'd received a black-edged card of condolence signed by all the staff. Her friend Brenda had been taking the children to school every morning and George had been leaving work to pick them up in the afternoon and deliver them back to their mother before returning to work for a further two hours.

At home, Callum and Marion were practically independent of their mother. Apart from being fed, the two of them had never seemed to need her as Sarah or Caitlin had. They lived in their twin world both physically and emotionally. Even in the bath they would pick up the flannels and wash each other's faces as though they were looking in a mirror. When Jane attempted to wash Marion's hair by pouring water over it with a jug, Marion's pipe-like voice would ring out, "Callum do it!" And the same with Callum. They never even minded if they got shampoo in each other's eyes. Then there was the secret language they had. They giggled surreptitiously behind their hands, laughing when Jane couldn't understand what had amused them. Ordinary words seemed superfluous to the two of them.

Jane rarely managed to get a cuddle with her young daughter. Marion was born self-contained, squirming out of her mother's embrace. Immediately after a feed she would push away and only really seem content once she was back under the dark hood of the big Silver Cross pram in the hallway. From there she would fix Jane with a scrutinising stare. Jane got the feeling the baby wondered who she was. If Jane tried to hold onto her after a feed, establish some interaction other than the functionality of feeding, Marion got rigid in her arms.

After Caitlin died, Jane's arms felt so empty. Callum allowed Jane to be a bit more tactile with him, especially when he was very tired. At bedtime, under the watchful gaze of his twin sister, he might accept his mother's patted invitation to climb on her lap. Relief flooded Jane as he consented to nestle there, however temporarily. She breathed the scent of her only son, burying her nose in his thick hair. She tightened her arms around him. Marion watched the two of them with a taut face. After a while it seemed Callum could take the bore of his sister's gaze no longer – it made him remove his thumb from his mouth and scramble down to sit quietly beside her on their favourite cushion.

Sarah, who had hovered anxiously at her mother's side throughout Jane's reading of the Peter Pan story, turned her lamp-like eyes to Jane with an expression that pleaded attention. Sarah was waif-like in appearance, but she was very much the older sister, always giving up things the twins demanded, rushing to help her mother when required; especially when the new baby arrived. But after Caitlin, Sarah made Jane feel uncomfortable. Her need was too palpable. Jane worried that she would never be able to meet it. The combination of Sarah's maturity and her little-girl needs were confusing. Jane wanted to 'forget about' Sarah in the face of all the other demands on her time, much of which was taken up with grieving. Sarah could be relied on not to make a fuss. Sarah would manage to tie up her own shoes, to tidy after the twins, and generally not to expect too much attention. But it didn't mean she didn't want it.

That state of relationship between Jane and Sarah never really changed. After her loss, Jane didn't feel capable of meeting anybody's needs, and more still after the death of Marion – in that, the mother felt her older daughter was a colluder. Or at least did nothing to stop it.

So, Jane read to the twins and Sarah from 'Peter Pan in Kensington Gardens' and Callum slipped off Jane's lap onto the cushion with his twin. Sarah stood pressed against her mother's shoulder, eyes pleading to be invited onto her lap. *Ask me, Sarah. Just ask me.* Supply meets demand: Sarah demanded so little that Jane felt she had to wring it out of herself on Sarah's behalf, and she didn't have the energy.

"Mummy..." Sarah finally ventured to interrupt (It was the part of the story where Peter flies back to his mother's window) "'*He went in a hurry in the end,*'" read Jane, "'*because he had dreamt that his mother was crying, and he knew what was the great thing she cried for, and that a hug from her splendid Peter would quickly make her to smile.*'" Here Jane stopped, took a breath. She was only too aware of how Peter's mother must have felt. "'*Oh, he felt sure of it, and so eager was he to be nestling in her arms that this time he flew straight to the window, which was always to be open for him.* "

Sarah's voice rang in Jane's ear like a tiny bell. "What is it, Sarah?"

"Please may I sit on your lap? –if nobody else wants it," Sarah added hastily.

Jane looked at Sarah and then at the expectant faces of the twins, watching to see what would happen. "Does anybody else want it?" Jane asked. The twins giggled and shook their heads. Callum jammed his thumb back in his mouth and snuggled closer to his sister. "Then you may," responded Jane. Despite her best intentions, she felt herself stiffening when Sarah settled her small bony bottom into place. She arranged her arms around Sarah with the book in front and leaned her chin on Sarah's shoulder.

" 'But the window was closed, and there were iron bars on it, and peering inside he saw his mother sleeping peacefully with her arm round another little boy. Peter called 'Mother! Mother!' but she heard him not; in vain he beat his little limbs against the iron bars.'" Jane wiped away tears with the back of her hand. Her children had got used to seeing her cry and waited patiently for her to regain control. She couldn't help thinking about Marion asking why Caitlin had been the one who got to 'fly away' but she would never have another baby.

Her attention shifted back to the child on her knee. Sarah never completely relaxed. She couldn't seem to accept that she was worthy of… of even this – sitting on her mother's lap.

GEORGE AND JANE waited anxiously outside the headmistress's office. Jane kept unfolding and refolding the letter. They had both been provided with a cup of coffee. Inside the office a child was being told off. Jane hoped it wasn't one of hers. Silly thoughts kept going round her head. Nothing really seemed to matter anymore. So what if she was going to be admonished in some way about Marion? Nothing was important anyway.

After Caitlin died, Jane's breasts were painfully engorged. She couldn't bear to express her milk once they took Caitlin away. The pain, the feverishness, the ensuing mastitis all seemed perfectly appropriate. Of course it should hurt! And so what if she developed an infection which could kill her? She refused to do anything to negate the physical manifestations of her loss, including swallowing the pills they were trying to give her 'to make the milk go away'.

•••

THESE THOUGHTS WERE still going around her head when Miss Carmichael let them into her office. An angelic-looking boy with bunched fists passed them on his way out. He stuck his tongue out at the headmistress behind her back and Jane felt a giggle bursting inside her.

"Mr and Mrs Wilde." Miss Carmichael re-established her position behind the imposing desk and reached across to shake their hands. Mrs Hobbs rushed in carrying some folders and flopped breathlessly into a chair the other side of Jane.

"Hello, how *are* you?" She asked pointedly of Jane.

"My husband and I," began Jane with dignity, but couldn't finish the sentence.

"My wife and I," George closed the fingers of his right hand over Jane's left one, "are bearing up." He tilted his chin, which Jane knew meant he was getting control of his emotions. She felt proud of him and squeezed his hand in return. Always, she was on the edge of tears. It would only take one seemingly insignificant thing to tip her over.

"Yes. May I offer again my sincere condolences for your loss," said Miss Carmichael. Jane's fingers dug into her thigh; that woman had only just remembered. But she and George each responded with a curt nod. Miss Carmichael shuffled some papers, picked up a fountain pen and replaced it immediately on her desk. "It's about Marion." The headmistress raised one eyebrow at Mrs Hobbs, who opened the top folder on her lap.

"Well it's about Marion *and* Callum, really," continued Mrs Hobbs, "but mainly Marion. I wanted to show you this." She turned the folder round so Marion's parents could see. It seemed to be a very neatly written story with some precise illustrations at the bottom. "There are lots more like these," Mrs Hobbs explained, turning pages and tilting the folder at them. They flicked their eyes over the words and pictures. "This one," Mrs Hobbs said, "is Marion's, and this one," she pointed to another, "is Callum's."

"Yes." Jane couldn't think of any other response and didn't know what Mrs Hobbs was getting at. Miss Carmichael watched their reaction closely.

"These children are five years old, Mrs Wilde," she said, as if she thought Jane might have forgotten.

"Yes," Jane repeated. She looked at George, who nodded in agreement.

Miss Carmichael asked Mrs Hobbs to get out another folder. She slid it from underneath the first two and took them on a similar journey through its contents, this time of repeated squiggly letters and very simple sentences. "You see," she said almost accusingly, "this is the work of a normal five-year-old. We are concerned about Marion and Callum, but especially about Marion."

"I don't understand," said Jane, "what has she written about that's so wrong?"

"It's not what the stories are about, Mrs Wilde," expressed Miss Carmichael, "it's that they are... like this."

"Could you please explain what you are getting at?" George put in.

"What I mean, Mr Wilde, is that it is not normal for a five-year-old – for two five-year-old children in this case – to be writing stories of this standard of grammar, with this depth of understanding of narrative and form. Young children should not have this level of perception. They do not generally use the kind of language and vocabulary we see here."

They sat for a moment in stunned silence. Mrs Hobbs looked apologetic.

"You're complaining that my children are articulate?" George wished to confirm.

"Or geniuses?" suggested Mrs Hobbs.

Miss Carmichael shot her a whiplash glance. Then her shoulders slumped a little. "I'm not sure what we can do with them – we have nothing to teach them as far as reading and writing are concerned," she finally admitted.

"Are they giving you any trouble in these lessons?"

"Oh, no, not at all. I set them a theme for a story, and they just get on with it." She gave Jane a quick, bright smile. "It makes my job easier really – I'm so busy trying to teach the other children their letters!"

"Then leave them to get on with it." Jane offered her face a delicate touch from her handkerchief. "There's really no point seeing problems where there aren't any." *As if I need any further problems created. There's only one problem of any importance, and that's the fact that my baby has died. Caitlin is dead. Oh dear God, Caitlin is really dead.* All in silence. It could not be sounded.

Miss Carmichael studied the couple in front of her for a moment. Jane knew that the woman saw none of the relentless activity behind her own composed countenance. Then the headmistress lowered her eyes. "Another thing about Marion." She paused. "I think Mrs Hobbs has already mentioned it to your husband?" She glanced at both George and Mrs Hobbs as she finished her sentence. Mrs Hobbs nodded. Jane's husband simply looked blank.

"Marion's communication difficulties?" Mrs Hobbs prompted. Jane looked at George, who continued to look blank for a few moments more before he obviously remembered. His face collapsed as he turned to her. "It was on the day that… I'm sorry, love," he said. Jane felt his arm come around her and give her a comforting squeeze. Jane nodded and made more use of the lace handkerchief, dabbing with it first at her eyes and then her nose. She wished she could place it over her face and not have to work so hard at creating an interested expression. Mrs Hobbs averted her own eyes and hurried back into the conversation as if afraid of Jane's emotion.

"Marion doesn't say a word in class," she said. "Never — she hasn't spoken since the first day she came to school, when she told me her name. She just gives me that peculiar stare of hers whenever I ask her to use her voice."

Chapter 14

Sarah

CAL LEANT AGAINST the banister, arms folded across his chest. Marianne halted like a frozen rabbit in front of him. Cal seized her hand, drawing her forward, grasping her with both arms. His closed-eyes expression was like when he last saw Marion. There was something Pre-Raphaelite about their pose, the way she hung limply in his embrace. By the time he released her, the cotton scarf she had worn around her shoulders had un-knotted and slid slowly down to fall in a heap on the floor. She put a hand out to the banister to steady herself. He had a set look to his face.

She bubbled back into animation, verbosely admiring the farmhouse table, the original butler sink, the old fireplace. There was something puppet-like about her movements, jerky and uncontrolled. I remembered that our Marion was never interested in the furniture or what things looked like. She only yearned for a spiritual connection with the natural environment. She wanted to withdraw from her very body and its base purposes. Marianne, though, was vibrant and physical. She kicked off her sandals, said she loved the feel of the cool tiles beneath her feet. She was enchanted by every doorknob, shelf and brick. Cal's expression developed into pained longing. The girl had set into effect an unpredictable chemical reaction in our home that I could only see would lead to an explosion.

"Please may I have a look upstairs? This is such an unusual house, would you mind if I had a look around – would you show me, Sarah?"

"Of course." I unpeeled myself from the doorframe. But Cal intercepted me.

"Come with me, Marianne, I'll show you where you'll be sleeping."

Sleeping? It made sense, it would have meant a lot of journey time for a one day visit, but for some reason it hadn't occurred to me. With a happy, backward glance Marianne followed Cal up the stairs. I threw some vegetables into the sink and turned the cold water on, listening out for them. I could still hear her chatter as their footsteps criss-crossed the landing above my head.

Her voice got muffled as they creaked over the floorboards in the three bedrooms. Transferring the washed vegetables onto the kitchen table, I placed an onion on the chopping board and selected my favourite knife from its hook. But as my fingers touched the handle the floor rocked beneath me, a veil of red came down like a mist. Pins stabbed the back of my neck; the cold feeling crept up over my scalp. The knife clattered out of my hand onto the table. It bounced off the edge, hit the floor. I watched, stunned, as it jammed itself between the tiles. The blade made a faint humming sound, vibrating on its point. I couldn't move.

Cal's voice came from far off. "Sarah, just bring some bedding up to the attic for Marianne, will you?"

I gave myself a vigorous shake, pulled the knife out of the gap between the tiles. I turned it over in my hand, caught sight of a ghost-like reflection in the blade but it didn't look like me. "Sarah!" Cal called again, and my breath caught in my throat. I laid the knife carefully on its side on the table. Grabbing bedding from the spare room on the way to the attic, I tried to breathe evenly as I struggled up the narrow staircase. A curtain of dust hung in the empty space. Cal and Marianne stood very close to each other by the far window, gazing across fields to the sea. Marianne had slipped off her shapeless cardigan and hung it over a horizontal beam, her arms and legs exposed by her floaty, faded dress. Light shone through it, casting her body into skeletal silhouette. Nausea engulfed me. I knew Anorexia's final act.

I crossed the large expanse of floor to the single bed nestled under the eaves, dropped the bedding on it. I'd planned to choose this place as my bedroom and painting studio when Cal and I moved in, but in the end the space was too vast; I didn't like being so far away from the windows, so I chose my smaller room downstairs where I could lie next to the window and smell the sea, and we had the brick building in the garden converted into my studio. At the creak of the mattress Marianne rushed across to me, her footsteps so light they barely registered on the floorboards. "You should have asked for help!" She shook her head at me. I was thrown by her attitude. She seemed to belong here, not me. Cal continued standing by the window, arms folded around himself.

"She gets paid for her work." He abruptly made for the staircase, his face like stone. He kept his gaze fixed in front.

HIS FOOTSTEPS THUNDERED down the stairs. Marianne looked at me, the edge of a sheet held up to her chin with both hands. I realised I'd been holding my breath. I exhaled and looked back into her strange, familiar eyes. The moment buzzed in the close air between us. A thick hank of hair had escaped from one of her plaits, and I wondered how it had happened. She ran both hands outward along the sheet's edges. Flicking her brittle wrists she sent it billowing in my direction. I caught it and together we spread it over the mattress. The oddness of the situation pressed in on me. She was panting slightly. She had pulled me back into the past; Marion was standing there with barely the energy to orchestrate her breath. I tried not to stare at Marianne's concave stomach, hip bones protruding through her thin dress. Sickening reminders of *you will die if you carry on like this.* And she had.

"I…" Marianne began, "It's great of you to let me stay. Thanks ever so much, Sarah."

"Stay?" I panicked. She looked over at the window and back again. The colour of her eyes changed from amber to green. "For the night, I mean, instead of me having to get the train home today. I'm… It's not very good at home at the moment."

She bent and tucked the sheet in under the mattress. I did the same on my side of the bed. The translucent skin at the back of her neck looked vulnerable. I still had the sick feeling in my stomach. Heaving the quilt awkwardly into its white cotton cover I picked it up, shaking it into the corners. I wheezed audibly. Marianne paused while I took a minute to steady my breathing. "It's a bit dusty up here. We'll have to open all the windows." *Why on earth didn't Cal put her in the spare room?*

Marianne smoothed the sheet and tucked it in more tightly with a brisk movement of her hand. She made a sweeping gesture with her arm. "This is an absolutely fantastic room, I love it."

I picked up the pillows from the floor and we grasped one each, eased them into their cases. Marianne gave me a smile, and then she took off across the floor, pirouetting like a ballerina. She paused for a beat before executing a series of breathtaking leaps, devouring the entire attic beneath her opening and closing leg spans. Her plaited hair lifted each time she left the floor, slapping down again onto her shoulders. She grunted each time she landed. The floor bounced, reverberating through me. Blinking rapidly, I pressed my hand to my chest and held it there, counting breaths.

"I took ballet lessons for twelve years." Her breath came in hoarse rasps. "I don't do it anymore." She performed another slow pirouette, escaped strands of hair an electrical halo in the light from the roof windows. "This room is a perfect practice space!"

I heard Marion's violin music in my head; saw her face as she played. I dropped onto the bed, weighed down by the memory and the reality of this girl's emaciated condition. The answer was obvious before I asked the question, but I wasn't sure whether she understood that I already knew the outcome of her story. "So, why did you stop?"

"Oh. My doctor told me I had to stop doing exercise. A while ago now..." Marianne twisted her long fingers, face blazing. She began to unravel the elastic bands from the ends of her plaits, releasing the trapped hair with her fingers into rippling waves. "Is it OK if I put some things in that cupboard?" She dragged her cardigan down from the beam, still panting. She opened the small oak cupboard at the side of the bed and placed the cardigan inside. "The carved edge around this door and the shape of the drawer handle remind me of the furniture that used to be in my grandparents' house," she said, stroking the wood. She seemed perfectly happy to hold a one-sided conversation and I was relieved simply to sit and listen. "At home I have a tiny room. I could have carried on sharing a larger bedroom with my sister Charissa. But we're so different."

When I didn't answer she shrugged, restless. She picked up seashells I'd placed along a horizontal beam after my first forages on the beach, years ago. She inspected them individually before replacing each one reverentially in the exact spot she'd removed it from. I straightened my back, digging my fingers deep into the muscles there, made an attempt at communication.

"So what's Charissa like?"

Marianne leaned against the beam. She rubbed her nose with the heel of her hand and screwed up her eyes. "Gorgeous. Everybody says so. Brown hair and lovely green eyes — she's really slim. She's been working as a model since she was seven. Mum pushed her into it. Dad never agreed with it. She recently got signed by a new agency." Shutters closed over her face. She pushed away from the beam, stretched her thin body with her arms above her head. "I'm gonna get all those windows open."

The sound of the sea, magnified in the upside-down boat shape of the roof, was as restless as she was; trapped inside instead of drifting in and out as it did at the open window of my own room. Another reason why I hadn't enjoyed sleeping up there.

CAL SEEMED TO have gone somewhere. Marianne offered to help me chop vegetables for the soup I'd planned to make. She hesitated before she lifted the knife and those tiny needles pricked my scalp again but I ran my fingers through my hair, brushed the premonition away.

Still, I was sure I noticed a tremor in her hand as the knife went through the onion. It may just have been a coincidence, or a mistake on my part. We finished making the soup and she suggested that since there was still no sign of Cal we eat alone but I was the only one who ate. She simply pretended to take sips off the end of her spoon. She picked up her bread and broke it, dabbing up miniscule crumbs and transferring them to the tip of her tongue from her finger. When I'd finished eating and Marianne had finished not eating, we cleared away in silence. Pink highlights emblazoned her cheeks. Where the hell was Cal?

Chapter 15

1970

Jane

JANE WAS REMOVING a tray of flapjack from the oven when Callum came bursting into the kitchen, slinging his school bag down on the floor. He went over to the fridge, peering inside. His mother took a moment to place the tray carefully in the centre of the kitchen table before wiping both hands on the apron tied round her waist. She gave Callum one of her looks.

"Oh, for God's sake!" exploded her son. But he closed the fridge and reached down to retrieve the blue bag as well as the tie he'd already pulled off over his head and flung on top of it.

Jane listened to his footsteps going across the living room into the vestibule which divided the front hallway from the back part of the house. It had leaded glass book cases on one side and the other half was a large cloakroom with ornate pegs around the walls. She hoped he wouldn't embark on one of his rages. Something could have upset him at school or on the way home – giving him one of her looks could have been enough to initiate meltdown. Her hand felt unnaturally tense;

Jane looked down and realised she was gripping the handle of the kettle far more tightly than she needed to.

Callum returned to the kitchen in a better mood. His mother was pleased to note that he'd divested himself of his school blazer, which she hoped he'd hung on a peg alongside the bag. She placed a cup of tea in front of her boy. He stretched out his hand and kept it hovering over the gently steaming flapjack, offering his mother a beguiling grin. That hank of hair, just like his father's, was flopping down over his forehead again. "Pretty please…?"

"Oh, go on then." Generally Jane's rule was that the children ate fruit when they arrived home from school but Callum could always get round her. By 'the children', she meant Callum and Sarah, of course. Marion hardly seemed to eat anything, but she would get over that. Jane washed the pots from her baking session and left them to drain while she cut up the rest of the flapjack and placed the pieces in a biscuit tin. She did the same thing with a cake she'd also made and found a third tin in which to accommodate a batch of scones.

"You've been busy." The boy licked his fingertips delicately. "Were you working at the library today, Mum?"

"Only this morning. It was my half-day. Tomorrow I have the whole day off so I plan to get the rest of the bathroom painted."

"You're a Supermum." Callum knew exactly which buttons to push to wind her up, but also which ones would make her feel appreciated.

"What did you do at school today?" She stepped onto a stool and lifted the tins one by one to the top of a wall cupboard.

"I thrashed Neil Peterson in the science test!" Callum banged a fist on the table. "Oh and Mr Piper told me I'm getting 'Man of the Month' award in debating society, for the third time in a row. Can I have another piece of flapjack, please?"

"No, but you may have an apple if you're still hungry." Jane gazed fondly at the top of her son's head as he reached for the fruit bowl. "Have you got any homework to do?"

Callum bit into the apple and spoke with his mouth full. "Just some geometry, I need to get it done quickly; I'm taking Lisa to the cinema tonight."

Jane stiffened. "What are you going to see?"

"Love Story; Lisa wanted to see it." He made a vomiting gesture. Not this already. Jane wanted to keep him young for longer. Her son was growing up so fast.

"Well, make sure you finish your homework first. That's more important. There'll be plenty of time for dating when you're older."

Fifteen years old. An ache pulled at her insides; he was leaving Marion behind. She wished she knew how to construct a conversation with her daughter. Callum looked up then and as if reading her thoughts asked if Marion was home yet. Jane reflected that she wouldn't know if Marion was. She crept in so silently, usually through the front door, which was far enough away from the kitchen for Jane not to hear her. Jane had even tried waiting in the front room looking out for her daughter but she'd never managed to be around when Marion came in. *I wish there was a co-educational grammar school the twins could have gone to together.* Jane worried that Callum's new relationship with Lisa would cause further problems for Marion.

Lisa was about as visual a contrast to Marion as you could get. Plump to Marion's thin, with an effervescent character that made up for Marion's silence. She had long hair, ironed straight although it had never seemed remotely wavy to Jane in the first place. As well as being friends since toddlerhood, Lisa and Marion played in the school orchestra together. Jane envied her friend Brenda, who had uncomplicated daughters with whom she seemed to get on so comfortably. Jane fretted that if the burgeoning relationship between Callum and Lisa developed and they one day got married, she might have to share grandmother-hood with Brenda, and Brenda would be better at it than her. "I don't actually know," Jane answered her son's question. Callum gave her an unfathomable look in much the same way as Marion did. An expression which always caused her to feel as though she'd disappointed her children.

The twins were still close, but whereas as small children they'd chattered in some sort of secret language, now she only heard Callum's low voice through the closed door of the room they called their office. They each had a desk with a typewriter on and reams of filled sheets of paper crowding the drawers. Sometimes Jane stood at the door of the room if it had been left open a crack, surveyed her twins as they worked. Watching Marion with her brother was like catching glimpses of a wild animal in its natural habitat. If Callum happened to comment or ask Marion's advice on anything, Marion would look up in an ordinary way instead of with that guarded expression which was her habitual countenance. She would smile and even laugh with her brother. Resentment wriggled inside Jane. *If Marion can behave 'normally' with her brother, why can't she do it with everyone else?*

Sarah was the only one currently allowed to read the twins' novels – that was how they described their work. Sarah had been appointed their editor apparently. And it seemed she wasn't permitted to divulge the contents of those pages.

Callum pulled his eyes away and said, "I'll go look then." He turned his head halfway back towards her as he reached the doorway: "Ta for the flapjack, Ma..." Jane took a deep breath after he'd left the kitchen. She was leaving it up to her son to retrieve his sister from whatever abyss she was falling into. And she knew that was wrong but she didn't know what to do about it.

◆◆◆

SARAH CAME IN through the back door. Jane had got a casserole in the oven and had just finished hanging washing on the ceiling-mounted clothes airer. She was struggling with the pulley and Sarah immediately dropped everything to help her. Sarah was sixteen. She was small for her age and looked a lot younger, a fact she hated now but her mother knew she would be grateful for later. Jane's eldest daughter was much prettier than she was aware of; she wore her blonde hair in a pixie cut which curved around her pointed face and made her blue eyes appear enormous. Jane was conscious that Sarah kept her inner self hidden away. She had thought of taking her to see someone professional, but she was frightened of exposing her own weaknesses to Sarah in the process of emotional examination that would be bound to be expected of both of them. She wanted to appear rational and sensible, a rock Sarah could grasp onto if the storm hit too hard. But how slippery that rock had become. If Sarah needed to reach for it – would she be able to hold on? Jane didn't even trust herself so why should Sarah?

Every time Jane looked at Sarah she thought of the sister who'd exactly resembled her. Caitlin would have been ten years old by now. This association was painful not only for the memory of her baby daughter's unnecessary death, but also because Jane felt she'd done a bad job of dealing with Sarah's loss. She told herself she'd cut Sarah loose in order to protect her from her own grief – but she knew she had really done it because she had nothing left for anyone else. Without George… she dreaded to think what would've happened. But Sarah had been strong, always looking out for her mother and the twins. She'd seemed to manage. Only now that she was a teenager, Jane was beginning to see the results of the damage done early on. Sarah was stuck in a role – the 'good' one. She was secretive and her only outlet for expression was her art.

Jane held the hanging clothes-airer cord in place while Sarah secured it on the wall hook. Sarah then went to retrieve her things from the floor where she'd dropped them in her eagerness to assist. Jane ran a slow finger up the tautness of the cord. The vibration transmitted through her body. She must hold on tightly. Her eyes surprised her by filling with tears. She sensed Sarah hovering in the doorway and turned to speak before an opportunity was lost. "Would you like a piece of flapjack?"

Sarah hesitated, but nodded and carefully placed her things in a neat pile on the dresser. She sat down at the kitchen table.

"Have you had a good day at school?" Jane removed the tea cosy from the pot that kept warm on the stove, pouring out two cups. The cup rattled in the saucer and some tea dripped onto the tablecloth as she passed it to her daughter. Sarah dabbed at it with the handkerchief from her pocket.

"Oh, we went on that field trip to the Wilberforce Museum…" Her voice petered out. Jane realised that she hadn't noticed Sarah wasn't wearing school uniform.

"For our History project." Sarah added. She didn't say *Remember?* But she hinted at it with the look on her face.

"I'm sorry Sarah," said Jane, "I should have remembered. Did you enjoy it? I hope you had enough money for your lunch. It's just that I had to get to the library earlier than usual this morning and, well…"

"It's OK." Sarah took a sip of tea and a tiny bite of flapjack. Jane worried she might be going the same way as Marion.

"I took a packed lunch," Sarah explained, "and I got a tea in a café on the High Street with Helen. We were allowed free time during lunch."

I wonder if she is still seeing that boy from Callum's school. Helen's mother had mentioned it to Jane at Church. But Jane didn't ask Sarah.

———◆◆———

WHEN MARION CAME in the kitchen Sarah felt the tension. She entered from the front of the house, still wearing her school uniform. She carried herself aloofly, like a dancer in performance. She made a noise pulling a chair out and then slid carefully onto it. She rested an elbow artfully on the kitchen table, putting her chin in her hand and fixing her gaze on Sarah until Sarah would meet her eyes. "What?" Sarah asked crossly in an undertone. Marion continued to pinpoint her gaze, until Sarah's eye was taken to the thinness of her sister's wrist, sticking up out of her deliberately ruckled-back blazer sleeve. Now Marion was satisfied that Sarah had noticed the perfect art of her bones. She swivelled the wrist slightly, with a sly, proud expression. Their eyes met again. Triumphant was the only word Sarah could think of to describe her.

Jane practically had her head in the oven checking on the casserole. "Would you like a cup of tea, love?" she asked, muffled by the oven's regions. With apparent effort Marion moved her body round to face where her mother was and when Jane straightened up with an enquiring expression Marion nodded. "Dinner'll be at about six-thirty." Jane put a tea without milk down in front of Marion. "How was school?"

Always, thought Sarah, Jane spoke to Marion in the expectation of getting an answer. It really annoyed Sarah, her mother refusing to acknowledge anything was wrong. She was convinced – or at least liked to demonstrate she was – that one day Marion would start speaking again as if nothing had ever gone amiss. Marion made an expressive movement with her mouth and raised both hands up at the same time from the table top in a slightly outward motion: school was OK. Marion's face then resumed its habitual shuttered expression. Sarah watched Jane separating eggs to make custard.

"It's your violin lesson tomorrow, isn't it?" Jane used her 'bright' voice. Marion nodded glumly. "What's the matter; are you not enjoying it anymore?" Marion shrugged and traced a pattern of spilt tea on the tablecloth.

Sarah noticed that her sister had somehow contrived to accumulate more tea in the saucer than she'd consumed.

"Have you done your practice?" Jane persevered, putting a pan of milk on the stove with one hand whilst continuing to beat eggs with the other. Marion had only been playing the violin for six months but her grammar school had already had to bring in a more advanced teacher to keep up with her accelerated progress. Violin was one of the few things Marion seemed happy doing besides writing. But she had given up many things she'd previously seemed to enjoy. Sarah wanted to warn her mother not to push Marion so hard, but Jane couldn't seem to stop herself. "Why don't you go up and have a practice before dinner, love?"

Marion narrowed her eyes and let out an audible sigh. Nonetheless she raised herself from the table, taking her own cup and Sarah's to the sink before letting the kitchen door swing closed behind her. A draught blew into the kitchen. "Make sure you hang up your uniform," Jane called after her.

Sarah got up and washed the cups and saucers in the sink, emptying the teapot and giving it a rinse. She took a tea towel from a hook under the sink and dried everything. Then she went over to the cupboards and put the cups, saucers and teapot away. When there was nothing else she could think of to do Sarah compelled herself to speak. "Have you seen how thin Marion's getting?"

There was no acknowledgement from Jane apart from an increased bustle of activity. Sarah forced herself to repeat the words, in an agony of apprehension.

"Mum?"

Jane had finished making the custard and left it on the cooker top with a lid over it. She usually made it well before they were going to eat it because the three children had always enjoyed it more with a 'skin' on top.

"Of course I have. I'm not blind," she snapped.

She took a whisk from the drawer and retrieved the bowl with the egg whites in. She poured in a measured quantity of sugar and then shot Sarah a warning look before beating frenziedly at the mixture. Her words were punctuated by the jolting movement of her body as she whisked. "You-know-what-Marion's-like-Sarah." She paused to pour in another half-cup of sugar. "If-I-go-in-there-all-guns-blazing-it'll-just-make-her-even-more-determined-to-do-whatever-it-is-she's-doing." She paused again, dipped her finger in the mixture to test its stiffness and then resumed beating. "She'll-get-fed-up-of-her-new-game-soon-enough.   She's-just-looking-for-renewed-attention-now-the-novelty-of-not-speaking-has-worn-thin." Jane stopped whisking and Sarah, standing by the dresser with her hands floating above her bag and denim jacket, couldn't decide whether to pick them up or not. She felt chastised.

"I didn't mean to snap at you." Her mother's voice softened. "I do know that you worry about things."

"It's not just that…" Sarah left the things on the dresser and came back to the table, where her mother had finally sat down. Jane held the bowl on her lap and the whisk poised above it in her other hand. Sarah stood at the further end of the table, gripping a chair back. Her knuckles were white.

"What is it then – what's the matter?" Jane asked, beginning to whisk again, but more gently. Sarah tucked a tendril of blonde hair behind one ear.

"Something weird happened…I saw Marion out in the garden last night."

"What do you mean in the garden?" Jane looked worried. "I mean, what time of night?"

The chair skidded in Sarah's vice-like grip and made a scraping sound on the kitchen floor, startling them both. "It happened really late – after everyone had gone to bed," she explained, recovering, "I was looking out at the moon, you know? Then I saw Marion. She was right at the bottom of the garden. Mum, it was creepy… she stood there, didn't move for ages. She was only wearing her pyjamas, and she had bare feet. You know how cold last night was – even when I came back from… from going to the pictures with Helen: I wished I was wearing my gloves then, my fingers were freezing. But Marion – she was standing perfectly still, she looked like a statue, and she stayed that way for about ten minutes, at least that long. It scared me. I didn't know what to do."

"What happened then?" Jane calmly put the bowl containing the whisked egg whites down on the table and Sarah tried to remember when she had last witnessed her mother displaying any emotion. Probably not since Caitlin died. Jane carried the whisk over to the sink and then bent to the cupboard underneath it, pulling out a baking tray which she brought back to the table. She began to drop spoonfuls of the mixture onto the tray and after a moment looked up. Sarah watched Jane's actions as though transfixed. She took a breath. "Oh, she – she kind of shook herself and started rubbing her arms, like she'd just woken up. She looked shocked. Do you think she was sleepwalking?"

"Possibly." Jane seemed non-committal. She bent to open the oven door and pop the meringues in near the bottom, then used a folded cloth to lift the lid off the casserole dish and check its contents. After closing the oven door she stood up again and turned the temperature down. She looked at Sarah with impassivity.

"Why 'possibly'?" Sarah was confused. "What else could it be?"

Jane ran a hand through her hair. She flexed her shoulders and sat down again rather heavily. "Well, it could be something else. Marion's started having these – sort of fits. She's only had them once or twice, as far as I know; something like what you described. Callum alerted me to it. I've been looking into it at the library. I think it might be catatonia."

"Oh no."

"Don't worry though." Jane continued. "I think it *is* a bit like sleepwalking; she's kind of awake but can't move. Marion may grow out of it. But I'm going to try and get her to go to the doctor with me to see about it."

"She won't go." Sarah felt despondent. Jane looked as though she agreed.

"Well, I can only try," she said, "and I can find out as much as possible about it and do my best to help her."

"She was crying!" Sarah blurted out. She let go of the chair abruptly and turned again to collect her things from the dresser. Jane got up with stiff joints and walked in Sarah's direction. "Marion." Sarah explained. "She was crying last night, when she came back in. I haven't heard her cry since she was really small, and then hardly ever." Sarah stood at the door with her things over her arm. Jane stopped in front of her.

"Your veins show right through the skin around your eyes, you know." Then she did something rare: she embraced Sarah. "Try not to feel responsible for everyone else's problems."

Sarah couldn't help but let out a sob, clasped like this. She was so unused to her mother's empathy. After a moment Jane patted Sarah's back and stepped away. Sarah felt awkward now they had to look at each other again, but grateful for the portion of attention. "I'll go and…" She tapped the stuff she was carrying.

Jane nodded. She stretched, her hands in the small of her back. She circled her head a couple of times. "I'm going to have a rest before your father gets home. When you've taken your things to your room, be a love and give the kitchen floor a sweep, will you?"

Sarah nodded. She took her things through the living room and the spooky darkness of the vestibule, where there was no natural light unless the door that led to outside was open. She went down the long, wide hallway and upstairs. Closing the door of her bedroom, she leaned her back against it. She'd moved into this room when she was five years old, the only place she could truly be just herself. She spent some time musing on the events of the previous hour, thinking about her mother hugging her and then asking her to sweep the kitchen floor, and wishing that it didn't feel as though some kind of payment had been exacted for that act of unaccustomed intimacy.

Chapter 16

1987

Sarah

SARAH, MARK AND Cal were in the garden in late July, early in the morning, much earlier than Cal was normally up. Sarah had hoped for some time alone with Mark before Cal arrived to agitate their tranquillity – something he'd been doing often.

Cal wandered down the garden clad only in white boxer shorts. "Parading himself," Mark muttered. Cal obviously wasn't even comfortable out there with next to nothing on. His arms and torso were goose pimpled, his eyes screwed into slits against the unfamiliar morning light. Mark pulled the cloth of the hammock completely over their two bodies. Sarah wore a soft towelling bathrobe into which Mark had slipped his hands, massaging her nipple between his finger and thumb, stroking her stomach in circular motions. She couldn't help pressing her thighs together, squashed up against his hardness. All hidden by the blanket covering them. Only Sarah's wet eyes told of the secrets below. But Cal paraded past Mark and Sarah nestled together in the hammock, strung between a sycamore tree and a hook on the side of the house. He reached the wall at the end of the garden and leaned on it, apparently absorbed in the shining mudflats, his back to them, thick hair lifting in the breeze. He seemed to be deliberately pushing out his buttocks in an animalistic display, territorialism.

Though she had the side of her face resting on Mark's chest, her fingers intertwining with the hairs on it, feeling his heart beating against her ear, Sarah still watched Cal. Mark was doing his best to focus only on Sarah. Even from the distance she was at, without being able to see his face, Sarah knew Cal was cold and that his bare feet hurt from the pebbles. She knew he was feeling ostracised and insecure. They shared an unconscious emotional transference, annoying as hell but inescapable. A symbiosis Cal brought over to his relationship with Sarah from his prematurely severed one with Marion.

Sarah rolled onto her back in the hammock and Mark snaked his hand across to hers and grasped it. Laying side by side they both gazed up into the ultramarine sky. Cal was only doing it because he enjoyed winding Mark up. He must have set his alarm especially to get up at that time, but it was beyond a joke. The tension between Sarah and Mark was growing. Cal was petulant when Mark was around. He said it disturbed his writing, and he made comments about Mark to Sarah which made her feel odd about her boyfriend. Mark counselled Sarah about her relationship with Cal and it put Sarah's back up. Mark had offered Sarah the chance to move away with him, he had even suggested they get married. But Sarah couldn't bring herself to contemplate it properly. Not only that but she wouldn't let herself explore her reasons. Perhaps she was afraid of leaving behind the security of her situation with Cal.

She was thirty-three years old but she still looked and felt twenty. Moving out of her comfort zone scared her. None of her relationships apart from with her brother had ever worked out. Not stepping fully into a life with Mark right then meant it could possibly happen later. Whereas if they got married and it went wrong, well then Sarah would know she had blown her chance to be happy, for good. She was tired of thinking about it. She turned her face towards Mark until her nose was practically in his armpit. She breathed in deeply the smell of his early morning sweat. Mark tilted her face up by the chin and kissed the end of her nose. She smiled when he hummed a snatch of the tune he wrote for her after he first met her, after she'd gone back to England and he couldn't stop thinking about her. He'd made it the introductory track on The Shanbos latest album and it had Sarah's name in the title.

The sound of gravel crunching heralded Cal coming back up the garden, walking gingerly on the pebbles and sharp stones, trying not to show discomfort. He kept his face averted from the two others as if he had not even noticed them, but he passed unnecessarily close on Sarah's side of the hammock. And as he did, she turned her head that way. She could clearly see the contours of his genitals, retracted from the chill, within his undergarment. She wondered what he was trying to prove. She didn't feel right nestled up naked with Mark at the same time as being confronted by her brother's almost-nudity, yet still she struggled with a rush of compassion for Cal. He was nothing but a silly boy, but she was convinced of his need for her.

A cacophony of bird noise started in the tree above. The leaves shook and a feather fell down from the branches. Sarah watched it drifting towards her face until it landed on her forehead. She picked it off and blew it away from her fingers, seeing it caught by a breath of wind. The squawking birds were a bad omen. Nothing about the morning was going right; she could not find the tranquillity they had sought. She pondered on her motives for wanting to wriggle out of the hammock and go after Cal – shake him even, discover the motives for his behaviour. But she didn't want Mark to think she was more concerned about Cal than him. Now that Cal had gone inside, Mark intensified his exploration of Sarah, exposed beneath her robe. This open air activity, sabotaged by Cal's appearance, was after all why they'd established themselves under the tree so early in the morning. Mark's fingers played her in the practised manner of a musician and she knew she ought to be reverberating like a violin string. But her heart was not in it anymore, no matter how she tried to shut out the thought of her brother's downcast face and concentrate on the actions of her lover. She couldn't make the appropriate responses. Mark's hands soon stopped moving. He didn't take them away, just left them inert on her skin. It took Sarah a while to notice, which was about the worst reaction – or lack of, that Mark could have expected.

"Honey," intoned Mark eventually in his gorgeous Irish accent. Sarah opened her half-closed eyes, bringing her vision back into focus, seeing the flitting shadows of the birds among the leaves beyond Mark's face above hers. His eyes were dark, like berries. They were looking at her with concern.

She didn't know what to do or say, but her hand of its own volition crept up and fitted around the back of his head in his springy black hair. Her other hand re-entwined itself in his chest hair. "Honey," repeated Mark, observing that her eyes had filled with tears. "Fair play to you if you're not in the mood, an' all. I'm not gonna force you, baby."

Sarah did love Mark. She really did – probably more than she had ever loved anyone, including her own family. And especially because, up to now, there had been no guilt or sense of responsibility involved in her love for Mark. Until the moment Cal walked past in his underpants and Sarah felt the need to protect Mark from the confusion of her feelings for Cal, as much as she needed to guard the attachment itself for Cal's, and her own, sake. And suddenly everything felt changed.

She cried in Mark's arms, told him that she didn't even know what the matter was. Nothing had changed – Sarah and Mark still loved each other and were happy, Sarah still had the security of Blackberry House, and Cal. But that *was* the problem; Sarah knew it and so did Mark. And so, probably, did Cal. Mark continued comforting her, but she could feel herself drawing away. She could no longer feel his hands on her body, her concentration drifting off like the feather she had blown into the wind.

❖

AND SO WITHOUT meaning to, Sarah made the decision in 1987 to put Cal before Mark. Her boyfriend hugged her until she could stop crying and then they both got out of the hammock. Mark couldn't look at Sarah, but when she was standing body-to body with him she regained her sexual arousal. It had returned too late. Mark stayed for the rest of the day, his mouth a tight line. He ate lunch with the brother and sister, gathered up the few things he'd been keeping at the house, went for a goodbye walk along the cliff top with Sarah and Jude. And then he drove away. There was not much else to do but head down the country towards Holyhead and the ferry to Ireland.

Chapter 17

Sarah

CAL REAPPEARED AT about four. He said he'd had to go into town to fetch a new ink ribbon for his word processor but that definitely wasn't true. On his specific request I'd collected two for him the week before on my way home from a teaching job. I wondered what he'd been doing instead. Marianne transferred her attention from me to him and I sighed. The babysitter had arrived to relieve me of the responsibility of her. A strange draught seemed to blow off his skin onto mine when he brushed passed me, raising goosebumps on my arms. I moved further away. My sense of unreality got stronger.

Marianne chattered at Cal about the act of writing. The two of them were standing by the window. From the other side of the kitchen I watched the tight muscles of his face relaxing. He responded by recommending a word processor, but Marianne cut him off. She insisted that writing by hand was best, or using the 1960's typewriter she'd inherited from her grandfather. It seemed she was crazy about hardback notebooks with beautiful covers. I was interested to hear that she considered herself a burgeoning playwright.

"Sometimes I illustrate the covers myself. Typing *is* impersonal, you've got to admit it, but at least you can feel the impact of the keys on the ribbon and in turn on the paper – you can *feel* what you're writing; you suffer – labour for it in a way as I think you should to produce anything…Whereas using a word processor is like walking along the ground without feeling it under your feet…like being on a hovercraft!"

I stood at the table, pressing my hands around a mug of tea. Cal had a flushed look, one I didn't recognise, or just vaguely remembered. He pushed his fingers through that floppy hair on his forehead and it immediately fell down again. He leaned towards Marianne to reply but she edged back, slipping away from him. His humiliation echoed in me and I gripped the edge of the table. She knelt down to stroke Jude, who gave her one of his goopy looks and rolled over. Cal tapped his fingers on the sink. He was restless in the way he became at public events, or in the past when he'd done something to upset Marion and she refused to acknowledge him. The outwardly fragile girl in our kitchen had an escalating power over my brother. He'd probably disappeared earlier in the day for a temporary respite.

Marianne took over organisation of afternoon tea. Watching the way I sliced and buttered scones with her lips pursed, she came over and took the knife out of my hand. Sun flashed on the blade as she turned it over. "It's much neater if you do it this way." I longed for the time when she would leave. Now that we had an approximation of Marion back in our lives she was as frustrating as ever; everything had to be her way. Pressure mounted in my head. Marion was dead, years had gone by. This was a different girl.

We went out into the garden where the sun still shone. I took a canvas lounger, Marianne took a deck chair and Cal climbed into the hammock. Closing my eyes, I let myself drift away, daydreamed about Mark. After we'd split up, Mark's band went to America. He'd asked me to go with him, offered me a second chance. The Shanbos toured for nine months. He wrote to me but I only replied to one or two letters. I deserved to be punished. On his return from the US, he'd written to Mum asking after her and me, and that summer she went to the music festival in Leitrim again, this time taking Dad, who enrolled on a Bodhran class. And while all this was going on, I'd been despised by my brother. Putting him first was not what I should have done. Cal would not have sacrificed another relationship for me, nor would I have expected him to.

Jolting me back to the moment, I heard Cal asking Marianne about college. He spoke in a deferential voice that reminded me of the way he had verbally courted his contrary twin. Marianne told him she got top grades in all her subjects. She spoke fervently, nibbling very delicately at the outermost edges of her scone. I could see the ripple of muscle activity under the strangely downy skin on her face. Cal's eyes met mine over her head. We were making a truce, I decided. Dissonant bird noise in the sycamore tree brought back that early morning in the garden with Mark on the day our relationship ended. A headache was coming on. I pressed my hand to the back of my neck.

———◆●◆———

I OPENED MY eyes to see Marianne assessing me with narrowed eyes. "Is your head hurting you Sarah? Do you want me to fetch you anything – just tell me where you keep the aspirin and I'll get it." She pushed herself out of the deck chair, moved closer, standing over me. In the hammock, Cal snored. How did men manage to fall asleep so quickly? By now I'd lost the vision in my left eye to jagged, flashing lights. Marianne's face splintered. She was too close. She looked all wrong, threatening. Nausea rose in my chest. I struggled to sit up but her hand on my shoulder persuaded me back. "Lie down."

Shapes swam across my vision. As they came together I saw Marion's hard-eyed gaze in Marianne's oppressive concern. "Tell me where you keep the aspirins," she repeated slowly, "I'll fetch you some."

My voice came out shrill, "I'm going to have a lie down upstairs with the curtains closed and then I'll feel better." I got up and stumbled over Jude on the ground beside me. He let out a yelp and jumped up and I tripped again. I squinted at the fluidly-outlined Marianne from the kitchen doorway. She had an aura of flickering, sharp-edged spikes of light. I pushed the door closed behind me and fumbled my way upstairs to my room one step at a time, moving as much by instinct and familiarity as by broken vision. Sinking onto my bed I reached out an arm and pulled the viridian curtains across to cut out the afternoon shimmer. Jude settled on the beanbag in the corner, watching me closely. My eyes closed as I listened to the river swishing against the shore. The low drone of voices drifted in. Awake again, Cal was quoting Tennyson to Marianne. *Mariana*, a variant of her own name. "*She said 'my life is dreary, he cometh not' she said. She said 'I am a-weary, a-weary. I would that I were dead.'*"

A PERFUNCTORY KNOCK woke me. Marianne approached my bed. She had a mug in one hand and a bottle of painkillers in the other. "I made you a cup of tea; Cal suggested I bring you these." She leaned over to place the mug on my bedside cabinet and I avoided the strong scent of her breath, turning my face to one side. "Shall I get some out for you? Would you like a glass of water as well? Cal said you get these migraines quite often."

"Not often, I wouldn't say. Sometimes." My vision was normal again but I had a thumping headache and felt dazed.

"Cal says you have to watch your health, what with the asthma and these migraines as well." Marianne shook two pills out of the bottle and handed them to me. She went over to my sink and got me a drink of water, then returned to the side of my bed to hand me the glass. The girl sat down in the armchair and watched. I thanked her and took the pills obediently, feeling like a hospital patient. I wondered at Cal's motives, sipping my tea.

"Cal's never shown any interest in my health before." I glanced out the window through the gap between the curtains, squinting to judge the time of evening, or was it still afternoon?

"It's seven-thirty," Marianne offered. Could she read my mind? My toes curled under the thin blankets on my bed and her eyes flicked over their moving shapes, intent as a cat. She stood up and brushed both hands down the front of her dress. She wore her lilac cardigan again and a worn pair of grey leggings, sagging at the knees. "I think I'll go and get my scarf, it's turning nippy. Are you going to get up soon, Sarah?

Cal was asking about supper – I can help you make it." After a pause, "Are you sure you're alright?"

"Just – give me a minute." It came out more sharply than I intended. Her flash of resistance was quickly absorbed back into a bland expression. I sensed she worked hard to maintain that. Again I had the impression there was more to her than met the eye.

Cal had spread hardback copies of his novels out on the kitchen table. He and Marianne were examining the photographs on the back sleeves as I clomped downstairs in my flip-flops. Marianne glanced at me with pinkly highlighted cheeks. "Would you mind if I cooked the dinner, Sarah?" The eager puppy look was back on her face. "I enjoy cooking, and Cal let me look in your cupboards for ingredients. Would you mind if I cooked you a vegetarian lasagne? I don't eat meat, you see."

Or anything much. Cal cast me a disdainful glance. Perhaps the two of us had not made it up after all. I kept my eyes narrowed against the brightness, felt my way over to a rocking chair near the open back door. Dusk was beginning to settle like a blanket – that strange, colour-bled quality of evening light when everything becomes less substantial. A blush of orange had just started to stain the sky, a lone seagull over the mudflats.

"I tend to do most of the cooking at home." She was already surrounded by piles of diced vegetables. "My mum gets annoyed because I refuse to cook meat, but if they want me to cook, they have to put up with vegetarian food."

Her voice floated over me. My auditory perception was drawn to the sycamore tree. The bird sounds resembled music for a change. All my senses had been heightened by the migraine. Pulling myself back I heard Marianne talking about her youngest sister Justine, in the remedial class at school. She refused to go anywhere without her teddy bear and cried at night if she misplaced it. Marianne was concerned about being away from home because Justine liked her to read a bedtime story.

"Justine's ten, but she's more like a seven-year old, really. She seems to be frightened of everything. Mum doesn't have a lot of patience with her, the poor thing." I saw Cal listening carefully. I wondered how different things would have been if we hadn't stood by and watched our sister pulling the plug on her own life. "Who'll make sure she's alright," Marianne asked, "if I'm not there to do it?"

There was a pause. Cal looked at me. He pushed back the wayward hunk of hair from his forehead. We both made an effort to smile. We would make things alright between us. Marianne closed the oven door and brought cooking implements over to the sink. "Let me do that," I eased myself out of the rocking chair. "You're supposed to be the guest and you've done enough work already." She protested, but even Cal must have seen the grimace on my face when another sledge-hammer blow hit the back of my head. He got up, said he would do the washing up. I stood disorientated for a moment, then thanked him and walked over to the table with Marianne. Jude nudged my knees with his nose and I put a hand under the table, stroking him to soothe myself more than anything.

"Will you let me see some more of your paintings later, Sarah?" Marianne broke through the blankness I'd sunk into. "Cal showed me that one above the fireplace in the living room. A seascape, it looks like. I love the colours you use, those deep blues and oranges. Cal said you've had loads of exhibitions."

"I haven't for a while. I kind of stopped getting inspired once I trained to be a teacher. The work you do then is mostly associated with your classes. Most of my old paintings are in the studio – it's that brick building near the bottom of the garden. We can have a look in the morning, if you like." I couldn't really blame my lack of recent production on the teaching. My classroom jobs were sporadic to say the least. Closer to the truth was that my inspiration was drained by Cal. I let it be. I was paid to do whatever he needed me to do and whenever he needed it. Before me, Cal had been in possession of a different personal assistant. In more ways than one, I learned from the tears and recriminations when her position was terminated.

"Did you always want to be an artist, Sarah?"

I realised I found it difficult to think of myself that way anymore.

"Did you do lots of paintings and drawings when you were a child?"

Childhood came back to me in a wave of memories, the three of us scribbling away in the playroom, working on our stories. I was being led by my twin siblings. When Caitlin was born, I created a new role as her protector. She was something I could be good at which distinguished me from the twins. This was a role I'd carried out so well that the loss of Caitlin caused the dissolution of my character. So I became the 'reliable helper' all round, defining myself by it.

"Sarah...?" Marianne urged. She looked impatient, jiggling her fingertips on the table.

"I kind of did, but I started off wanting to be a writer. Anyway it turned out I was better at the illustrations so I started to do them for Cal and M... OW!"

The sharp pain in my forehead wasn't a symptom of the migraine – I recognised it immediately. Cal, in the process of putting away saucepans, had given me one of his glares. The twins used to interrupt each other with a concentrated glance like that. I registered the shocked look on Marianne's face, her gaze snapping over to Cal's.

"What's the matter Sarah? Is it your migraine?" Her forced voice reminded me of when she was first introduced to Cal. Only last night. Unbelievable as that seemed. As then, I now got the feeling she was playing dumb. But her expression was also full of confusion. She breathed quickly, on the edge of panic. Cal seemed frozen to the spot, saucepans suspended in mid-air. So I did my usual thing and elected to play the 'everything's normal' game.

"Dinner smells delicious! Would you like a drink of anything? We've got beer, wine, maybe some vodka. Haven't we, Cal? Or we have some juice if you prefer."

Marianne seemed mortified. "I, well, I'm not sure. How much do you think... what calories does vodka have? I can't... Do you have any slimline tonic?"

I hadn't expected that. I shut my mouth quickly and tried to smile. "I don't reckon vodka's very high in calories. I'll go and have a look in the office and see if we've got any slimline tonic."

MARIANNE CONSENTED TO drink vodka with ordinary Schweppes – the merest splash of it, and lots of ice. She ate no dinner. I was fascinated by the way she disguised not eating. Anyone could have sat with her and believed she'd eaten a meal. Even the food left on her plate could be explained away by a small appetite. She was clever. Just like Marion. She served large portions of lasagne to Cal and me and then placed the dishes of vegetables on the table for us to help ourselves, detracting our attention from the tiny portion of lasagne on her own plate. She moved her food around, would lift a forkful up to her mouth, stopping half way to make an observation or a joke, during which time the fork would be lowered discreetly back on the plate and the food tucked into a neat pile. By the end of the meal the amount of food I had left was roughly the same as Marianne's, only I'd eaten a large dinner and Marianne hadn't imbibed much more than the smell it.

"This is good." Cal kept his eyes on his own food. "Is there any more?"

"Here, you can have the rest of mine; I'm full," Marianne laughed, pushing her plate towards him. "Was that OK for you, Sarah? Are you not very hungry tonight? Perhaps you're still feeling a bit poorly. Here, let me take that away for you."

Crafty, Marianne. She served a fruit salad, hers smaller than the rest. I saw her consume only a few morsels of grape. Cal offered to wash the dinner pots. He'd never done this, even as a boy – Mum never expected him to. I let him get on with it, calling Jude for a walk. An owl flew overhead just as I opened the back door, its shadow huge in the slice of artificial light that followed us out. Jude gave a restrained bark. We went out of the garden gate and I took a deep breath, filled with the same hushed reverence as in a cathedral, a sense of my own irrelevance. Everything was stained inky-blue and a choir of voices came from the surrounding water. The tide lapped in over the mudflats, its gentle slosh set against the hoarseness of the ocean from the other direction. I pre-sentimentally missed my home, even though I hadn't yet made a specific plan to leave. Walking along the curved bank above the estuary beach, feeling carefully with my feet in the darkness, I shivered with excitement, not knowing what was going to happen.

Finding a sheltered spot I sat hugging my knees, absorbing the sound of water and the echoing horns of distant boats, Jude's comforting body pressed against me. Orange lights pinpricked the distant opposite bank. The dark had truly fallen by the time we arrived back at Blackberry House, Jude my guide on the uneven path. The clear sky spilled out a million stars.

Jude bounded into an empty kitchen. The pots were washed and put away, the table wiped. There was only one dim light on. I closed the door and pushed the bolt across, then did the same to the back door. I could hear the Beatles and Cal's and Marianne's murmuring voices from the living room upstairs. Turning off the light, climbing the wooden steps I had a strange feeling this night was never going to end.

❧❦❧

CAL HAD LIT the paraffin lamps Mark gave me as a present when he first came over to visit from Ireland. I don't know why I'd allowed Cal to persuade me to put them in the living room. They were placed on identical carved tables Cal had brought back from a book tour in Africa. *She's leaving home* was on the stereo. Cal had Marianne in his arms, their reflection replicated in the tall black rectangles of the two seaward windows, framed by red velvet curtains. Their outlines were so blurred you couldn't tell one from the other. A shudder went through my body. *I walked into the office to find Marion and Cal standing unnaturally close to each other, the same song on the record player. They broke apart, looked guilty when they saw me, well, Cal did. Marion just gave me one of her stares.*

That was a long time ago. I collected a drink from the sideboard, sank into the depths of the tattered armchair near the door. This was a party for two. Cal had drunk a lot of whisky; I smelt it as he passed by dancing a slow, circular dance with Marianne. He lurched unsteadily, Marianne either clinging on to him or holding him up despite her seeming frailty. The song ended and Cal stumbled backwards, ending up just about in a sitting position on the floor with Marianne in his lap. "You don't have to go home, you know. You could stay here with us. Couldn't she, Sarah?" He swung his head towards me. He looked vulnerable, a teenager again.

"She could." I was leaving anyway. I was leaving home. Marianne looked tearful. *Never mind that she's a frail-looking seventeen-year old. There's something stronger in her than in either of us.* I forgot about Jane Eyre or whoever she reminded me of when I first saw her. Marianne wiped a hand across her eyes. Then she smoothed the floppy lock of hair back from Cal's face, a gesture that caused a tightening in my chest.

"It's kind of you both." Her bottom lip trembled. A few seconds later she added, "I'm not sure if I'd be able to leave Justine, though." She struggled out of Cal's arms into a standing position, looked down at him. Then she turned and went over to the record player. "Can we have this on?" She held up a record. Cal's head dropped into his hands. U2's *War*. When *Drowning Man* came on it had the expected effect; staggering to his feet, he started pitching around the room. By now I was half asleep, head resting in the wing of my chair, feet curled under me.

I was brought alert by something Marianne did. Propped in a corner of the room sipping her drink, she put it down and moved decisively towards Cal. She placed her hands on his forearms. There was something mechanical about her movements. The skin on my arms went cold. I opened my eyes fully and watched her hands slide up behind his elbows, heard her speaking to him in an undertone. She stood on tip-toes, her mouth close to his ear. I couldn't hear what she was saying but I picked up the insistent tone. Cal appeared spellbound, either by her words or her grip on his arms, I couldn't tell. It could have been the intent way she was looking at him. Whatever she was saying, there was something so assured about her it startled me fully awake. She had the hard look of Marion again.

As when Cal had first embraced her, her body suddenly went loose, sinking against him. Her bony arms crept around his neck, long fingers linked at the base of his skull. In a slurred voice, muffled by her hair, Cal mumbled along to the music. By the time the song finished they were kissing each other. Dread weighted my joints, made it hard to move them. This all felt so wrong. But I floundered in indecision, how could I stop them – physically drag them apart? This must be wrong. If she was somehow Marion then the wrongness was because she was his sister but if this Marianne was a completely independent spirit – I mean had never been

Marion, then the situation between the two of them was still unorthodox. Marianne herself had pointed it out: he was old enough to be her father.

Weren't they both vulnerable? Marianne because of her age and anorexia, Cal because he wanted his twin back. But the way Cal was holding her was in no way fraternal. His hands moved roughly over her hip bones. I feared she might break. But he pulled her in tighter against him, kissed her face. It made me hold my breath, wondering how he could bear the bitter smell of hers, but he didn't seem to notice. She ran her hands up and down his spine; her head tipped back, eyes closed. This was a different Marianne altogether from the one we had met the previous night. I suddenly saw how manipulative she was, not nearly as vulnerable as I'd believed.

I escaped to my own bedroom, pulling the living room door shut behind me as I left. In my room I studied my reflection in the mirror above the basin, trying to connect to something familiar. But choosing my own image was a mistake. My eyes looked smudged, my face pale. I could hear music thudding through the wall. I got into bed, pulling the covers up over my head, wondering what Cal and I had invoked with our curiosity.

Chapter 18

MY RACING MIND was trapped, my body pinioned to the bed. But eventually the sleep paralysis eased and I managed to move one of my fingers. Sensation returned to the rest of me. I fumbled for my inhaler on the bedside table but my fingers closed over nothing. I'd knocked it with the back of my hand and heard it crash to the floor. Before I could bring myself round I fell asleep again, as suddenly as dropping over a cliff. I dreamt about Marion, wearing pyjamas with little flower buds on in our old garden. She reminded me of someone, but my sleep-drugged brain couldn't think who.

The next time I opened my eyes there was a hint of light. Something was wrong. The quiet felt excessive, made my ears ring. I sighed noisily, if only to be able to hear a solid sound. I wished I'd brought Jude up to bed with me. Just as I was about to swing my legs out I heard the back door click closed, followed by the skittering of my dog's toenails. He let out a politely restrained 'woof' – enough to inform me something was amiss. I peered out the window, was sure that I glimpsed a pale figure heading in the direction of the sea. When I pulled my bedroom door open Jude shoved his wet nose straight into my crotch.

"What's going on, Scooby-dude? Have you come upstairs to tell me?" He positioned his face so he was staring intently into my eyes, cocking his head on one side and then the other. Damn. I would have to wake Cal up. Snoring rattled through the floor as I approached warily, mentally steeling myself for his reaction. I prodded him through the quilt. "Wha-uhhh?" He shot bolt upright, hair sticking out at frightening angles.

"I think Marianne's gone out. In the dark. You need to get out of bed." I continued prodding. "Cal, honestly. Wake up!"

He rubbed his eyes with the backs of his hands. "Sweet Mother Mary! Can't you deal with it?"

I bit my lip. "I don't know what's been going on between you and her but I think she might be really upset. I heard her pacing about earlier and now I think she's gone. Don't you even care? Just get up, check the attic. Please!" I still had that weird feeling that this night was never going to end. I continued to push my mind and my limbs through viscous unreality.

"Fuck." Cal threw the quilt off the bed with a violent swing of his arm, pushed me to one side. I rubbed my shoulder and followed him out of the bedroom. The door at the top of the attic staircase hung open. Out of the lamp's range was all shadow and hidden spaces. When Cal reappeared from the dark corners he was shaking his head. He refused to meet my eyes. Now I had to tell him. "I think I saw her," I panted, hurrying after him down the curved stairs. "She was going towards the road."

"Are you sure?" he said. "Maybe you were only dreaming." I could have been. But the fact remained she didn't seem to be in the house. This was confirmed by a check of the rooms on the first floor and the kitchen, office and cloakroom.

"Oh fuck," Cal's face had turned white. "Jesus. We can't leave her out there on her own – Christ, she could be sleepwalking. She could go on for miles…she could end up falling off a cliff. You should have woken me earlier!"

Marianne wasn't in the garden. I had a stich in my side as I pushed open the gate, flashing my torch to the left and right in the opaqueness of dark over the mudflats. I was sure I'd seen her go round the front of the house. It *must* have been her. Back in the house my hands trembled when I lifted the kettle, spilling water as I tried to fill it. Cal pushed past me to search the office for another torch. As his shoulder bumped against the sore place on mine I had a strange feeling that my flesh-and-blood brother had gone. Nothing felt like it should. We both went upstairs to get dressed. When I came down again I carried extra clothes in a plastic bag. I got a flask of coffee ready, if she was really out there in her pyjamas she would be freezing when we found her. Cal jerked his chin at me, keeping his eyes averted. "You'd better bring some whisky as well."

I wondered how many calories it had and if we'd be able to get her to drink it.

⬤

MY FEET PLODDED along the hard road to the sea. The parts of my body felt disconnected from each other. Jude bounced ahead, plunging his nose into the early morning scents of the hedgerows. "We'll walk along the cliff top," Cal said, "then we'll be able to see her whether she's above or below."

Cold, salty tongues of air rasped against my face. I huffed and struggled to keep up. I was shaking. I wanted to wake up from this bad dream, yet at the same time I knew I was awake already. When I managed to speak I could hardly hear myself over the pounding waves. We were standing looking over the beach. "Marion used to have, you know, trances. Mum said they were a bit like sleepwalking. Maybe Marianne's the same."

Cal shot me a sideways glance and kept swinging the torch from side to side. We stopped, searched the dunes to our left on the cliff path. I had no real idea of where the young girl that we had lured into our lives could be. I could only hope her sleep-walking feet might have retraced the route she'd taken the day before when she met me coming back from my walk with Jude, and we'd find her there now. We continued on past the caravan site, Jude raised his head, sniffing the air. He turned to look at me in a strange, conspiratorial way. "He knows something..." But Cal had gone on ahead.

She could have been anywhere. There were no signs of a lost girl. We kept scanning the grey beach and the even darker sea. There was a band of lighter sky on the horizon but any details in the landscape were indistinguishable. In the distance the futuristic structures of the North Sea gas terminal loomed from the early morning fog. The sea boomed. Just as the tide advanced and receded, so did the shifting sand it tried to swallow up. The sea song reverberated around us in a range of deep and hollow voices, a percussive hiss topping the thrum of every bass line. Its music resonated into the fog and I shivered, pinpricks on the back of my neck. Suddenly Jude began scrabbling down the clay slope. Cal followed him.

"You stay up here. Keep scanning the beach but look around up there as well."

If only I had called out to her from my bedroom window. The shock of her youth now seemed to outweigh the strength of character she'd projected. I felt guilty as hell. I placed the polythene bag of clothes and the flask on the ground. *Shit, shit. What are we going to do?* But walking towards the cliff, minding my steps on the crumbling edge, I saw her at exactly the same moment Jude started barking. I could just make out his streaking black shape with its flashes of white, running towards the pale figure that seemed suspended somewhere between the cliff edge and the sea.

"Cal!" I shouted as loud as I could, my voice battling the sea, "Cal, she's over there!"

Cal was in the other direction but he finally heard me and started making for the area indicated by my outstretched arm. But when I returned my gaze I saw Jude, running back towards Cal. I couldn't see Marianne any more. "Oh shit," I muttered under my breath, "did I imagine that?" I scrutinised the area again but even though the light was getting stronger I couldn't see Marianne anywhere.

Cal walked up and down the sea's edge in the direction I'd pointed, turning to stare at me from time to time, his whole body questioning. I forced my eyes to do another inspection, taking in the beach and the sea, but I came up with nothing. In the end I opened my arms in a gesture of defeat which had him heading back towards the cliff. I worked on controlling my breathing, stepping back instinctively as he began climbing the cliff. By the time he'd regained the path, he was irate and filthy. He stamped the red clay off his boots, stood over me punching out forceful breaths.

"She *was* there," I attempted to defend myself. "I saw her. Jude saw her as well. That's why he was barking, he went running towards her just as I started calling you. I don't understand what happened…" I held out a cup of hot coffee. Cal, shivering violently, accepted it.

"Sweet Jesus," he pushed out through chattering teeth. "Get the whisky, pour some in will you?" I tipped a plentiful amount of whisky into the coffee and then screwed the cap back on carefully. His eyes had turned dark in the early morning light. "Why the hell did you take your eyes off her? For fuck's sake, she's under eighteen! Does her mother even know she was staying with us?"

I decided not to reply. What was the point of reminding him of his stupid actions the night before? Instead I attempted to wrap a jumper over his jacket but he shrugged himself out of it. I said, "I had to take my eyes off her to try and get your attention."

He didn't speak but continued sipping, his breath blossoming in front of his face in the chill air. Then he said, "I just can't understand where she's got to. *Jesus*. We'd better get back to the house and see if she's somehow made her way back there and if not we'll have to call someone. Jesus," he repeated, "what's it gonna look like if we don't find her?"

I gathered up the jumpers and flask, stuffed them back in the bag, and we set off along the track to the road. Cadmium highlights defined the horizon now. My eyes, trained to observe, flickered between the white boxes of the caravan site and the broken concrete cubes, remnants of war defences, on the beach near the road. I was confused – I *had* seen her on the beach, hadn't I? Way over to my left in the broad empty part that led to the gasworks. Unless she'd ascended the cliff beyond us and then doubled back and passed behind me while I was still looking out at the beach, but it would have been difficult for her to get back to the house before us or without being seen.

⬩●⬩

THE HEDGES BESIDE the path reached out to snag my clothes. We didn't speak. Cal's face when I sneaked glances at him was impassive. Our hard breaths punctuated the air. My legs shook so much that on reaching our front door Jude nearly knocked me over. As soon as we got into the kitchen, the dog started sniffing the floor. He ran about in excited circles then lifted his head towards the top of the stairs, barking sharply several times. He turned and met my eyes, gave me an imploring look. I was afraid to go up – even though I wanted her to be up there, obviously. Everything about this night – even the day before, and the night before that – was too strange. I was so tired. I tucked the polythene bag under the stairs and sat down. "We'll have to go up." But neither of us moved. Jude's hackles were raised, his back ramrod straight. A ripple of trembling made his black coat shimmer. Why did Marianne not call down if she was up there?

"Oh come on!" My voice snapped the otherwise silence. Cal shook himself. Sweat glistened on his face. His skin looked pasty. I hoped he wasn't going to be sick. He bent and removed his boots one at a time, dislodging each of them with the toes of his other foot. I waited a moment and then pulled mine off too. We stood looking at each other and, as if we were counting in our heads, moved forward at the same time. Jude followed, his nails clicking on the wooden stairs.

Half way up the attic staircase Cal surprised me by grabbing hold of my wrist. The sudden movement sent a shockwave through me, but I was glad of the contact despite his unnecessarily firm grip. By unspoken agreement we moved forward again simultaneously. Jude let out a whine. Changing his mind; he turned back and went downstairs, tail low, ears flattened to the sides of his head. She was there, Marianne, in the attic beneath the open window. She didn't move. The white silk pyjamas she wore belonged to Cal, too big and pulled in tightly at the waist; the cloth stuck to her skin. She looked like a marble statue; translucent folds carved onto her body. Her chin tilted up and her arms were raised slightly away from her sides. She was a vision that to me seemed both shocking and familiar.

Her hair hung in moist strands, weighed down by water. Her eyes were wide open.

"Cal." He flicked on the light, but Marianne didn't move. "Go on," he said. Could it be a trick? I took a step forward, transfixed by her waxwork presence, but my legs refused to move further. "You do it." Memory riveted me in place. So Cal moved forward, one careful step at a time. It didn't look like an act. He said her name and laid the palm of his hand on her arm, drew his fingers all the way down to her wrist. "She's freezing. We need to get her warm. Marianne…" He leant towards her and wrinkled his nose, "She smells of the sea. It's weird. Come and touch her Sarah."

"I don't want to. What's the matter with her?"

His face twisted in a disturbing kind of a smile. "She's been on the beach, or even in the sea. Yet how…? This is so weird." Like one of his novels: the same type of character, the same inexplicable circumstances. He cupped his hands, called her name through them. But she didn't even twitch. "Marianne..." This time the way he said the word was hypnotic. It reminded me of the twins' secret language.

She seemed to waver in front of my eyes. Cal was a magician and Marianne his plaything. I was in a nightmare. I dug my nails into my upper arms to try and stop the shivering.

"You saw something like this happening to Marion, didn't you Sarah?"

Marianne screamed. The sound filled the attic, bouncing off the walls, soaring into the rafters. Cal and I pressed our hands against our ears, cowering under its onslaught. The scream, coming out of her oval-slitted mouth, overrode everything. By the time it stopped I'd fallen to my knees. Cal was paralysed as well. Sorrow pressed me into the ground, primeval, elemental. I had to claw my way into the present: *where am I?* Once I was aware of who I was again, I dragged in a series of shuddering breaths and looked around. Cal's face was ashen. This was no trick. *Oh God.*

Marianne subsided, crumpling in slow motion. When her body hit the floor she sounded like a bag of bones emptying out. Cal crawled over to her, gathered the loose bones up in his arms. I could have sworn he was humming that U2 tune he was obsessed with. His voice was fractured, gaps between each word. "Help me get her into bed." We got to our feet awkwardly with the burden between us. Together we arranged her on the bed. I had to take a rest, hoped my wheezing would subside of its own accord. Marianne settled into the pillow with a burrowing movement but did not wake up. "Jesus, look at her."

I glanced at Cal, pushed the hair off Marianne's forehead, checked for a bump where her head had hit the floor, but there was only a red mark. We peeled off her damp pyjamas, they clung to her cold skin as if they didn't want to let go. Her hair stuck to her in long tendrils. I tried not to look at her emaciated body and didn't want Cal to, pulling the quilt partly over her. I used the towel Cal passed me to try and rub some warmth into her. The motion made her breath judder. She whimpered in protest and tried to turn over onto her side again. When her hair was dry I tucked the quilt up under her chin. "I'll go and get my dressing gown. Try and keep her warm."

I found it hard to pull myself away, yet at the same time I fought disgust. I wanted my mother. Me. I wished we had never met Marianne, or invited her to Blackberry House. But Cal, now he had let go of her, stepped back, "I don't want… to be alone with her. You stay with her while I get it. Shall I bring anything else?"

"Get some socks and err, oh it doesn't matter, just bring the dressing gown and socks – and my crocheted blanket off the chair."

I forced myself to put my arms around her, to imbue her body with warmth. I couldn't stop thinking of Marion on her deathbed. Grief for my two dead sisters brimmed up from the current that ran permanently beneath my every-day life. This was somebody else's baby, and yet she seemed as dislocated from her own physical presence as Marion had been. I didn't think we were the people who could help her. I now realised that one of the reasons I'd been frightened of committing to Mark was the idea of us having a baby and potentially losing it. The possibility of further grief was too huge a burden. After all, my mother had lost two of her children – it could easily happen to me. I'd never have to face sorrow again if I didn't set myself up for it in the first place. I heard a low cry come out of my own body. Grief had come to us though, despite our sheltered lives. Cal and I were being punished for our greed in wanting to know Marianne.

"Sweet Mother Mary!" He returned with the dressing gown, socks, and the knickers – too big for Marianne – I hadn't wanted to ask him for. "What the hell do we do with her now?"

I wiped my eyes on my sleeve. "I'll manage to dress her by myself," I said. "You go down to the kitchen and put the kettle on. She'll need a hot water bottle." It crossed my mind that we should have considered calling an ambulance, but as far as I could tell Marianne was only sleeping. There'd be too many questions, how would we answer them? This girl was a stranger to us. *We brought her home because she looked just like our dead sister, Officer.* "Look in the chest in the office," I called out to Cal. "There's an extra quilt in there." We'd just have to keep an eye on her. My gown was soft, a deep rose-coloured velour that would have wrapped around her twice. While I worked I sang 'Chickadee' in a soft voice, a rhyme that could bring both my mother and me to tears any time we heard it. At the same time as I dressed Marianne I wrapped the grief up tightly and pushed it back down inside me. She was somebody else's baby, not ours.

In the kitchen, Cal said he'd take the hot water bottle up. When I started to hand it over to him he startled me with an awkward hug. My nose got squashed against his chest and I resisted at first, then I gave in. The hot water bottle warmed both of us. Every catch of his breath seemed to echo mine. "I shouldn't have…" Cal choked on his words, pulling away.

"SHE'S FAST asleep; she looks really peaceful." Cal came down and stood next to me while I poured water into the teapot. It felt eerily similar to the night Marion died, except there was no white-faced woman clutching a photograph at the table. No Dad to tell us what to do. And it wasn't over.

"Je-sus," said Cal. "This must be how parents feel. When their kid screams in the night and there's nothing you can do to help them."

We sat down and I poured him a cup of tea, passed it across the table. He curled his hands around the mug, saying he had never registered what his agent John was going on about. "I guess I always turn off when people start talking about their kids. But now I think I've got some idea of how they must feel."

It struck me that Cal and I had both been thinking like parents about Marianne. And yet only the evening before, Cal had been kissing her passionately. I hoped to God he had gone no further than that. Now I could almost forget that Marianne had a family of her own; it felt like she was ours, the same as she'd always been. A sister. After a long pause Cal said, "Do you think we should tell her?"

I didn't have to ask what he was talking about. "God, I don't know. I mean, what would we say? Do we ask her outright if she remembers; what do they call it, a previous personality? How could it work, if she is – was – Marion? Why would Marion come back again: she bloody hated being alive, didn't she?" I was glad we were talking about it. We hardly ever discussed our dead sister. Strange: I could think about Marion and Marianne being one and the same, and yet each a separate personality. Marianne, up there, was a vulnerable child – a different generation. And yet she was also someone familiar, rediscovered.

"She didn't hate being alive." Cal sniffed, wiped the back of his hand underneath his nose before meeting my eyes. His knee jiggled under the table.

"I beg your pardon?"

"She didn't hate being alive." He ran the edge of his thumbnail into a well-worn groove, looked down at the table again. I watched his pushed-back hair slide forward. "She just couldn't cope with it. She actually thought the world was beautiful. She loved it, we both did. Perhaps she thought…"

I twisted my hands together on my lap, waiting. "What?"

"Perhaps she thought it would be easier, in a different body." Cal brushed the table top lightly with his fingers. We hadn't had a conversation like this for a long time. I remembered as children – me, Helen and Lisa, Marion and Cal, playing Ouija board. Trying to 'contact the spirits'. Marion had the idea. Mum discovered us. She told Helen's parents and we were all sent to Confession.

I wished I could contact Marion's spirit – the real Marion – and find out what we were supposed to do about Marianne. "Maybe this was meant to happen, us all being together again," Cal looked up at me, reading my thoughts. "I've missed her so much. Marianne's made the wound raw again."

My chest tightened. "Oh God." I went cold imagining Marion starving herself to death and then choosing to get born again less than a month later into another family. Had everything been leading up to this? And it wasn't even as if her new body was finding life any easier – Marianne's anorexia told its own story. "No." I had to make it definite. "She can't have chosen this!"

Cal curled his fingers inside his hand and rested his chin on the knuckles. He looked at me steadily. "OK, what if coming back wasn't intentional, what if she made a mistake and kind of slipped, into… Jesus, Sarah, I can't bear the thought of it. What if she's trying to do the whole thing again? What if she had to come to us to do it?"

"Stop it!" I said. "We could imagine anything, but it wouldn't necessarily be true. Right now, she's just… Marianne. She has a different mother, father and sisters. Even if she was our sister – before, well, she has another life now. She's been around all this time without us. Without you." I looked directly in his eyes. "You have to start living your own life, without always having to depend on somebody."

It would be a terrible mistake, Marianne coming to live here, drowned in our history. He stared back as long as he could and then dropped his eyes. "I was one of a set. We were part of each other. Sweet…how could it all have happened? I relied on her. Marion made the important decisions." He picked up his mug and swilled down the rest of his tea. *They were fifteen; it happened just before Marion stopped talking. I walked into their office and they were standing very close to each other, her arms on their way down. But only Cal looked guilty.*

"Her being the way she was made me the way I am. She was always the one who drove us. If she hadn't become the way she did I would never have written the first novel, and yet if I hadn't had it published the way I did she might not have deteriorated so much."

We'd been over that a million times and as far as I could see there weren't any new turns to take, so I held my own counsel. Outside, the sun had fully risen and the kitchen was now flooded with golden light.

Chapter 19

THE LAST TIME I saw Marianne before I collapsed into my bed she accepted a glass of water from me, drank it down, but her eyes had a far-away look in them. So I was surprised when I came downstairs at noon to find her in the kitchen rolling pastry. She glanced up and smiled, but there was an unnatural quality to it. She wiped the back of a floury hand across her forehead. "I'm making a cheese and mushroom pie for lunch."

I went down the last few steps, avoiding the pale reflection that loomed at me from the glass over the front door. I asked her how she was and she produced a laugh. "I'm fine, Sarah. I must say, you and Cal are late up this morning, I was expecting you to be an early riser; I thought you were that type. Although I suppose I shouldn't make assumptions. Sorry. Anyway, I took Jude for a walk, I hope you don't mind." My dog was stretched under the table at her feet. I leant down to him and he gave me a guilty look and thumped his tail weakly but did not get up to greet me.

I considered what to tell Marianne.

"We *were* up early Marianne. We were up in the dark, both Cal and me. We had to go out and find you, you were sleepwalking or something. We were worried about you. I'm not sure, but I think you went all the way to the beach."

She digested this. Her guile had left her now. She seemed to be struggling not to cry, staring at the coating of flour on her hands. "Not again." She sat down at the table, wrapped her hands around the rolling pin, her body bent forward.

I moved closer. "This has happened before?"

Still staring at me, Marianne said, "Apparently. I never remember anything. But Charissa told me she saw me standing in the garden one night. And there was the time…" She looked as though someone had just punched her and she was struggling to breathe. Jude stretched again. I saw him give Marianne's ankle a lick. His new friend. He wasn't so keen on her the night before, in the attic. She gripped the rolling pin harder. She was still looking at me. Her face crumpled and then she straightened it. She said, "I don't know what to do. It scares me."

Then something occurred to her. "Oh, that's why I woke up wearing someone else's dressing gown. Did you put it on me, or did…?" She looked perturbed. "What did I, I was drinking last night, wasn't I? I hope I never – I can't actually remember what happened." She picked at a shred of skin on the edge of her thumb. She'd done the same thing in the café bar. I could hardly believe that was only two nights ago.

"I don't know what you did after I went to bed. You and Cal were all over each other." I had a sudden suspicion that there'd be terrible repercussions from this whole thing. We would never be able to walk away from it. I'd seen the way she directed Cal, her hands gripping his arms.

She sucked in her bottom lip, pressed her upper teeth down on it. Her pupils flicked from side to side. "As for the dressing gown," I continued, "I put it on you. Your pyjamas were damp." I decided not to say anything more. I waited to see if she would ask. But she changed the subject.

"I thought we could have lunch together and I'll get the train back this afternoon. I've had a really great time here, Sarah. I don't know what it is about this place, or about you and Cal. I feel I've known you for ages." She got up, her shoulders rigid. The day before, her movements had been fluid, her dance training evident in the way she carried herself. But now she moved with apparent effort. Oddly automated.

Arranging the pastry in a pie dish she tried again to say what she meant, jerking her chin up to look at me. "I don't know what it is." But we both did. Something about the set of her mouth changed when I still didn't answer. She poured the filling into the pastry and put the pie in the oven. Then she collected utensils and mixing bowls off the table, her expression frozen. There was a strange absence of animation in it, implacable as the face of a marble statue. I went over to the sink to help her, but static shot between us making me jump even though she hadn't touched me. Sweat broke out on my forehead. She gave me a helpless look. Silence stretched, taut as a wire.

At lunch Cal could hardly look at her either. When he sat down I almost let out a cry of shock. "What…?" I said, but there was no way to articulate what had unnerved me about his appearance. It was more something I couldn't see. Like he had hardened up, become somehow heavier. I said I would drive Marianne into Hull.

"I'm sorry, I need more sleep." Cal still couldn't meet her eyes. To me he muttered, "I don't feel that well and we've got to… you know." He didn't say 'face the parents'. The thought of Mum and Dad ever finding out about her was intolerable.

How could this phenomenon be explained? We had to stop this now. Forget it ever happened, deliver her home. At least the girl was still in one piece.

•••

AT THE RAILWAY station, light flooded through glass panes in the ceiling, mixed with the sounds of brakes screeching; the relentless rumble of engines. I backed away from Marianne, pretended to fish for something in my bag. I couldn't help it. All I could think about was what a mistake we'd made. Her train pulled in. As I led her into the throng of train boarders there seemed to be a great pair of beating wings at my back, Marianne's panic getting a hold of me. Her voice cheeped like a hungry fledgling. "Will I be able to visit again?"

"Of course you will." *But why do you want to?* I had to fight a powerful urge to run away before she even got on the train. We edged towards her platform, my fists clenched tightly against the sensory offence of her bag with its pointy corners still bumping against her hip. She leaned towards me before she got on and I met her eyes. Sun from the glass ceiling overhead glanced off her hair and I saw how real she was. But she had arrived seventeen years too late. I could do nothing to help her. The same rage welled up as when I watched Marion slowly killing herself. So I said goodbye and walked away. Once she was safely on the train she would be somebody else's responsibility.

In my car the tension finally broke. Around me car doors opened and closed, people pushed between the gaps in the lines of vehicles. They loaded and unloaded their luggage, got in or got out of their cars, arrived or drove away. I sat there for ages, crying as unobtrusively as I could.

On the drive back I could barely stay awake. My eyes were red and sore. I drove whole chunks of distance without remembering how I got from one village to another. Once or twice I nearly missed a sharp bend in the road. I counted off the villages in my head to try and stay alert: Rosengold, Lockington, Otterton, Cammington, Michaelton, Wellgood, Corningham and Skangton. After the gas terminal at Restingham I was on the final stretch of road leading to Pottersea. On the gravel in front of Blackberry House I parked the car at a skewed angle, flung myself out; slammed the door.

"Maybe we should try not to think about – you know." Cal said as I got in the house. "Not until after we get back from the parents' at least. You go up and get some sleep and we'll aim to head off about six-thirtyish. I'll drive, we'll take my car."

Chapter 20

Marianne

SARAH HAD BEEN in such a hurry to get rid of her. It had felt like there was a glass barrier between the two of them when they were in the car. The barrier was still in place when they arrived at the station. The sleepwalking thing she had, it scared people, she could understand that. Sarah had been evasive from the moment she walked into the kitchen that lunchtime, and Cal wouldn't look at her at all. She had told Sarah she didn't remember anything about the night before but elements were coming back. Not all of it. But what happened between her and Cal, the inevitability. The impossibility of resistance – not that she had wanted to resist. But Cal had tried, half-heartedly.

His hands. Long fingers like hers, but browner with coarse hairs on them. The touch of them made her feel alive, woke her up. They brought colour and form to the merest scribble her body had turned into, the thing she'd most wanted to disassociate from. Without this physical vehicle in which she moved though, without its mouthpiece through which to speak, she could never have reached him. Being a solid thing finally made sense. But at the same time it meant that she would have to let her body have its say, abandoning her 'real' self to the cruel control of the physical one.

She scribbled furiously in her notebook as the train hurtled through the flat outskirts of Hull, speeding through industrial estates, brushing against clumps of grey-looking urban woodland, breaking out at last into open air right alongside a choppy brown river which, she came to realise, was the one at the end of which Cal lived. The train stopped briefly at Brough. Afternoon sun deepened the red-coloured coat of an Irish setter sitting patiently on the platform with its owner. It seemed to catch her eye through the window and she thought of Jude. Some gently rolling hills poked up out of the level landscape. The train resumed its motion and the landscape became greener, more awake. Marianne went back over her last few sentences. She had written '*I could never have reached him.*' But it didn't feel complete. She wanted to add 'again'. But she didn't mean again from the night of the TV recording; this 'again' went way back before that. *But how can that be? I'm only seventeen, when could I have known Callum Wilde before?*

Something stirred in her consciousness. Like the first moment a foetus stretches in its mother's womb, not that Marianne would know that. Not yet. But the thing uncurling in her cognizance was similarly both alien and familiar. Hitherto unknown but recognised immediately. She knew beyond doubt that she had known Cal before. *I knew it anyway.*

She put down her pen. A glazed look came into her eyes. Other passengers fidgeted, looked at each other questioningly or focused attentively on their books and newspapers. There was something wrong with the extraordinarily thin girl in the corner seat, but nobody wanted to be the first to get up and check. Her pen rolled about on the table. Her eyes, unblinking, stared straight ahead and her mouth hung partly open. Her neighbouring passengers averted their eyes. But a little boy climbed off his mother's lap and went to stand by Marianne, putting a hand out to touch her. His mother gasped, got out of her seat and snatched him up just at the moment Marianne uttered a choking breath. She rubbed her eyes with the backs of her hands, looked with surprise at the woman withdrawing quickly back into her seat, child tucked securely under her arm.

Pain shot through Marianne's muscles. She was vaguely aware of a jump in time. Something had just happened. *Please don't let it be…* She looked down at where the pen should have been in her hand but it was no longer there. It had rolled onto the floor and was now out of reach under the table. Marianne delved into her bag for another. She uncapped it and words immediately sprang from its tip onto the pages of her notebook.

I remember the day he told us he'd had his novel accepted for publication. I was completely shocked: he'd never said anything about this before, he'd never even told Sarah or me about this particular novel at all. He'd been working on it secretly, in his room at nights, while all the time he and I were preparing our 'first' novels simultaneously in our office, with Sarah acting as editor. He looked at me sadly after he'd made his announcement to the family. He said he'd just wanted to do something for himself and by himself for the first time ever. Later on he brought the manuscript to my room for me to read. He seemed anxious, his hands hovering over the pages like moths. He said I wasn't to take it personally and I thought he meant about going ahead without me, until I read the novel. And then I understood what he'd really meant by that.

She snapped the notebook shut without reading over the words, pressing the heel of her hand down hard as though to prevent them from jumping out and confronting her. She was trembling as she slid the notebook into her bag without looking at it again. Then she twisted her long fingers endlessly around themselves for the rest of the journey. She was very cold and couldn't think of anything that could make her warm again.

❖

THE NIGHT BEFORE, Cal let go of her at the bottom of the attic staircase. When he closed his bedroom door behind him, Marianne stood where she'd been left and stared at the doorknob, hoping to see it turn again and Cal to emerge. But he didn't, and it wasn't long before she could hear his snores from behind the closed door. And then all she could do was swivel round and ascend the attic stairs.

Up there, she paced from one end of the room to the other and back again. Her sub-consciousness filled with the experience she'd had that evening with Cal. Consciously though, she couldn't stop thinking about the food she'd eaten at dinner and how she'd succumbed to so much vodka. She wanted to make herself sick but was afraid she would wake Sarah or Cal if she used the bathroom which was on the floor below, so instead she tried to calculate how many steps she would have to take to negate the added weight of all the foreign matter her body had taken on board.

She must have walked herself into a kind of stupor and then made her way downstairs and out of the house without realising it. Because as the train careered from station to station, she recalled the feel of cold, gritty sand under the soles of her feet, sore after a long walk. Memory put her back on the beach below the path she'd met Sarah on earlier that day. A grey sea sucked sand out from under her and then spat it back again. She remembered darkness and the sea's repetitive voices. But she couldn't recall getting to the beach in the first place.

Somehow, the sea had become Cal's bedroom door – no, something even more desirable than that: the means by which she could be erased. The sea would wipe her clean and transform her into what she was supposed to be. That was right. She needed to get through the door that was the sea, but the sea kept on receding and she couldn't get close enough. So she walked forward and kept on walking, stumbling on the dipped, gravelled sand. The waves came at her, crashing and taunting and she was filled with overwhelming exhilaration. *Come and get me.*

Pebbles rained onto her feet. Sharp spray stung her skin. The noise battered the inside of her head. An experimental symphony of cymbals and percussion, a cacophonous chaos that she needed to be absorbed into. Waves snatched away the sand, caused her to stumble; knocked her backwards. She scrabbled back upright and threw herself forward. *Take me.* The sea opened its throat and swallowed her in the curve of a savage wave which slapped her hard into the gravel and then siphoned her back up in a fizzling swirl of pebbles and shells, lifted her high into the air, held her poised there for an infinitesimal moment.

It gulped her back in, sucked her into itself and then hurled her forwards again, crashing her into the grit and foam. She felt exhilarated: brought alive by agonising, beautiful pain.

She could feel the bruises forming on her hips and ribs. *Yes.* Water forced itself into her lungs. Involuntarily she retched and heaved but didn't try to fight back. But then the sea rejected her, spewing her out the same way she had vomited an unwanted intake so many times. It disgorged her many metres further down the beach than she entered it. It left her shivering on the sand, grains embossed into her thin layer of skin, regurgitated by her expected, so longed-for oblivion.

The flow retreated and then washed over her once more before she pushed herself first to her elbows and knees, and then to her feet. Sand and water deluged off the narrow slopes of her shoulders and hips, the pool at her feet quickly reclaimed by the tide. The choice had been made. It would not take her. So, by then electrifyingly alert, she staggered, dripping, up the beach towards a shallow cliff directly ahead.

Scrambling up to the path above, she was much closer to the road than she'd been before. A hard breeze buffeted the wet silk pyjamas, pulled half undone by the sea, into the grain of her cold skin. She was being blown dry. A seam chafed the top of her thigh as she walked. Heavy, salted ropes of hair slapped against her face and neck. She didn't even wince at the puncturing stones under her bare, leathered feet. The walk back to the house was as surreal as a dream.

THE CONCOURSE OF Leeds railway station seemed impossibly vast. Her limbs were stiff, her body felt heavy. She could hardly carry her bag. Friday afternoon was busy, full of commuters and students returning to or leaving for their home towns – London, York or Edinburgh. Marianne didn't feel as though she was returning home, more that she'd been rejected from hers. She couldn't leave things this way, the brief but impossibly intimate encounter she felt certain Sarah and Cal had no intention of continuing. She had to find a way to break through their wall.

She had to admit she didn't want to discover the full truth of what had happened. She didn't feel in control of her own life, something she had striven so hard to achieve for the past couple of years by trying to cancel out her body.

Too many strange things had started happening. More than her brain could digest. There was only one place that felt right and that had been in Cal's arms. She didn't even know why; he was a man old enough to be her father – and yet. Marianne could see the boy inside, it made no difference that his physical body was older than hers. She *knew* him, that was what mattered, and when his arms were around her, his face buried in her hair, when he pulled back to look in her eyes which mirrored his – she was sure he knew her in exactly the same way.

<hr>

"I FEEL SO safe with you," is what he'd told her last night after Sarah had left the room, when the two of them sank down onto the pile of cushions in the corner. After Cal tenderly removed Marianne's clothes and wept on her skin. "Now I finally have you back again. Now everything is alright."

And she comforted him by stroking back that wayward lock of hair. She'd kissed his eyelids, swollen with tears, and held him tightly, not even bothering about being naked, that he might think her too fat. He had made her grateful to be in her own body.

⬥

AND THIS WAS why Marianne knew she had to make him take down the wall he'd erected between then and this morning. She'd ring him later, when everyone at home had gone to bed. It would be okay.

Her legs were so tired by the time she had urged them as far as the ring road, a part of her feared they would stop moving of their own accord. But she denied this to herself. The heart inside her carried on beating weakly. Forcing her feet up the steps to her front door, she inserted her key in the lock.

Justine flung herself into Marianne's arms. "I thought you were never coming back!"

Marianne slipped the bag off her shoulder and stroked Justine's lovely blonde hair. "I told you I would."

Justine regarded Marianne from under long eyelashes. She took her thumb out of her mouth to say, "Mummy was angry that you never said where you were going, so she looked in your room."

⬥

"WHO'S THIS CALLUM Wilde?" Geraldine demanded at the dinner table. "You've written his name all over your mirror." Marianne was thrown off balance by the fact that her mother had prepared a meal: chicken, mashed potatoes and peas with instant gravy. Haughtily, Marianne helped herself to minuscule portions of the vegetables. She toyed with a pea on the end of her fork and tossed a scornful glance at Geraldine. She couldn't believe that woman. How could she have forgotten he was the author of *The Shell*? She was relieved Charissa wasn't there; she would have recognised the name immediately. But her sister had gone for her weekly appointment at the tanning studio, having eaten her salad earlier.

Geraldine was still staring at her. She knew Marianne hated being watched while eating.

"A friend." She'd reveal as little as possible.

Geraldine frowned. "And for God's sake where did you get to last night? We were worried sick."

At this Marianne put down her fork and met her mother's gaze with a withering look. The only person Geraldine would ever be 'worried sick' about was Charissa. "I stayed with friends. I was quite safe," she finally offered.

Everyone knew she never stayed with friends. Did she even have any friends? She hardly ever went out. She pushed her chair away from the table with a request to be excused.

"I have a writing assignment to complete before Monday." She addressed this to Joseph but Geraldine hadn't finished with her.

"You're a rude, ungrateful girl to go off like that without telling anyone; your dad sat up half the night waiting for you to come home."

Joseph raised a feeble hand but Geraldine had a relentless look. "Not to mention your little sister, crying herself to sleep because you weren't there to read her bedtime story."

Marianne stared at Geraldine. "It's a pity her real mother isn't able to meet her needs then isn't it? Anyway, I did tell

Justine." She said this more quietly. "I told her I wouldn't be home last night."

She glanced at her little sister, whose mouth hung open. There was gravy on the grey jumper of her school uniform. Marianne went over with a flannel and encouraged her to wipe her face with it. "Use your knife and fork properly, Justine."

Geraldine watched. Marianne's words must have stung. "You're only seventeen and already sleeping around. Oh my God!" Marianne saw it dawn on her face. "You really are, aren't you?"

Geraldine seemed half admiring and half disgusted. Marianne guessed that the fact anyone would want to sleep with the daughter she had heard her mother describe as 'scrawny and obdurate' was beyond her understanding.

Geraldine left it at that, returning to the food on her plate with which she had a better relationship. Joseph said nothing. Marianne felt him staring at her back as she exited the room. She went furtively to the telephone in the hall, one ear cocked to the low level bickering between her parents at the dining table. She had Cal's number etched in her brain, never mind on the mirror. She imagined the dark-painted office at one end of the huge kitchen in Pottersea, where the telephone sat ringing to itself. It rang on and on and nobody answered. She put the receiver at her end down. *Maybe they've taken the dog for a walk.* More likely Sarah would have taken the dog for a walk and Cal couldn't be bothered to come down from his room and answer the phone. She would try again later.

Chapter 21

Sarah

CAL REVERSED HIS dusty red car into our parents' driveway next to Dad's clean black one. We sat looking at each other. Cal's face was as familiar to me as my own but as I gazed at him the younger, starker visage of Marianne Fairchild was superimposed over his, his interrupted twin. I wondered what Marion would have looked like by now. The traffic on Beverley Road gleamed in the evening sun, which lighted the roofs of the houses opposite. My parents' home was built in the nineteen-thirties, two storeys high. The house was small and detached with a broad drive and a square front lawn surrounded by an herbaceous border. Completely different from the imposing Victorian terrace on Hull's famous Avenues that we'd grown up in, I could never think of it as home.

Mum opened the front door as we got out of the car. She and I gave each other a tentative hug. Then I watched as she melted into Cal. He was miles taller than her. They stayed hugging for a long time. They'd always been relaxed together, but this time Cal was acting. He had more to feel guilty about over Marianne than I did. His scared eyes reminded me of the little brother who used to try and stop Marion doing crazy things, like when she climbed out the window onto the roof. But he was never successful. Marion did what she wanted, just as Marianne had done the night before.

⋆

"WHERE'S DAD?" I asked on the way into the house.

"Just in the shower," said Mum. "He's been in the garden for hours, I persuaded him to take a day off work for his birthday."

A black and white cat wound itself round my legs. "Leo!"

"He can smell Jude on you," Mum commented. "He's never forgiven you for getting that dog." When I straightened up she smiled. "You're looking tired." She meant well but whatever she said to me always felt derogatory. My eyes did that stupid blinking thing of theirs.

Dad was on his way downstairs. I managed a grin. "Happy birthday, sweet sixty-one!" *You took me around the dance floor after my birthday dinner. We danced to Neil Sedaka's Sweet Sixteen and I was so proud. Cal tried to persuade Marion to dance with him but she refused.*

Dad looked older than he ought to. He'd carried the weight of my mother's grief as well as his own. But he still had the floppy hunk of hair over his forehead that had been inherited by his son. There was an awkward hug between him and Cal. Whereas Cal's eyes were agitated I now floated on a sea of calm, almost dreamlike.

Cal and I both went up to our old rooms. Most of my memories in that room were of holidays and later short stays between flats or house-shares. Cal lived there full time until he bought Blackberry House in 1984, so it was more his home than mine. I showered and dressed in jeans and a peasant top. Downstairs I found Mum in the kitchen and asked if she needed any help. A few guests had already arrived. Most of them stood chatting at the French doors of the dining room looking out at the garden. Dad had lit outdoor candles and a string of fairy lights hung across the garage roof. It looked comforting, pretty.

"You don't have to always offer help, Sarah, you're a guest here. Why don't you just enjoy it for once?"

I can never do anything right. I let the feeling show on my face. But Mum told me not to be silly. She wore an unreadable expression. "I've got a confession to make."

"What is it?"

Mum bit her lip.

"What is it?" I was getting impatient.

"I invited Mark." She said it in a rush. I was confused. For a minute I couldn't think what she meant. Then: *Oh my God.*

I had to sit down. Mum sat next to me with a kind look as though she'd just given me some bad news.

"But.... You said Mark was in Europe. How can he be coming here?" My chest tightened. I'd forgotten to bring my inhaler and felt slightly panicky.

"Mark's European tour finished two weeks ago."

"How though...?" I asked again. "How can you have invited him here?"

"Easily. Mark's a friend of ours and your Dad wanted him here."

You did, you mean. She'd fancied him right from the first time we met him. Then I couldn't believe I was thinking like this about my own mother. Mum got up and slid a couple of trays out of the oven. "He's not able to get here 'til late. Your Dad was hoping we could have a bit of a session at the end of the evening."

A bit of a session – she acted like she thought she was some kind of musician herself.

My knuckles went up to my mouth. It dawned on me that I was really going to see Mark. That night. "But you can't invite him here. Oh fuck." I felt my face reddening at the escaping expletive but Mum chose to ignore it. "I just mean… look at me – look what I'm *wearing*! You never told me – I expected it to be all *old* people. It's Dad's party, for heaven's sake."

"Calm down, Sarah." Mum gazed steadily at me. "You know, you look lovely."

"Maybe to people in…"

She interrupted, "You look lovely, but you're not wearing that outfit for your reunion with Mark."

Now she was getting sinister. She continued smiling and went so far as to take hold of both my hands. My mother took a deep breath. "I've got you a new dress. It's on the bed in my room."

All the things that had happened over the last few days were emotional, and now this. "Why?"

"Because you're my only daughter and I ought to make the most of you. I should appreciate you more; don't think I don't know it." She hated talking about Marion, whereas if you allowed her she would talk about Caitlin too much – Caitlin the innocent one. But she was evoking both of them in her statement that I was her only daughter. If she knew what had been happening recently… But how could I possibly tell her I believed her second daughter had been reincarnated?

"The feeling's mutual." I withdrew my hands.

She wiped her forehead with the back of her arm. "Are you going to have a look at the dress – put it on I mean?" Mum looked pretty with a smile on her face. She looked young again, standing in the kitchen with a finger-mark of flour on her cheek. "I'm just going to pop this next lot of cheese-straws in the oven. They're your Dad's favourites."

My most comforting memories were of her making us something to eat. As a mother of young children, baking had been her sole creative outlet. Since that penny whistle class at the Irish music festival she'd taken up the flute, and she'd told me she'd begun experimenting with watercolours as well. A woman of many interests and talents. Shared activities which had kept her and Dad's relationship moving along. I thanked her and she looked up from the oven with flushed cheeks. A new bunch of party-goers was arriving. "Get the dress on!" She mouthed it with a grin.

THE DRESS WAS made of red jersey, low-waisted with a scooped neckline. Mum had also provided a filled make-up bag, red nail varnish and a red glass necklace and earrings as well as a pair of extremely high-heeled sandals. I couldn't believe she'd gone to so much trouble; then I was sad for not thinking I was worth it. I pulled the dress over my head, smoothed it down over my breasts, hips and stomach. It fitted me perfectly and was exactly the right shape to flatter me. I'd been so lazy with my clothes, maybe Mum knew me better than I realised. But while I was delighted with my makeover I couldn't deny being a tiny bit hurt that she hadn't considered me good enough to attract Mark as I was. What my mother had essentially done was gift-wrap me for a man.

Cal was on the landing when I came out of Mum's room. His tired face stretched open when he saw me. "Fuck me!" Vol au vent crumbs sprayed all over the carpet. He ran his eyes from the top of my head to my high heels. "Sweet Jesus, what's happened to you?" His colour was already heightened. It wouldn't take much to send him crashing over the cliff he was paused on the edge of.

"Is that your way of saying I look nice, Cal?" The red dress made me feel like someone else, which was no bad thing; it had altered Cal's perception of me as well. Just then I noticed Helen coming in the front door with Lisa. Helen was married with two children, and I didn't think she was happy. She looked thin, her vitality somehow compressed. A stark contrast to the girl all the boys had fancied at school. Lisa was the single mother of a seven-year old daughter. She had roses in her cheeks, doll-eyes, and long, naturally blonde hair, styled in some kind of twist rippling down her back. She was plump but not overweight. I had a soft spot for her because of her being the one friend who'd stuck by Marion through the last year of her life. None other of Marion's peers had been able to cope with the actuality of starvation, the poking-through bones, bulging eyes; the bad breath of it.

Lisa wore a grey angora dress which enhanced the creamy colour of her skin. It had a low neckline and the calf-length skirt swung around her legs. She led Helen in by the elbow, both of them peering around anxiously for something or someone familiar. Cal and I leaned over the banister to see them better. "Je-sus!" Cal exhaled. He forced his eyes away from Lisa, made them meet mine. A light in them seemed to have gone out since yesterday. There was still that dark halo around him. But his eyes contained reflections of my young brother, kissing a girl for the first time. The girl was Lisa at her thirteenth birthday party; Helen and I giggling behind our hands, Marion's eyes hardening in disbelief. It took her a while to get used to it, but Marion grew to approve of the relationship between her twin and her best friend. She was upset when Cal cheated on Lisa and finished with her.

With that helpless look Cal was asking my permission – or rather my blessing, to cancel out whatever happened between him and Marianne the previous night. It didn't occur to me to take any plans Marianne might have into account. I just nodded silently. Here we were in our parents' home. My mother's contented face made me realise it would destroy everything to bring the ghost of Marion back into our lives, and that was all Marianne could ever really be. Marion was dead, she really was. Even if she'd been born again, our Marion was still dead, her body was in the ground. That was indisputable.

At the bottom of the stairs Cal approached Lisa. His bearing was unnaturally submissive; it came to me that she was his potential salvation. Whereas he was tainted by darkness, she glowed with a faint warm light. She offered her cheek to him but he kissed her on the mouth, his hand on the back of her neck. She was left pressing two fingers to her lips as though she didn't quite believe they were still in one piece. I stopped on the stairs. A whooshing feeling ran through me. Everything in front of my eyes seemed transparent, a veil of the present I could see straight through into the past.

Lisa's blue eyes were glazed as she turned to greet me. Cal had gone to fetch drinks from the kitchen, pushing his hair off his face. I saw him cast a glance back at Lisa. He seemed afraid she might disappear. Helen surveyed me. "You look effing amazing, Sarah!"

"You look – what do you look, Helen?" She seemed like a shadow of my friend.

"Like I feel, I guess," Helen mustered a smile. "Peter's being awful. I don't know how much longer I can take it." I linked my arm through that of my friend and drew her into a quiet corner by the coat-hooks. "Do you have to take it?" I was unsure how difficult it was to get out of a marriage that contained children.

She sighed, tucked my arm tighter in the crook of her elbow. "It's really good to see you, you know. Really good. Especially looking the way you do. You're – radiant. What's happened?" she demanded, "not that you aren't always pretty, of course. But this is a new look for you, isn't it?"

"It's my Mum's look actually," I giggled. "She's planned this down to the last detail. It's a kind of gift-wrapping for Mark." Helen picked a long blonde hair that looked like one of Lisa's off the sleeve of her jacket and sent it floating down to the floor. She showed a lot of interest in the pale tracery of the flower pattern on the buttermilk-coloured wallpaper before turning back to me with a frown. "But I thought you and Mark split up ages ago?"

"We did, but tonight is to be our reunion, according to my mother." I put a hand over my heart, watched it rise and fall over the red dress. Helen looked down at my glittering fingernails.

"And you want this?"

"Oh God, of course." *I see Marianne again, screaming in the attic. Falling to the floor like a tower of poorly-balanced bones. Cal gathering up the bones, humming that U2 song.* "Everything's been so weird, lately, I wish I could tell you but I can't. I just want something real to happen. If I have the chance to get Mark back, I'm going to take it. I need to get out of my stagnant life."

My eyes filled up. Helen grasped my arm. "Take it then, Sarah, for God's sake. I always liked him, he was lovely to you. It's about time you did something for yourself and not for that self-centred brother of yours."

She frowned as my self-centred brother came back with the drinks. I was probably the only one who noticed the peculiar stiffness of his movements. He looked feverish, the smile he gave Lisa brittle. Maybe I should warn her to be careful. On the other hand, I wanted to be able to let go. Lisa was an adult; I was not my younger brother's keeper. Helen laughed. "You know, I should stop being such a misery! It's really great to be here and I plan to have some fun for once. Are there any more youngish people here? It looks like your gorgeous, demanding brother's appropriated my sister for the evening. I just hope Lisa knows what she's doing, she's never really got over him, you know." The truth of her statement was reflected in the hollow look Lisa flashed her sister as Cal swung her away, his hand pressed into her back. *Be careful with her Cal — you never mean to hurt people, but you do…*

As if in answer to Helen's question, Kevin Whitley and Vincent Gormley arrived through the front door; school friends of Cal. It seemed Mum had made a big effort to make Dad's party enjoyable for Cal and I. But then I realised that our contemporaries who'd stayed local might simply know my parents as friends in their shared community and not just because they were somebody else's parents during our school years. "Cor blimey," enthused Helen, "Vinny gets better-looking every time I see him. And I've heard he's divorced now. I might… if you don't mind, Sarah?"

With a laugh bubbling out of me I released Helen and gave her a delicate push forward. "Go ahead." I was excited that this party had turned out to be something more than a duty-visit. Coming here was the best thing that could have happened to Cal and me. Our neighbour Sue was looking after the dog at home so there was no need for either of us to return to Pottersea that night.

My large glass of red wine was gone already. I turned towards the kitchen to get some more. It would drown the butterflies in my stomach. *I'm going to see Mark. Here, tonight. Oh God.* Music thumped from the tape deck in the dining room as I made my way back from refilling my glass in the kitchen. In there, I'd seen Cal with his arms around Lisa, his face buried in her blonde hair. He'd been in the process of releasing it from its braid. Lisa had been sliding her hand up and down his back in a comforting way. I hoped that he wasn't just using her as a distraction from Marianne. *It could work, it could really work. Lisa and Cal are both grown up now – being with Lisa could bring Cal back to where he was before Marion died, without destroying the life of a young girl in the process.* The strange day and night with Marianne seemed so long ago already. Perhaps I had imagined the whole thing. If only I could convince myself of that.

The floor seemed to be moving. I peeped into the dining room and saw the next generation up performing rowing motions to *Oops upside your head* in a column on the floor. Mum was right at the front of the snaking line of seated bodies. I took a few steps backwards, feeling a bit wobbly on my feet, and nearly fell into Dad.

"Easy, Baby." Dad caught me in his strong arm. Then I realised I'd just about finished my second glass of wine already.

"I need some more of this, Papa." And funnily enough he happened to be carrying one of those boxes of red wine in his other arm, presumably to top up the oldies while they rowed.

"Come and have a sit down in the front room." Dad steered me helpfully by the elbow to the living room sofa. "Marion used to call me Papa." He refilled my glass as I held it out to him. "Even after she stopped speaking generally, she would call me it sometimes, never when anyone else was around though."

Wow. I hadn't realised Marion continued to speak to Dad even when she'd become silent with everyone else. My blurry brain forced me to consider that there might have been some truth in the things Cal said to me the other night. *Marion never got a look in with Dad because of you.* Maybe she had wanted – or even had the kind of close relationship with our father that I'd always cherished as my exclusive privilege.

❦

"DID YOU LOVE Marion, Dad?"

He flinched. "Of course I loved her! I think about her every day." I was ashamed for asking such a stupid question. Would it be better or worse for Dad if I told him about her? *Oh God, of course it would be worse.* He would probably be angry with me for telling him something he'd find impossible to believe but which would upset him nevertheless. Marion – the original one – could never be brought back, or that fundamental grief be undone. I had to keep telling myself that. *It's better to let the grief lie – in more ways than one.*

Mum and Dad were happy enough in the life they'd maintained together, who was I to disturb their equilibrium? Dad wiped his eyes on the sleeve of his silk shirt. I put my arm around him and rested my head on his shoulder. Right at that moment, Marianne really did seem like a figment of my imagination. We were in a different world, the children again of Mum and Dad. Marianne didn't belong in this world. Cal had kissed Lisa on the mouth; there was great tenderness in the embrace I'd witnessed in the kitchen. The last few days had been a terrible mistake. *We don't have to speak about it again. Pretend it never happened.*

"What's the matter, Sarah?" Dad slid his arm around my shoulders in return. *Don't tell him anything.* I looked across the room at the abstract painting I'd given him for his birthday, focused on it while I asked "What about Mum?"

"What about her?"

"Does she think about Marion, do you think?"

"Sarah, she's a bereaved mother, of course she does. Both of them were her babies, Marion and the little one. They were our children, the same as you and Cal."

"So. Do you – do you still love Mum, or do you just – not want to have any more upsets?" I didn't know why I was asking all this. I was the one who didn't want any more upsets. Perhaps the wine was loosening my tongue. I swallowed another mouthful. Maybe it would cancel itself out. Dad took a while to consider his answer.

"I worked hard to make sure we didn't have any serious upsets other than the tragedies we suffered, Sarah. If I hadn't been determined to do that, I don't think your mother and I would have been able to carry on together. She wasn't strong enough to put any effort into our marriage for a while, not the second time especially. The first time she had to focus on keeping herself strong enough to raise the three of you, but the second time it must have seemed to her the effort hadn't been worth it; not on Marion's behalf anyway. It took her a long time to forgive Marion, but it didn't mean there was one moment that she didn't love her or think about her. And there was never a moment I didn't love your mother even though I found it hard to like her in the dark days. But she's made up for everything in the last few years. She tries very hard to make things good for me."

Cal had been witness to 'the dark days', while I'd gone off to university soon after Marion's death. I wondered what it had been like at home. Cal had been thrown into the publicity for his first book in the months following her funeral. He'd also had to cope with moving to a house we had no affection for, and my departure. All that time he must have been wrestling with his guilt over Marion as well. He'd been unable to produce the second novel his publishers demanded and for a while, it had seemed he would be what the reviewers had suggested: a one-hit wonder. Through all this, he'd had to watch Mum in the depths of her depression and Dad struggling to keep it all going. And yet in the end Cal had managed to carve himself out a career as a writer, getting a job in the local newspaper office while working on his second novel during the evenings, exactly the same way as he had written the first. Perhaps I'd deserved some of his vitriol.

Dad's cheek was so close to mine, I could see every pore and blemish on his weathered skin. I smelt his favourite soap. Although he'd worked in an office most of his life he was happiest outside in the garden; I always pictured him there. As he hummed along to the music blaring through the wall, the box of wine jammed between his knees, I fidgeted with a loose thread poking through the shoulder seam of his new silk shirt until I managed to pull it free. I took a noisy swallow of wine, emptying my glass again. "I know I'm being a pain, Dad," I persisted, "but I just need to be reassured on one more thing – you do love Cal, don't you?"

At this Dad stood up, tucking the wine box under his arm. He pulled me to my feet. He had a perplexed look on his face. "I love you both equally Sarah. Each in a different way, but equally." His skin was flushed. But still he chucked me under the chin and peered into my eyes with concern. "Stop worrying now; enjoy my party. I've got to get back to your mother."

Dad seemed to have shed ten years from his appearance as he pulled me out into the hall. There we bumped into Mum. She smiled happily when she spotted me in my red dress. "Doesn't she look gorgeous, George?" Her face also seemed to be getting younger by the minute.

Dad winked at me. "She's nearly as gorgeous as her mother." He kissed her on the lips, right in front of me. I pushed my way back through a group of people in the hall to top up my wine again, while they hurried to join their friends on the makeshift dance floor in the other room. I had the sensation of being far away even as I greeted familiar acquaintances in the kitchen. I answered questions from several of my parents' friends about my current marital state. I cleaned up some wine I spilt while pouring myself another glass. But I was doing everything from a distance.

I found myself unexpectedly alone in the hall. Time seemed to fall out of place. When the doorbell rang I came to sitting on the bottom stair gazing into the liquid in my glass. An image seemed to waver in it: a white face with an open-mouthed scream. The scream echoed in my head, I heard the sharp crack as Marianne's skull hit the attic floor. I wondered if Cal was suffering from similar flashbacks. I couldn't feel myself breathing but I could hear the air whistling in and out of my lungs. *Pull yourself together, Sarah.*

The doorbell rang again and this time the sound registered properly. I looked up and saw a hazy image in the front door glass. My body became aware of who was standing on the other side of the door before my mind caught up. Mark had arrived. I struggled to make sense of my tangled thoughts. The things that had recently happened needed to be consigned to the past. It had finished now: the first part of the story had been concluded. Wipe the slate, turn the page; fit a new reel of film into the projector. My future, I hoped, was about to begin.

Chapter 22

Marianne

EVERY HALF HOUR Marianne tried to telephone Cal and Sarah. Speaking to either of them would have done. By this time all she needed was to have her own existence reaffirmed. She looked down at her trembling hands, the long, unhappy fingers with ripped edges that shook continuously, the bone-thin wrists. She held them in front of her eyes, which had by this time darkened to the colour of burnt treacle. She hardly recognised those hands as her own. She felt more dislocated than ever.

Voices she'd heard in her head before had started to crowd back overwhelmingly. Unseen presences hovered. One of them, most terrifyingly, was her own, but more like a shadow, herself and at the same time not quite, almost out of reach. Something was wrong. There was a little boy and it seemed to be the boy in her dream – the one she had urged Charissa to pretend to be when they were both small.

"Marion," the boy kept saying. That name Sarah had called her by, the night they met at the TV studio. A name so similar to her own and yet different enough to be someone else. And Cal had called her by it as well. Who *was* she to them?

You know who. You know exactly who. Stop pretending.

Marianne lifted the telephone receiver again and held it to her ear, its soft burr drowning out the insistent little boy's voice. Her finger dialled the number burning in her brain and she listened for a long time to the hypnotic repetitiveness of it ringing in a far-away house.

"Cal." Her voice cracked the darkness. Everybody in her home had by now gone to bed. Nobody answered in Blackberry House. She longed to be there, in the house with the mud flats at the end of the garden. Marianne listened so hard she could almost hear the slosh of the tide creeping over mud. The distant whisper of the sea. When she had no hope left, she put the receiver back in its cradle, the same as she had every other time that evening.

"Cal..." A breath only.

In the hall mirror a glow of light from the streetlights on the road outside reflected from the stained-glass panels of the front door. Raising her head from those despairing hands Marianne seemed to catch the flash of an image; small, with a shock of what might have been reddish hair, a little boy, all ready for bed in his pyjamas. So utterly familiar.

"Cal." She whispered it. But he was hiding from her. She knew there was a little girl there too – a much more taciturn creature that would never show her face. Close on the heels of her brother, egging him on.

Marianne was so tired, but she wouldn't be able to sleep.

THE NIGHT BEFORE, once Sarah had left the room, Cal had wept on Marianne's bare skin. She'd finally discovered the purpose of the body she was born into, inviting him in. But Cal had remembered himself and tried to restrain the engulfing need, turning away.

"We can't do this, *Marion*."

That name again which wasn't really hers. So she had pulled him down with arms that were stronger than they looked, she wanted him to discover the real her that was hiding inside this body. The one she knew he wanted.

She kept an insistent whisper going on in his ear, gripping his arms with long fingers, winding her legs around his, arching her dancer's body up towards him even as he tried to disentangle himself. But not for long. Soon his teeth were grazing her neck, his hardness pushing inside her, he finally forgot himself; and then she had him. But he *would* still call her Marion, and his tears continued to fall all over the skin that covered her. Those were the things she couldn't alter.

The sentences she said, she didn't even recognise as coming from her own consciousness. "*The Shell*…it was about me, wasn't it Cal? Well here I am, the shell that you wrote about, and now you are filling me like the sea, like you made him do to Maria, in the story…You are only the same as him, Cal, but you always knew that, didn't you?" Her aggressive whisper aroused him further; deeper he drove, crushing her bones, gasping and crying. She revelled in the bruises his gripping fingers would make on her arms.

His eyes were elsewhere. She clung on, all the while understanding he was as lost to himself as he was to her. His body jolted the way it would if an electric current ran through it. His jaw opened wide, face stretching until she was afraid his skin would tear. She thought he was going to die. He shouted out as if he had been shot, then moaned like a wounded man. A while later he pulled her into his arms and said her proper name. Their amber eyes met. She smoothed back the lock of hair clinging with sweat to his forehead and he caught hold of her hand and pressed it against his lips.

"Marianne."

Hollowness opened up inside her.

"Marianne…"

Don't say it. I want things to stay just the way they are.

Then she felt him relax, the hand that held hers dropped down onto his chest and she realised he had fallen asleep. She nestled there, afraid to move, her execution stayed. All the while the familiar insistent voice was in her ear. "We are the same, you and I, the sooner you admit it the better. You can never win." She knew that was true. Then she fell asleep too.

When he roused her, Cal was gentle and kind. He slid back into his clothes and gathered up hers up in one arm, wrapping a throw from an armchair around her with the other. He led her to his room holding her very close against him. In a drawer, he found a pair of white silk pyjamas and suggested she put them on. Cal helped her tighten the drawstring waist, while she sat on his enormous bed he rolled up the legs of the pyjamas so she wouldn't trip over them. She thought he was going to take her into his bed, but instead he took her hand and led her to the attic staircase.

"We can't do this again, Marianne." At least he had called her by her proper name. He bent to give her a final kiss. "You said it yourself – I'm old enough to be your father. You're sweet and beautiful, honey, but this really shouldn't have happened. There are too many…complications."

Marianne had her turn to cry as she watched him walk away from her and close his bedroom door. "It wasn't even you that he wanted," said the voice in her body. She would have to find another way to get to him.

———◆◆———

MARIANNE ROSE FROM the floor in the hallway of her home in Leeds. She pressed the heels of her trembling hands into her eyes, removed any vestiges of tears. The mirror reflected coloured light from the front door, but she would refuse to acknowledge the shadow that had come to the fore of the glass. It stood beside her reflection, the same size and shape, but less defined. She turned away, the echoing voices quietening.

Cal not answering the phone was a more emphatic message than any words. He'd had time to think about it, remember the body she'd offered him and by now he must be feeling disgusted by it, as she herself was. Cal must have instructed Sarah not to answer the phone as well; Marianne had noticed the influence he seemed to have over his sister.

She pulled herself wearily up the stairs, hanging on to the ornate banister. It felt more like a mountain than a series of fourteen steps to have to climb.

The stupid woman, Geraldine, had got a new prescription for the same kind of sleeping tablets Marianne had used last time. She'd left them in the exact place in the bathroom cabinet as before. Even without the voice instructing her it seemed like a message to Marianne – a mother who didn't care.

This time Marianne added a third of a container of aspirin and the three quarters remaining of a bottle of cough medicine she'd been giving Justine recently to the concoction she swallowed. She would never acknowledge it as suicide – she only wanted to get some sleep, but she was hoping that sleep would last for a long, long time.

Chapter 23

Sarah

"IF IT ISN'T me lady in red." But he hadn't quite managed to cover up his uncertainty with his confident greeting. His black eyes were full of questions. His hair was longer now, wiry curls snaking down into the collar of his blue shirt. I forced out some strangled words, barely able to hear my own voice through the drumbeat in my ears. He put a tentative hand on my shoulder. I twisted the stem of my glass in both hands. We stood in the doorway, eyes locked on each other's faces. I wanted to raise my arms, let the outside air cool my armpits, my hot back. Behind me in the house clamoured the buzz of excited voices, thumping music, the clinking of glasses; in front of me stood Mark, the enveloping evening, a cool breeze. The sky was just getting dark.

When Mark pulled me towards him, my arms responded by creeping around his body, the wine glass still in one of my hands.

"Shall we go in?" His voice interrupted the strange suspension of time. We slipped into the empty front room, pushed the door shut. Clack. Before I had time to think, Mark pressed his mouth onto mine, his fingers making the nerves in the back of my neck tingle.

"You look fecking gorgeous in that dress, but the awful thing is, Sarah, I just wanna take it off you, by God!"

"Later," I forced out. Mark sat down on the sofa, pulled me into his lap. I remembered the last time we'd been together; his hand under my gown in the hammock. It seemed fitting that we were more or less resuming where we left off. But I had to remember we were in my parents' front room. His teeth toyed with the skin of my neck.

"Mark, we need to talk…" I pushed him off gently. Struggling into a standing position, I put my hands on his shoulders, savoured the texture of fine cotton and the heat pulsing off his skin beneath. I wanted to keep touching him forever and never have to go raking over the past. "You look so beautiful."

He put his arms around me again; I stroked his hair. "I still love you," I admitted.

The awareness of his breath on my skin was exquisite, covering me with goose bumps. Eventually he looked up. If I wasn't careful I would fall right into those blackberry-coloured eyes of his and never get out. "We could go over what happened," he said, "and we probably will, but I don't want to now. I have you here – Christ, I can't believe I have you in my arms again." His voice was husky. "What I wanna know, gorgeous girl, is where do we stand right now? Are we together again, Sarah?" His grip on me tightened. "'Cause if we're not, what the bloody hell am I doing here – why am I holdin' you like this?"

"We are…" I whispered. "We are together, Mark. Please?" I swallowed a sob. "I'm so lucky to be given this second chance. I do want to be with you. I was stupid before, and then I had to punish myself. I've realised that now." Mark tugged me in even closer, if that was possible. His voice was muffled by my cleavage.

"Ahhh, me gorgeous Sarah… this feels so good, and me little feller's getting that excited he's about to explode! Are you sure we can't go and do something about it right away?" He grinned wickedly. "Can't you take pity on me Sarah? I might be able to forgive you if you do…" His hands ran over me. I had to pull away, get my breath.

"I don't know…" But Mark dragged me down into his lap again, recovered my mouth with his own. I no longer cared that we were in my parents' house. "Come on then." I hardly recognised my own guttural voice. When we stood up I realised I'd spilled the last of the wine from my glass. Oddly, I didn't feel that bothered. I bent to tug the corner of a hearth rug a couple of inches to the right, covering the stain. While I was bending down, Mark made the most of my position with his exploring hands. "Oh God, come on," I repeated when I'd collected myself, "We've got to get up to my room without being seen."

The front part of the hall was still miraculously empty. Peering down the other end I could see that all the action was taking place in the dining room and in the kitchen, which was bursting at the seams. I spotted the chestnut and gold heads of Cal and Lisa close together amongst the melee. The *Odyssey* music bonanza was still in full swing: *If you're looking for a way out* playing on the stereo. I caught sight of Helen, slow-dancing in the dining room with Vinny.

I slipped off my sandals and held them in one hand as we snuck up the stairs together, me pulling Mark behind with my other hand. I couldn't help laughing at him arranging the front of his shirt over his tell-tale bulge. He had a sheepish look on his face. "You don't know how hard – if you'll excuse me pun – it is to walk, Sarah."

An old female friend of my parents came out of the bathroom as we passed it. She peered short-sightedly at us. I don't think she recognised me although she'd known me since I was a teenager. Whether she did or not, she decided to offer us both a beaming smile before proceeding carefully down the stairs.

"I hope you don't mind…" Mark said; his back against my bedroom door once we were inside. "I've brought a condom. Well, a whole box, actually. I was hoping…" he paused and took a breath. "Feck it, Sarah, I knew I was going to be seeing you, so I thought I'd better, you know, just in case." He cocked his eyebrow in a quizzical manner. I burst out laughing, fought down the sharp corners of hysteria poking up through the joy of having Mark back.

I had to convince myself the last few days were a dream. I had to forget Marianne existed. Even if she was a reincarnation of my dead sister, she was still a separate person in her own right. She was a young girl who needed to live the life she seemed to have been given a second chance at. And Cal needed to move on as well. Perhaps the attachment he'd briefly formed to Marianne would finally enable him to lay the ghost of Marion to rest. *Please God, let it be so.*

I pushed all those thoughts away. Mark locked my bedroom door, sliding across the bolt I'd clumsily screwed on myself when I was eighteen. I'd wanted to hide from the world then, not have to hear Mum crying every night through the thin walls of this unfamiliar house. I didn't want to have to look at her walking around like a zombie during the days either. But the time had come now to put away every sad memory of when we moved to this house. I went over to the window, drew the curtain against the reflection of my pale face, my eyes that looked like black wells in the dark glass, denying what I might see in them. I would not look at myself, or the ghosts that had inhabited me for so long. Tonight was a new and hopeful start.

The red jersey dress was easy to slip off over my head. I left it in a heap on the floor. Together, my hands and his released Mark from the shackles of his jeans. I held his penis in both my hands. His breathing was laboured in my ear. Faintness swamped me, the feelings, emotional as well as physical, overwhelming. "We don't have to… You know, it seems mad to bring it up like this, but…" He drew back to look deep into my eyes, and then continued speaking in a soft, serious voice. "I wanna marry you, Sarah… we talked about it once, remember? Darlin', I really want us to take this chance."

Mark sat carefully on the bed, keeping me close with his hands circling my wrists, my hands still holding him. His fingers continually stroked my skin. "Fair play to you if you don't agree, but we don't have to use a condom, is what I'm saying – if you think you could consider…?"

I held close the memory of my sisters, the babies my mother had lost, nodded blindly at Mark. All this was very sudden, but sometimes you could spend too long making decisions. My life had been on hold for such a long time. I put my nose into the hollow at the base of Mark's neck, breathed in the scent that made me feel I inhabited my own body for the first time in ages, suddenly aware of how empty the air around me had been until he had placed himself back in it. It occurred to me that I had to be prepared to risk loss in order to stand a chance of winning. I slid my wrists out of his hands, went over to the light switch and flipped it off. Mark followed me and we stood skin to skin, his hardness again in my hand. I stroked his shoulders and back with my other hand, re-imprinting him in my sensory memory. He pulled us both back onto the bed. I fitted myself onto him and we moved in a practised dance. I nearly passed out at the moment I came. When his stomach muscles tensed just before he erupted inside me, I somehow knew for sure I was going to get pregnant.

Chapter 24

Geraldine

"DON'T FRET ABOUT it, Love, she'll be alright in the morning." Joseph gave Geraldine's arm an awkward pat but she didn't think she was ready to be mollified yet. Her dinner-time exchange with her daughter continued to rattle around her head.

"And what would *you* know about saying 'Boo' to a goose?"

Her irrational reply prompted an offended silence from the other side of the bed. But Geraldine wanted her husband on-side. "I did try with her at the beginning, you know. But she was never an easy child."

"You're not wrong there, Love."

She hadn't wanted to be pregnant in the first place. Then she had the most awful postnatal depression. She had to take the tranquilizers for so long that her baby girl was beginning to speak in complete sentences by the time things started to clear in her head. Marianne was only just over a year old, but Geraldine had missed the most important parts already.

She thought back, wondering what she could have done differently. What would have prevented Marianne becoming so sick? Geraldine admitted it to herself: the girl was ill.

"Mari-*anne*" She remembered leaning over the cot. Her daughter was gripping the bars, fixing a stony gaze on Geraldine.

"No!" the child shouted right back in her face. "Not Mari-*anne*."

Geraldine shook herself and tried again. She must have misheard. "Marianne?" She put out a tentative hand, as to an unpredictable animal in a cage.

But the child startled her by replying in a high voice, "What have you done with my brother?"

After that, Geraldine backed away quickly, wondering if she was experiencing the after-effects of the medication she'd been on.

It only got worse. Geraldine found she was pregnant again a few months after Marianne's first birthday. She could hardly remember how it had happened, until she recalled the Young Farmers barn dance. Joseph's parents, who'd moved out of the farmhouse into a cottage on the land after their son got married, had babysat for their strange little granddaughter that night. Geraldine remembered dancing with a local gamekeeper for most of the evening. It was very 'Lady Chatterley', at least in Geraldine's mind. When they got home she'd for once not resisted Joseph's advances in the bedroom. And look where it had got her.

Once she'd managed to accept the new pregnancy Geraldine found herself wondering if she could be carrying the 'my brother' that Marianne had mentioned at such a young age. But when the baby came she was a girl. She took to her second daughter Charissa, lusty and more substantial than her older sister. However Geraldine nevertheless suffered from a second dose of baby blues and the children's grandmother had to take over much of their care.

In bed next to the recumbent form of her husband (who'd had the effrontery to fall asleep), Geraldine remembered how Marianne had denied her identity when she was a small child. The grandmother encouraged Geraldine to attend a mother and baby social group in the village hall, she said it would help her daughter-in-law bond with her children. She gave them a lift there in the Land Rover and picked them all up afterwards.

"What's your name?" one of the other mothers asked Marianne. She also had a baby and a little boy around Marianne's age. Marianne seemed fascinated by the little boy. She stayed close to him and copied everything he did. She was confused when he began to scream and push her away. Marianne was just over two years old. The woman, (Jenny, Geraldine thought her name was) placed her baby in a carrycot on the floor and took the little boy on her knee. He stopped screaming and snuggled in close to his mother, his thumb lodged in his mouth.

Marianne came to stand by the woman's knee, looking up at the boy with an expression of such longing that for once Geraldine experienced maternal empathy, and that's when Jenny asked Marianne her question.

"Marion Wilde," Marianne replied promptly. She glanced with puzzlement at the child on Jenny's knee. "Is that my brother?"

"No dear, this is Jeremy; he's not your brother I'm afraid. But you have a very pretty name, don't you?"

Geraldine could see the look of distaste on the other mother's face. She tried to take hold of Marianne's hand but her daughter slipped out of her grasp. "Her name's Marianne Fairchild, actually, she always gets it wrong for some reason. Maybe Marion Wilde is just easier to say."

Geraldine would never forget how Marianne turned then from her fascination with the boy on his mother's knee. She gave Geraldine a look of such contempt it made her feel physically cold.

"I am *not* Marianne Fairchild," the child announced in a very clear voice. "My name is Marion Wilde, and you are not my mother. When are you going to take me home to my family?"

That wasn't the only time Marianne had embarrassed her in that way. Her whole life she'd made Geraldine feel completely ineffectual as a mother. It was no wonder, thought Geraldine all these years later, tossing from one side to the other in the bed in Leeds, that she'd never been able to make a successful relationship with the child who'd rejected her so early on. Not to mention that she hadn't really been cut out to be a mother anyway.

She was happiest in her apartment in London. There everything was placed just where she wanted it and she stored her personal possessions: the things she'd kept from her childhood, the modelling shots she'd had done just before she met Joseph. She was a sleeping partner in a business she part-owned: a glamour publication called Gadfly. She couldn't continue her previously active role when she got married to a farmer, but she took Charissa on regular visits to the office. Somehow she had got trapped by a series of unplanned pregnancies into this life with Joseph and three daughters, only one of whom she had ever really managed to forge some kind of connection with. Even that was because Charissa submitted her own individuality to Geraldine's shaping. And Geraldine did sometimes feel guilty about this.

Marianne believed she didn't notice anything, but she was aware the girl had been sneaking to the telephone throughout the evening, coming away each time after a few minutes with a despondent set to her shoulders. Geraldine guessed that the Callum Wilde her daughter seemed so obsessed with had something to do with her mood. In the morning, she decided, she would get up as early as she was able. She would apologise to Marianne. She would say that she had been unfair in accusing her of sleeping around and that if Marianne had a boyfriend, her mother would be interested in hearing about it. In fact, Marianne having a boyfriend might be just the thing for finally kick-starting a relationship between them. At last they'd be able to communicate about something Geraldine understood. Soon after making that decision she turned over in bed one last time – with her back to Joseph – and fell quickly into the sleep of the righteous.

She woke up with the same good intentions from the night before and came down to the kitchen, expecting to find the early-rising Marianne, but only Joseph was in there.

"She's not up yet." Joseph nodded towards the stairs.

So, knotting her linen house-robe more securely around her waist, Geraldine made for Marianne's room at the end of the hall. *Cupboard is more like it.* Rapping on the door, she felt nervous, just as she would if she was embarking on any other new relationship. But Marianne didn't answer and it wasn't long before Geraldine's nerves transmuted into irritation. Typical Marianne; refused to give an inch when Geraldine was clearly offering a mile. Then she considered that there might be more similarities between herself and her daughter than she'd realised. Stubbornness was a shining example. If only Marianne could get over that 'scarecrow' look. Maybe Geraldine would offer to take her down to London on the next visit. Geraldine's knuckles, newly determined, hit the door several more times, but still Marianne didn't answer, even when Geraldine called out her name.

So she took hold of the doorknob and pushed open the door. She had a strong sense of dread as she began to go in. There had been a drama to the first occasion they'd found Marianne unconscious – her head flung over the edge of the bed; vomit all over the book she'd been reading. But this time, everything appeared spookily natural. Marianne could have been simply asleep, curled up on her side under the crocheted daffodil bedspread, another of the possessions Marianne had accrued from her paternal grandparents' effects.

Geraldine wanted to pause time, have a think what to do. She wanted to wind back and start again from the beginning of Marianne's life. *When you were born I was only a young girl myself. I'd had such hopes for my life and you put a stop to that. I hated the weight of pregnancy, the way I was taken over not just by you but by the obligations I was now under. Your birth terrified me. It seemed that I had nothing to do with it. You were pulled out of my body and laid in a plastic crib. I watched your father checking you over as though you were one of his newborn lambs. And all I could do was cry. But I am your mother. Nothing can ever change that.* Was it too late? Marianne's face was bleached of colour, one of those wax death-masks Geraldine had once seen with Charissa at a museum. She couldn't hear any breathing sounds. She was afraid to feel for her daughter's pulse. On the dresser were the empty packets and bottles of medicines that Marianne had used. *She means it this time. This is not a cry for help; Marianne really means it.*

She screamed for Joseph.

Chapter 25

Sarah

A FEW MOMENTS passed before the physical and emotional realisations hit me simultaneously: I wasn't alone. Mark's warm back pressed against mine, the rumble of his breathing was in my body. Sun stabbed my eyes through clumps of make-up; I tried to unstick my dry throat, coax life back into limbs that didn't feel like they could be mine. I was vaguely aware that below my sunshiny contentment something negative was ruffling its wings. But I must have fallen asleep again because the sound of my parents' doorbell roused Mark and me at the same time. Without speaking we smiled at each other from adjacent pillows.

I put on a long t-shirt and went out onto the landing. I was startled to see Cal and Lisa just coming through the front door. Even more surprising was that Lisa's golden-haired daughter, who I hadn't seen since Helen's anniversary party two years ago, was clutching Cal by the hand. This was something I had never expected to see. Black bin bags bulging with empty bottles and cans were stacked up by the front door. The house looked and smelt clean thanks to my efficient mother.

"Sarah," admonished Mum, obviously having spotted me with the eyes in the back of her head. "Put some clothes on for goodness' sake."

"Sorry Mum. Hi Lisa, hi Cal." My brother looked up. There was a mixture of trepidation and relief in his eyes, possibly the tiniest trace of a threat. *Don't say anything; the last few days never happened.* I dragged my gaze away, arranged a smile on my face for the little girl. "Hello Alice." The child was growing up into the spitting image of her mum. At the bottom of the stairs I pulled the t-shirt down with both hands and sat on the step in front of Alice. "Is Cal being nice to you?" I asked. "You make sure you tell me if he isn't."

She gave me an endearing smile, took several breaths before declaring in a raucous voice, "We have been having a sleep-over at my house."

"A sleep-over? Hmm." I gave Cal a raised-eyebrows glance, surprised that the look he returned had developed into one of naked pleading. My heart jumped. Though both Cal and I seemed to have moved on so utterly in the space of a few hours, I could see something in the way he carried himself, in the bleakness that lay at the back of his eyes, behind the smile of gratitude he gave Lisa. I could see it in his flushed pleasure at the child's attentions: the fear that mirrored mine. Marianne knew where we lived. She could return at any time.

Hurrying along the corridor I heard Mum hustle the three of them into the front room. "That little girl is so sweet." There was a gushing tone to her voice as she followed me into the kitchen a few minutes later. "Do you know she's actually sat on Cal's knee right at this moment, reading to him? Amazing isn't it? Our Cal."

"It is amazing," I agreed, slipping past her in the doorway. Talking about Cal with her made me uncomfortable. If Cal and I got caught in a room together with our perspicacious mother I was afraid she would get the truth out of us. As only a mother could, she would ferret out the discomfiture that flitted between us. Eventually she would notice the shifting presence of Marion in our exchanged glances. Dad had said that he thought about Marion every day; I wondered if Mum did too. Seventeen years was such a short time in retrospect. Grief settled, but it took only a slight disturbance of the still pool to set off a new tidal wave. I experienced again the weight of the fallen-down girl in my arms the other night, heard the words of that funny childhood rhyme Mum and me used to sing to Caitlin in my head. *"Chickadee, Chickadee…"*

"Oh, Sarah,"

"Yeah?"

"I'm so happy about you and Mark." She gave a deep sigh. "It looks as though my children are finally settling down. That Lisa could be good for him you know, especially with the child. She'll need security and having to provide it could make him finally grow up. Don't you think?"

"Yeah, I guess you're right." There was no way we could ever let her find out about Marianne. Something made me turn back towards the kitchen. I placed the two mugs I was holding on the work surface nearest the door so I could tug the t-shirt down again. "Mum?"

She paused in her arrangement of cups and biscuits, wiping her hands on her jeans and looking up at me. "Yes?"

"Mark asked me to marry him, and I said yes."

Her face went loose and her shoulders slumped. It looked like all the air had been let out of her. She made an involuntary noise, a kind of "fwhumph." In her hurry to get to me she knocked her wrist on the corner of a cabinet and she rubbed vigorously at the red mark before putting her arms around me. She squeezed me tightly. I was finally the daughter she wanted. "Sarah," she said. "I can't tell you how happy this makes me."

"Oh Mum," I said. "I can probably guess."

——◆——

BY THE TIME Mark and I came downstairs showered and dressed, Cal was getting ready to leave. Lisa's doll-eyes looked to be filling with tears. "I'd hoped we could spend the weekend together."

Cal stroked her hair. "I'm sorry, honey; I have to get back to my writing. I'm already behind. Oh, and there's the dog to get back to as well."

He gave me a hard look. We both knew our neighbour Sue was looking after the dog.

"Oh wow, you've got a dog. I wish I had a dog." Alice had such a strange croaky voice.

"You can come and see him soon, I promise." Cal knelt down, giving her a fifty-pence piece. "If your mum doesn't mind, you can buy some sweeties with that."

"Thank you." Alice gave him a beaming smile. She slid one hand into Lisa's, turning the coin over in the other. Cal went to say goodbye to Mum. It seemed Dad had gone out to his allotment.

"Are you alright for a lift home, Sarah?" Cal had already moved towards his car door, Lisa following after him with Alice in tow.

"Sure she is." Mark gave the impression of being determined to assert himself over Cal in the hierarchy of my affections, and I sensed the importance of letting him establish the boundaries this time.

Cal's body sank against Lisa's; she was holding him up. I was glad. I wanted to blot out the memory of Marianne as much as I'm sure he did. *Forget it, forget her. It could only bring pain into any of our lives. Look at how happy we can all be if we let ourselves.*

I half-slept during the first part of the drive back to Pottersea with Mark. We'd been for lunch at a riverside pub and I was full with emotion and food. In the passenger seat I was aware of his warm thigh beneath my hand. Everything on the road seemed clearer, more sharply defined when I opened my eyes and drank in the views than it had done the day before. I remembered driving back after dropping Marianne off at the station, the heavy feeling of dread in my stomach. All gone now, I tried to convince myself. I pictured those worries blowing away on the wind like the seeds from a dandelion clock.

The first day of June felt exactly as it ought to. Cow parsley bowed and dipped at the edges of the road. A field of rape stretched startlingly yellow as far as I could see on one side, a herd of black-and-white cows grazed close to the fence on the other.

"When do you want to get married?" I snuggled my face into Mark's shoulder.

"Ah, as soon as we can, me sweet girl, don't you think?"

I'd been testing him to check that he really meant his proposal.

I dreamed of the cottage in Ireland he had told me about. "It's in County Leitrim right at the foot of a mountain. Not far from where you stayed with your mam. We can go swimming in the lake; you'll love it, Sarah. I've been doing it up for the past two years, I bought it just after we split up, knowing you'd come back to me one day."

I was ready to drop everything now, leave everyone behind. Two years of regret were enough to convince me. *And Marianne will never find you there.* Over the sea and far away.

JUDE HURTLED OUT of the open kitchen door, wriggling and making his half-laughing, half-crying whimpering sound. "Silly boy. Aren't you a silly boy, eh Scooby-dude?" But I was thrilled to see him leaping into Mark's arms. He must have remembered him. If Cal wanted a dog after I'd gone he'd have to get himself another, I planned to take Jude with me when I moved to Ireland. A strange, still atmosphere pervaded the kitchen. Cal sat at the table, his head in his hands. When he lifted his face I saw how drawn he was, his eyes hollow. I squinted into the gloom; certain I could see a grey shape looming behind him. But when I blinked there was nothing there. I flicked on the light. "What on earth's the matter?" But I didn't really want to know. *Everything is supposed to be alright now.*

I hesitated by the cooker, Mark's hand on my shoulder. Cal pushed back the hair from his forehead, coughed, took out a ragged piece of tissue; wiped his nose. "There's been a phone call."

"From who?" But the dread was back, lodged firmly in my stomach. *Just tell me.*

"M... Marianne's mother. Sue took a message when she came in here to get some dog food. We need to ring her back."

Marianne's mother. Oh God. How incongruous, why would her mother telephone our house? My fingers tingled; that horrible sensation crept up the back of my neck. It settled over my head, the beginnings of a premonition. *Of course it wasn't going to be that easy to escape. I should never have looked for her after the recording.* I was doomed to go over and over this, I realised it now. Oh shit. "Did she say what... why she was ringing?"

"Something terrible's happened. Marianne... I don't want to say it in front of him."

Cal gave me a hard stare, transferred the gaze over my shoulder to Mark. Static seemed to crack in the air between the three of us. This felt private between Cal and me, yet I couldn't keep it from Mark. His fingers gripped my shoulder. I cleared my throat, reached up; grasped Mark's hand. I pulled him towards the table. "Come and sit down." When we had arranged ourselves knee to knee at the table I leaned over and kissed him. I said to Cal, "I'm going to marry Mark, and I'm not going to have any secrets from him anymore. He has to be told everything."

❖

IT WAS STILL light when we reached Leeds. I'd been willing for Mark to come along but on the other hand Cal and I needed to sort this out by ourselves; this mess we'd got ourselves into. Whatever was about to happen I would have him to go back to and that made it easier to face. I asked and answered my own questions in my head as I negotiated the Saturday evening traffic into Leeds. How many days since we had last made the journey to Leeds? Only four; it seemed impossible. What had we caused to happen, me and Cal? A devastating effect on the life of a young woman we'd felt a connection with because of a tragedy in our past. It wasn't all our fault though, she had a mesmeric effect on us; she was the one who made that phone call the next morning, insisted on coming to visit. I was doing a good job of convincing myself she was just an ordinary girl who happened to look like our dead sister: she had manipulated us, not the other way round. I managed for a few moments, then all the doubts and recriminations came back. It was our fault, *my* fault, of course it was. Why had I gone running out into the audience looking for her after the show? If I hadn't, that glimpse of her would have become only a poignant memory.

As was usual during a journey, Cal and I didn't speak much to each other. I drove his car. The time filled with a tangible block of cold space we were forced to cross. Once on the other side of it I could crawl into bed with Mark. *Let us just get through tonight.*

"Junction 2, you're looking for," Cal said, stirring himself with the map. "We need to merge onto the A643."

The map negotiation occupied us for the next few minutes. We came to a roundabout and Cal shouted, "Take the next exit, no, the third one, onto the A643, damn, you missed it. Jesus Sarah, can you not pay attention?"

"It's you being confusing," I muttered. "You said 'the next exit' and then changed it to the third one!" He made me feel flustered. I had to follow the roundabout all the way around again, relieved in a way because it delayed our inevitable arrival.

"That's it, the third exit," Cal directed with mock patience. We came to another roundabout pretty soon afterwards. "Look for a sign to a hospital; we should be merging onto the A58." My brain was tired, my vision slightly blurred. Maybe I needed glasses for driving. "This steering's dodgy," I murmured as I hauled the wheel round, "you should get it looked at."

Cal shot me a cold glance. "Err, that's your job, Sarah."

"Not for much longer. Mark and I are getting married, and I'm going to live in Ireland." I stared fixedly ahead, looking for the turn onto Park Lane. But I could almost hear Cal's brain ticking over.

"We'll talk about it later. Turn right onto Hanover Way and then left onto Woodhouse Square. There. Now you want to go down Clarendon Road and then turn right onto Hyde Terrace. Here we are. We're looking for one of those tall houses with the steps leading up to the front door."

I slowed the car to a crawl, while Cal searched for the house number. We were both subdued by the time I manoeuvred with difficulty into a cramped parking space between a tiny car and a huge van. I couldn't believe what we were about to do, after everything I'd vowed to myself since dropping Marianne off at the station in Hull. We sat still, looked at each other for a moment before I opened my door and got out. After another moment I heard the passenger door slam shut. We walked up the steps together but he was the one who put his finger on the doorbell.

I heard running footsteps and the door was hauled open by a plump girl of about ten. Staring up at us, she thrust a thumb in her mouth. Marianne's fondness for her youngest sister came back to me.

"Are you Justine?"

She nodded, but a harsh voice called out from the end of a tiled passageway, "Justine, get up those stairs to bed, I've already told you."

A woman with swept-back pale auburn hair tapped her way towards us on high heels. Her appearance caused the child to scutter up the red patterned carpet in the centre of the staircase. "Charissa," the woman yelled upwards. "See that Justine brushes her teeth." Standing in the still open front doorway, I caught a glimpse of a swish of dark brown hair, long legs in tight-bottomed jeans moving across the landing at the top of the stairs. The woman looked Cal in the eyes and made a small gasping sound; stepped back infinitesimally. But she gathered herself quickly.

"Would you come in?" In a cold voice but with impeccable manners, she introduced herself as Geraldine Fairchild.

She clicked before us down a long corridor to a dining room at the end. A man with grey-sprinkled hair was standing in there. He had sideburns on his cheeks like a character from a seventies detective series on TV. He greeted us with a nod then disappeared through a doorway that I assumed led to a kitchen. This was confirmed a moment later when he popped his face back through the door.

"Tea?"

The woman indicated us to sit down. She took a shuddering breath, looked at her hands in her lap, long clean white fingers with polished nails. I was fascinated that she was

Marianne's mother. I could see no resemblance either in looks or demeanour. Red earrings like heavy drops of blood swung angrily against her neck as she whipped her head round to glare at Cal.

"I wanted to say this to you face-to-face, so you're under no illusions that you have any other option but to leave my daughter alone." She paused, twisting her snake hands together in her lap. My eyes started up with their usual activity, which I couldn't help. I could see Cal similarly struggling to control his trembling leg.

"I'm sorry about what happened, Mrs Fairchild," I managed, "I was shocked to hear the news. I'm… I hope Marianne will recover from this." I nudged Cal, underpinned by the frozen glaze of Geraldine Fairchild's slitted eyes, but he seemed to have gone dumb.

"What she did was your fault; you should be ashamed of yourself for getting involved with such a young girl, a man of your age!" she almost spat the words at my brother, but Cal still sat motionless apart from his leg, his only other sign of life the quick catch of his breathing. He reminded me of a rabbit transfixed in front of an oncoming car.

Mr Fairchild, "Call me Joseph," came in with the tray of tea just as Geraldine leaned towards Cal, her face cold and pale. "I could have informed the police about you, and I will if you have anything to do with her again."

Chapter 26

I GOT THE impression Joseph Fairchild would avoid conflict at any cost, a characteristic I was all too familiar with. He handed out mugs of tea and I had to withdraw my prayer-posed hands from between my knees to accept the offering. He gently grasped his wife's arm. I noticed how strong and brown his fingers were, such a contrast to hers. "It's not the first time Marianne's done this." He dipped his chin. Maybe he thought Mrs Fairchild had overestimated Cal's guilt. "She's taken an overdose before. Now Geraldine, it's only fair the pair of them should know, isn't it?"

Her voice came out on a high arc. "And it was his fault the last time as well! She did it after she read that book — written by him."

"Don't upset yourself, love." Mr Fairchild moved his hand soothingly on her arm. A mournful expression turned the corners of his mouth down. To us he said "It's a horrible thing to have to go through, finding your daughter uncon-scious like that."

As when I'd tended her after her collapse in our attic, it hit me that Marianne was somebody's baby. She was not Marion. She was not Marion now, at least. Cal and I had been utterly selfish in our need to claim her. The realisation weighted me down like sand. She must have been searching for an answer to the puzzle of her life. She'd attempted suicide before, when she had been disturbed by reading *The Shell*. Had she deliberately sought us out? Sought Cal out? *Did she know?* My grip tightened on the mug I was holding. I felt cold. *God, what have we done?*

Geraldine sniffed into an embroidered handkerchief, avoiding everyone's gaze. After a few moments her husband leaned closer to her. "Hopefully she'll be home in a couple of days."

"Oh I doubt that very much," said his wife, "they're not going to let her go that easily this time, are they?"

This time. To think she had done it before, when we didn't even know of her existence. *It was his fault the last time as well.* Some tea spilled out of Cal's cup. Mrs Fairchild needn't fear that we would bother Marianne again. The whole experience had turned into a horror story. Terrible as the girl's suicide attempt was, the best thing we could all do was stay away from each other now, for the sake of everyone's mental health. I could only hope Marianne would be able to get over her ordeal, that meeting us would suffice as closure.

Cal and I needed to get out of her home, realign ourselves with our new, comforting futures. It struck me again that meeting Marianne had released us from the past, allowed us to say a final goodbye to Marion as well as to our troubled teenaged selves. But what had it done to her?

Half-way through my mug of tea I deemed it a suitable time to end the excruciating visit. Joseph accompanied us to the door, mumbling apologies for his wife's curt behaviour. When his hand touched my shoulder my skin crawled. He should have been angrier. Marianne needed parents who were prepared to fight for her. I was grateful for Geraldine's wrath, a sign that she wanted to hold onto her daughter. Pathos would never win in a battle for identity, I should know. Recognising my own past behaviour in his reaction to his daughter's crisis was what disgusted me. *Don't rock any boats.* When the front door closed I turned to Cal on the top step and it was like watching a speeded-up film of a frozen corpse thawing back to life. His shoulders clicked as he straightened them. "Fucking bitch!"

"Are you up to driving?" I asked. "Because if not, I don't mind driving home."

"Why wouldn't I be?" Cal put his hand out for the car keys.

✦

MARK MUST HAVE already gone to bed. The kitchen was tidy, a plate of biscuits left out on the table. I hadn't realised how hungry I was. I grabbed one, poured myself a glass of milk from the fridge. "You want anything?" I asked Cal. He looked exhausted. "Do you want to – y'know, talk about anything?"

"Jesus," he said. He stood with his shoulders hunched over. He was staring at his jacket on the floor where it had fallen when he missed the hook. "What are you, my counsellor or something? There's no point in fucking talking, it's all been said already." He gave the jacket a kick. All his pent up anger was back. I reminded myself that my incarceration with him and his anger would soon be over.

"Fine. I'm just off to take Jude for a quick walk."

He gave me a dark look and I had no idea what he was thinking. As he went towards the stairs I had the weirdest feeling there was something ragged hanging off one side of him, like a torn piece of fabric, all down his arm and torso and leg. The blood in my veins froze. But when he moved under the light by the front door I could no longer see any of that. His footsteps receded onto the landing carpet and his bedroom door closed. That was when my legs went from under me. I grabbed the edge of the table, lowered myself into a chair, grabbed two handfuls of my hair and pulled on them. I must have been hallucinating. God, what had we stirred up by getting involved with Marianne? Fear flapped like a white-sheet ghost in my chest. I took my hands out of my hair, rubbed furiously at my face, reminded myself that Mark was waiting for me upstairs. Everything was going to be alright.

A whine from Jude brought me back to myself. He rested his chin on my knee. He'd dropped his lead on the floor at my feet. I stroked his head, pushed myself up from the chair on shaking legs. "Come on then, boy."

I had my hand on the door handle when the phone rang. Jude and I looked at each other, his waving tail coming to a hesitant stop. "Shit. I'd better answer it, sorry Jude." Long-suffering, he flopped down onto his stomach with a grunt, resigned to a patient wait. I was annoyed to hear Lisa's voice.

"Hi Sarah, sorry to ring so late. I fell asleep in the bath would you believe? Is Cal there?"

"Cal's gone up to bed," I told her, "I don't want to disturb him, he's just had some bad news I'm afraid."

"Bad news?" There was a mixture of fear and curiosity in her voice. "Are you sure I can't speak to him, I may be able to help."

"Why don't you try again tomorrow? Or I could get him to ring you. He's really not up to it tonight, sorry Lisa."

"Oh. Would you mind telling me what's happened?"

I struggled to keep my feelings level. She'd only been back with Cal five minutes; was acting like she owned him already. "It's difficult. A girl we recently became acquainted with tried to commit suicide. She took an overdose. When Cal got back here there was a phone call from the girl's mother. She wanted us to go and see her – not the girl, her mother. We've just got back from Leeds and Cal's exhausted. I'll get him to call you tomorrow and explain more, OK?"

There was a short silence punctuated by Lisa's quick breaths. "A girl… why did she? I don't understand what this has got to do with Cal."

I let another silence fall and then roused myself to speak again. It wasn't up to me to explain this to Lisa. I needed to get to bed. I was still shaking from that weird experience with Cal. "Look Lisa, I'm really tired. It's been an exhausting couple of days and to be honest I just want to go to bed. I'll get Cal to ring you tomorrow when he's had a good night's sleep. OK?"

She sounded disgruntled. I could almost see the pout on her pretty doll face. "OK then. I'm sorry to have bothered you, it's just, I did promise Cal I'd call. Still, I'm sorry about the bad news. Goodnight, Sarah."

The line clicked. I'd probably offended her but it wasn't my business to wrap her in cotton wool. "Goodnight, Lisa," I said into the stillness of the dark office.

<hr>

I TOOK JUDE for an early walk the following morning, leaving Mark asleep in my bed. I couldn't get that vision of Cal with the ragged, flapping outline out of my head. Something had been torn away all along one side of his body. Was it an aberration in my mind or something real?

Don't think about it, Sarah. I left the garden by the back gate, followed the green bank curved like an arm around the land on one side, the wide sweep of river lapping the other. The sky was impossibly blue; it gave a cerulean tone to the water below it. While I walked I fed my eyes on contrasting textures of slippery green rocks against rippled mud; swathes of mossy seaweed spread like marmalade on the toast coloured beach, sunlight blazing silver on all the wet surfaces. *Close your eyes, Sarah. Breathe it in.* Ireland would surely be beautiful, but I wanted to keep the memory of this place inside me forever. I had to accept that this was Cal and Ireland was Mark.

Cal came down while Mark and I were eating. I kept my eyes on the plate, dreading that I might see him again like I had the night before. But I remembered the phone call. "Lisa rang last night. I said you'd call her back." The atmosphere in the kitchen was strained. Cal opened cupboards and fiddled with boxes and tins. In the end I think he shook some cereal into a bowl and helped himself to coffee from the pot Mark had made. After that he went into the office and shut the door. I relaxed. "What do you…?" I was suddenly shy with Mark, but we needed to talk about this before he left. "What kind of place would you like to get married in?" Neither of us were church goers, but it would break Mum's heart if we didn't celebrate our vows in some sort of consecrated space. Mark knew Mum well enough to consider this.

"Ah now, I take the idea of making me vows to you seriously enough to do it in a church, if that's what you want, darlin'."

"Well, I think it would make my parents happy." I let my shoulders go. I asked him if his father would come over. Mark's mother had died from cancer when he was fourteen and he left home not much more than a year afterwards, never getting on with his dad. "I'll let him know about it," Mark eventually said, "but don't hold your breath."

The timbre of Cal's voice rumbled out through the gap in the doorframe of the office. I felt awkward sharing the house with the two of them, knowing they were unlikely ever to be friends. Yet though I didn't want to acknowledge it, I was frightened of being alone in the house with Cal. I had seen him flawed, mangled. I mean, I'd known it anyway, that he was irrevocably damaged by his twin's death, but I'd never seen it so graphically. It might just have been my tired brain, but I couldn't shake off the feeling we had disturbed things that should have been left buried.

"Are you alright, honey?" Mark examined me with a worried expression. My eyes came back into focus and I was flooded with the realisation he would be gone soon.

"We have one more day together for now." I slid my arms around him, leaned my head on his chest. "What would you like to do?"

"I'd like to get out the way of me laddie-oh," he nodded over at the office. "How about we walk down to that newsagents shop by the caravan park and get us an ice cream? Then I can paddle me feet in the sea. And maybe this afternoon we could go for a drive, have a look at the church over in — what's it called — Michaelton, is it?"

❦

CAL CAME DOWNSTAIRS just as I was pouring water onto teabags. "Want a cup?"

"No thanks." He made towards the office.

"We're off down the Rose and Crown for a slap-up supper, Cal." Mark cleared his throat. "Would'ya fancy joining us?"

The two men looked at each other across the kitchen. "No thanks." Cal thrust his hands into his jeans' pockets. He wore a thick flannel shirt over a white t-shirt. He still didn't look quite himself. There was sweat on his forehead. I tried to catch his eyes but they flitted about like two mice in a trap. *Oh, Cal.* If Mark hadn't been there I would have tried harder to break the glass wall between us.

"Aren't you hot?" I couldn't think of anything else to say.

"No, I'm fine." Cal nudged open the office door with his shoulder. "Oh and by the way, Lisa's coming tomorrow. She's coming here to stay with me." He wrapped his arms tightly around his waist, one foot in the office and one in the kitchen. He let his eyes meet mine. There was a strange emptiness in his gaze. My heart thumped and I looked away quickly.

Chapter 27

Marion

SENSATIONS HAVE BEGUN to get through to me. I think I've been dormant for a long time. I don't know where I am. Sometimes I feel myself turning within the cramped body I was forced into after the freedom was over. Sometimes I find myself loose, formless, but not free: trying to reattach to the tattered scraps that have hung off my brother since we were born. I nibble at them with my imaginary teeth. I'm sure he is aware of me. But I want to be free again.

Let me go.

Chapter 28

Sarah

LISA HAD INSTALLED herself in Cal's lap on the sofa in our kitchen. They'd been kissing for almost an hour. I kept to myself; afraid of what I'd see when I looked at Cal. I almost felt sorry for Lisa: did she really understand what she was taking on? Mark had left early that morning. I'd cooked breakfast for Cal, but he'd hardly eaten anything. All the time I sat opposite him light prickled at the edges of my vision, or was it around the edges of him? But as soon as I looked away again everything seemed normal.

Lisa's child was being looked after by her father and his new wife. They had a two-year old daughter themselves, named Charlene. Charlene, for goodness' sake. All this Lisa had explained as she bustled her way into the house with a huge rucksack on her back, a cake tin in her hands. She then proceeded to take over my kitchen.

I went down to my studio to work up some sketches of Mark, incorporated the figurative images into abstract designs, his eyes combined with the ripples of the sea, the line of his naked shoulder and hip just visible under the curves of waves. I became totally immersed in the physical process of the pastels and the putty rubber.

Later I went to the fish and chip shop on the caravan site. I ate sitting on the beach in the shelter of a tall red cliff, damp blossoming up through my skirt. I shook the salt off my clothes and was glad to be able to refuse Lisa's offer of a cooked meal when Jude and I returned.

She and Cal canoodled at every opportunity, his hands rudely fondling her breasts without any attempt at discretion. He appeared desperate, losing his self-awareness in her sexuality. What was it, only three nights since he'd lain with Marianne? Both he and I knew that hadn't even been about sex. It niggled at me that Lisa didn't know anything about what had happened over the previous week. I wondered whether Marianne was recovering from her overdose. And then my brain grew too tired to think about any of it.

I fed my dog, retreated to the living room upstairs, switched on the television. I stared more at the view out across fields to the sea than at the screen. When my attention wandered back into the room it fell on the various articles placed around. Everything in the room had been put together by me. The long red velvet curtains at the two tall windows, my painting above the fireplace; the ornate rugs on the floor. I'd take as much as I could to put in my new cottage in County Leitrim, re-form the home I'd come to love in a new country. My gaze fell particularly on the twin paraffin lamps that Mark had originally given me. I suspected that Cal would be moving Lisa in as soon as I'd gone, I couldn't imagine he would live here alone.

It was impossible to tell whether he would love her. I could see how easily he could take physical delight in her, escape in her body. Healthy and plump, she was the antithesis of the starveling-twin replicant he'd seduced, or who had seduced him. Pretty in an unthreatening way, comforting, Lisa would look after him. She was a mother figure, which to be honest was what I'd indulged him by becoming. And at least he could guiltlessly fuck her. But whether he had any passion for her I would probably never know. After I'd watched Eastenders without taking in any of the storyline I switched off the television and went to my own room.

THERE WAS A KNOCK on my door just as it was just getting dark. I had an uncomfortable flashback to Marianne's visit, expected for a moment to see the glass of water and the container of painkillers in Lisa's hand as she moved towards me across the floor. But instead she was holding a letter. In the dim light from a bedside lamp I could see that the envelope was slightly yellowed. My heart thumped.

"I'm sorry to disturb you," Lisa whispered "But I thought you would want to read this. Marion sent it to me a month before she died."

She watched my face as I pulled the letter gently out, smoothed it over my knees. Marion had tried to explain her life to Lisa. 'The only time I feel truly myself is when I have these out-of-body experiences, then I recognise the essence of being in its absoluteness. That's what I want to hold onto more than anything.'

A surreal feeling overtook me. First Marianne had shown up to remind us of Marion, and now Lisa had brought this letter. What could it all mean? I could only keep trying to convince myself that the purpose was to persuade Cal and I to move on, take any opportunities that were offered, achieve our own perceptions of happiness. *As long as Marianne can do the same.*

"She really cared about you," I managed to say, folding the letter ready to slip it back into the envelope. But I smoothed it out again, reading it one last time. Finally I refolded it, slid it into the envelope and handed it back to Lisa. I fiddled with my earring until the sharp pin at the back pierced the skin of my finger. Surprised, I looked down and watched a spot of blood blooming. Lisa looked away, pressing the letter between both of her hands.

"I'm sorry Mum stopped you from coming over that night." I cleared my throat. "She shouldn't have done that. Reading this, I think Marion would have wanted you there."

"I knew she was going to die that night," Lisa said softly. "I was so lonely after she died, but everybody kept saying it was a blessing. My friends and me, we were in the first year of our A Levels, all they wanted to do in their spare time was have fun." She turned and looked me full in the eyes. "I'm not as shallow as you think, Sarah. I learnt a lot from Marion, from her silence."

It came to me what we should do. "I think we should publish Marion's first novel, even things out a bit between her and Cal. What do you think?"

Colour came into her cheeks. "Well, from what she says in the letter it would make sense. She was hurt he had done it without her wasn't she?"

"I have all her work. It's in the loft at Mum and Dad's. I could get it."

I don't know why it hadn't occurred to me that she would have wanted her work published after all. I'd assumed that in abdicating her life, Marion had abdicated the desire to be a recognised author, but now I realised that leaving her work to me had probably meant exactly the opposite; she'd expected me to continue my role as her editor, immortalise her. "Will you help me collate it all?" This had been the reason for Marion, in whatever form, coming back. "She called her first novel *Spirit Wings*. I think there's enough material for a second novel as well. If there's not quite enough we can get Cal to fill in."

Chapter 29

THE DOOR AT the bottom of the attic staircase was open. *The last time I came up here was the night Marianne scared the life out of us. I forced myself to go up again. This is not that time. Marianne has gone now, Cal is with Lisa. Everything is safe.* A trail of sunshine spilled through the open door, halfway down the stairs.

Lisa was standing in the middle of the huge space, turning around slowly. She jumped when she heard my foot creak on the top step. "Cal's asked me to move in with him."

She swept her thick blonde hair away from her neck with one hand, twisted it into some kind of bun. Holding it in place she took a leather hair-slide from a pocket in her dress, stretched it over the bun; poked a small stick through two holes in it. The smoothness of her actions fascinated me. I'd always kept my hair short but I admired the sophistication with which long-haired women created artful hairstyles. I let out a cough. Cal had acted true to form.

"He says we can convert this space into a room for Alice. The kind of room she can grow up in. So… he must be serious then?"

Alarm bells. No. I sensed horror in the thick attic air, just like on that night. "Why this room? It's huge for a small girl like her. You'd be much better decorating the spare bedroom for her downstairs. Or even my room, it's large enough. I don't mind, I won't need it anymore."

What was Cal thinking? This room was as good as haunted. I would never be able to get the picture of Marianne standing here frozen in the moonlight out of my head. But Lisa looked uncertain. Making a circle with her foot on the floorboards she lifted her chin. "I don't know. Cal says she can have her own bathroom up here, a playroom as well as a bedroom."

All tucked nicely out of the way at the top of the house so she wouldn't be too much of a bother to Cal.

Lisa was wearing a blue Indian-cotton dress. It shimmered with tiny mirrors and bells that tinkled as she moved. She went over to the first window and looked out. "I'll have to think about it. Let Alice have a look and see what she thinks."

"You've decided to accept his invitation to move in then?"

Standing next to her at the window I smelt her light perfume mixed with the scent of her body. Even I could see why Cal found her so sexy. She was one of those women who intoxicated men without any effort at all.

"It's mad, isn't it?" But Lisa's eyes sparkled. "I'll have to give up my job and everything, find another one round here. Alice would have to move schools. But I'm going to make some phone calls this afternoon, see what my options are, before I make a decision."

Just as she mentioned the phone Cal's voice bellowed up the stairs. "Lisa, Alice is on the phone!"

She reacted was as though someone had shot her. "Oh Lord, I hope she's alright! I don't know why she'd call at this time of the morning… she should be getting ready for school!"

✦

"THEY'RE GETTING her a puppy. She's so excited about it. At this rate she'll never want to come back to me." Lisa's voice wobbled. Cal pulled her against him, kissing the top of her head.

"We'll get her a puppy as well, and a pony and some guinea pigs too."

"Oh Lord, I haven't even told her about us yet."

He smoothed the long hair out of Lisa's eyes. Liberated from its hair-slide he had it all gathered at the back of her neck. He put his nose there and drew in a breath; I could hear it from where I sat at the table on the other side of the kitchen. I concentrated on my cornflakes and coffee. The two of them stood in the office doorway.

"I love your hair," Cal murmured against her ear, but loud enough to reach me. "I love your hair and your skin, your beautiful round blue eyes as well." I kept my eyes down but sensed the growing urgency of their movements. His voice got rougher. "Jesus, Lisa, you're so sexy."

For goodness' sake. I wasn't even sure if either of them had noticed me but I scraped my chair across the floor; collecting my cereal bowl and coffee from the table.

"Come on, Jude!"

My dog and I went into the garden. My brother didn't seem to have any of the normal kinds of boundaries. He had always been determined to feed himself the moment he got hungry. But I'd seen a new darkness in Cal and it frightened me. It had been getting worse since the night we had to go and see Marianne's mother.

◆◆

THAT AFTERNOON I drove into Hull, stopping at the garage in Restingham for fuel.

"Stay in the car." Jude sat with his ears pricked, a breeze ruffling his fur. I went in to pay and came out with a chocolate-covered ice lolly which I finished off quickly, letting Jude lick the remaining slivers of chocolate off my fingers. When we reached my parents' house, I said "Stay out here in the front garden." I dragged the gate closed behind me. The dog gave me a bored look. He ambled over to the laburnum tree in the corner. "Don't nibble anything over there, it's poisonous." Jude offered me a short bark in response then heaved himself up and went to lie down in the opposite corner instead.

Mum was out on her hospital visiting scheme, one of her many church activities. Dad had got the boxes of Marion's writings lined up in the hall. My fingers itched to go through them there and then, but if I started I would probably carry on until it got dark.

"Now are you sure about this?" Dad said. "It's a lot to take on what with your wedding as well." Mark and I had got a cancellation for a Friday in early August. "You know your mother would have preferred a Catholic service – but she's thrilled you're at least doing it in a church. Thanks for that, Sarah; I know it wouldn't have bothered you, but I'm grateful you considered her feelings."

LISA AND I worked together at the kitchen table every evening for the next week, collating the pages of *Spirit Wings*, Marion's first novel. Every now and then Cal would peer over our shoulders, bristling. In his socks I couldn't hear his footsteps on the quarry tiles but I sensed his approach like a cold shadow. I didn't know how to talk to him anymore. We couldn't seem to stand being alone together. If Lisa wasn't in the room Cal would cast me a guarded glance and leave. He gave me the impression I'd done something wrong. The same thing as always, probably. I was just the wrong sister.

"I don't think this is a good idea," Cal said when we first told him what we planned to do with the book. But then Lisa showed him Marion's letter and it must have brought back all his guilt. His skin tightened; that same static crackling around him I'd felt before. I'd got a similar shock off Marianne the last day she was at our house. But all that seemed so long ago. This period of me, Cal and Lisa living together at the house was like a break between the two sections of mine and Cal's lives.

The following day Cal had a long phone call with his agent, who agreed to represent Marion's work on the basis that Cal would be prepared to write an introduction to each of the two novels we planned to put together. He would also have to do publicity engagements for her books, talking about his dead sister with the media.

During the days Lisa and I were both busy on other projects. I packed up my stuff: it would be transported over to Ireland in the big lorry that was hired for the beginning of July. I planned to get back to work as a full-time artist as soon as I had established my studio in a derelict barn at the back of the cottage. I was soon going to see my new home for the first time; spend two weeks settling in before coming back to England for the wedding at the beginning of the following month.

Lisa came into the kitchen from the office with a flushed, satisfied look on her face the day after I collected the boxes from Dad's. "I've got a school place for Alice in Restingham," she said. "There's a school bus that collects children from all the surrounding villages apparently."

"Have you told Alice yet?"

Her face fell. "No, and I'm really nervous about doing it. She still thinks I'm coming home at the weekend and that everything will go back to normal. Oh Lord, I don't know how I'm going to break it to her."

While I pondered this, I discovered I was holding my hand over my stomach. The night Mark and I got back together I had accepted the possibility of motherhood. It was too early to tell if anything had happened yet, but I would know in another week or so whether my period was late. I was startled out of my thoughts by the phone ringing. It was for Lisa and she went back into the office to take it.

"I have to go out and catch a bus, it's in five minutes." She came out pulling on a pair of battered-looking sandals. She sounded out of breath. "I've been offered a job interview at the Tourist Information Centre in Wittersea." The town was a small seaside resort a few miles up the coast from Pottersea.

It was really happening then. Cal and Lisa were establishing a future together just as I was with Mark. Marianne's face came into my head. Would she ever be able to resume a 'normal' life like we were?

———◆◆———

ALTHOUGH WE TRAILED around quite a few bridal departments, I ended up buying a dress from an ordinary fashion shop. Helen had made a big show of pressing a hanky to her eyes every time I came out of another dressing room in a different creation but Mum was brisk. My dress had a low-waisted bodice and three quarter length sleeves with a lace trim. When I came out wearing it, Mum smiled.

"Well, you're cheap anyway, I'll give you that! Come on; you need some expensive shoes to go with it."

Helen sniffed. "You'll need some ivory-coloured underwear too."

"And you can borrow your grandmother's pearls." Mum gave me a satisfied smile.

———◆◆———

FINDING DRESSES FOR the two girls was easier. Alice and her cousin Phoebe, Helen's daughter, were going to be my bridesmaids. Mum insisted on taking us all for lunch once we had unanimously settled on matching party dresses in a deep rose colour.

"You're all going to look so pretty together," sniffed Helen.

"What are you wearing to be my Matron of Honour then?" I asked.

"My shout," Mum threw in, though technically it was Dad's credit card.

❧

"I'D LIKE TO ask you and Cal to sign the wedding register as my witnesses." I decided to offer Lisa this as we drove back to Blackberry House. It hadn't been that difficult to put a smile of gratitude on her face after all. Back at the house Alice went crazy running around the attic which was already marked out in tape with some partition walls half-erected. No amount of persuasion on my part had been able to convince her that my room or the spare bedroom on the first floor landing would have been better for her.

"This is going to be my sleeping room and through this door here is the corridor, and this bit will be my bathroom," she explained in her incongruously raucous voice, dragging me into one partitioned space after another. I had to admit the rooms were going to look good, and I could see Cal's point about designing a space for her in which she could comfortably grow up into a young woman. Best of all the building work was a clear indication of his intention to keep Lisa and Alice in his life. I only hoped Lisa would be able to put up with his moods, be stronger about standing up to him than I had been.

"Sarah, Sarah," shouted Alice from the other end of the attic. I peeped around the partition wall of her bathroom.

"Yes?"

"This bit, you've got to come and look – this bit is going to be called my library!"

Chapter 30

20ᵗʰ of June 1989

THREE DAYS BEFORE my visit to Ireland I was alone in Blackberry House for the first time in ages. Alice was at school. Cal had taken Lisa into Wittersea on her first morning in her new job. The phone rang in the office just as I came into the kitchen with Jude. I hung up his lead first, checked he had water, kicked off my sandals. The phone rang on and on. Cal had mentioned several 'wrong number' calls over the past few days, but this time there was a voice on the other end when I answered. Something about the voice was familiar, but that feeling came more from the chill on the back of my neck than anything else.

"Is that Sarah?"

"Yes."

"Thank God. I've been trying to get hold of you for days. Not that I really wanted to but I don't know what else to do."

The chill spread up into my scalp. It couldn't be... Why would she? The woman breathed unevenly. I said, "Who is this?"

"I'm sorry to bother you. I certainly didn't want to have to do this. But... I'm Geraldine Fairchild. I'm ringing about my daughter, Marianne."

No. No. all this was supposed to be over. The first thing I should have asked was 'Is Marianne OK?' But I couldn't. I started chewing at the skin around my thumbnail before realising I was replicating Marianne's habit. Her mother carried on talking.

"She has a preposterous idea that… I can't say it. It's imperative that she never sees or speaks to your brother again but I thought you…"

The sound of Jude lapping from his bowl by the back door carried through to the office. I curled my bare toes into the worn carpet.

"I want you to convince her that… she isn't what she thinks she is. She has a ridiculous notion… do you know what I'm talking about?"

I struggled to swallow. "I'm sorry, you'll – you'll have to explain."

Jude stopped lapping and I heard his loud sigh as he collapsed into his creaking basket. A silence crumbled and cracked into place. Then she spoke again.

"Marianne is obsessed with your brother. Callum Wilde." His name sounded like poison coming from her. "She seems to think – she says that she knew him before. She couldn't possibly have done, since she's only seventeen." There was a short pause. "She is very confused, deeply depressed. She does not seem able to come out of the melancholia caused by her overdose."

Melancholia. Such an old-fashioned word, I pictured Marianne again as a Bronte heroine, tramping across the moors, cloak flapping. I didn't know what Geraldine Fairchild wanted from me. My whole body prickled with what felt like tiny arrows, I had to sit down.

"Are you still there?" Her voice sharpened, like when Cal and I visited her house.

"Yes."

"I rang you because I sensed you'd be willing to help. I don't know what else to do, I'm asking you to go and see her; convince her that she's wrong. The anorexia, you know, it plays tricks with her mind. The doctors have explained this to me."

A long time seemed to go by. Marianne's face came to my mind as I had first seen it under that white spotlight. The same adrenalin rush went through me. My heart gave a few irregular thumps. *You're getting married Sarah, soon you'll be far away from all this. It'll seem like it never happened.* It was our fault Marianne had gone home that night and taken an overdose. *Cal's fault.* If there was anything I could do to put Marianne's life back on track I should do it. I had to pay her a visit. I wouldn't be able to live with myself otherwise. "Where is she?"

I heard Geraldine's expelled breath. "She's in the psychiatric unit at St James' Hospital. I will give her caring team your name so they will know to expect you. I still think…"

I picked up the heavy black telephone and walked over to the tiny office window, pushed it open, snatched a deep breath of early summer air. The incoming tide played its hypnotic tune against the river beach and the screeching cries of a pair of seagulls evoked eternal mournfulness. I had to fight an urge to burst into tears. Geraldine seemed to collect herself before continuing.

"I still think," she repeated in a careful voice, "that your brother behaved abominably, inviting my daughter to his home."

I didn't feel like reminding her it was my home too. *Not for much longer though.* "He took advantage of an impressionable girl. He is old enough to be her father. But I appreciate that you are willing to try and help. If at all possible I'd like you to visit her tomorrow. She is being moved onto a programme of treatment with restricted visiting after that, so it may be more difficult. Have you got a pen and paper ready so I can give you the details of where to go?"

⸻❖⸻

I COULDN'T FACE the drive to Leeds so soon after the last two visits. Instead I took the train, leaving my car at Hull station. I would take a taxi to the hospital in Leeds. I'd told Cal and Lisa I was doing wedding-related errands, mentioned that the dog would need walking and hoped one of them would do it. Geraldine needn't have worried about keeping the visit to Marianne secret from my brother. What I hoped to do was close this episode in our lives forever. We were doing the right thing by Marion, working on her books. And all because of Marianne. I owed her and her family the peace of mind I'd expected to get for myself when I dropped her off at the train station in Hull. Since then my brother had become a stranger to me. He was trailing the unfinished seams of his severed duality like a wound. The wound needed to be healed. Possibly setting Marianne's mind at ease was the way to do that.

On the train I tried to read but couldn't concentrate. The window above me was open and air blew over my skin. I looked out at the framed views of fields racing by, tried to imagine what it would be like to be locked in a room, unable to feel any breeze. I supposed Marianne now felt trapped in the hospital, terrified. I remembered her eyes, so similar to Marion's, and the way she had changed during her time in our house. I wondered what I was going to say to convince her she was just herself; that she belonged in the Fairchild family, not in ours.

WALKING DOWN THE smooth-floored corridor, glancing through the open doors of small rooms and larger bays divided by curtains, I noticed most particularly those thin girls like her with huge eyes in wasted faces. I saw a young girl, maybe no more than thirteen, reading on a window-seat. Two older girls were playing a board game in a glassed-off room. I passed a young woman on a bed, hunched miserably over folded knees which she could have wrapped her wire-like arms around twice.

The last time I saw Marianne she'd been keeping up appearances, seemed fit to burst with energy, despite barely eating and with hardly any sleep. So I was shocked to find her in bed wearing pink pyjamas that were decorated with white hearts. They made her look like a child. She was on her side with her face towards me as I entered the cubicle, but her eyes were closed. The skin on her face was sallow; there was a rash of spots on her cheek and chin. The thin blanket on the bed was pushed down to her waist revealing rigid arms, hands tucked between her drawn-up knees. Her bed was in one of the larger bays off the ward, partitioned by stiff blue curtains. A young nurse with the name-badge 'Jessica' explained that

Marianne was about to be moved into a room shared with one other girl. Jessica bustled into the cubicle with me.

"Come on Marianne, you need to get up now. Snack time soon."

Turning aside Jessica whispered to me, "We try to keep them in a routine, get used to eating at certain times."

"That seems a good idea." But I didn't like Marianne being referred to as one of 'them'.

Marianne, lying with her face half-buried in the pillow, must have heard the whispered exchange. She bolted upright in the bed, pushed limp hair away from her face.

"Don't fucking talk about me behind my back." Her amber eyes were narrowed into slits but they opened wide when she realised it was me that Jessica was talking to. "Sarah." The sudden animation in her face died down like a candle going out. "How did you know I was here?"

I decided to be honest, explaining that her mother had telephoned and asked me to visit. I sat down on the orange vinyl chair, my hands on the seat either side of me. They squeaked as I slid them forward. Hesitantly, Marianne shuffled to the edge of the bed, hugging her knees. Jessica propped herself up in the doorframe, taking mental notes I guessed. But Marianne said she would only talk to me if Jessica left the room.

"OK," agreed Jessica. "Half an hour." The girls were expected to be in the social room for snacks and drinks at the regulated time. Marianne pulled a cotton robe on over her pyjamas. She kept her eyes averted, constantly pushed back the hair from her face, a gesture so similar to Cal's. Her movements were weighty, ponderous; I wondered if she was drugged. "They've given up telling me to get dressed. But I think I will tomorrow. I don't want them to think they're in control, that's all."

She spoke in a mumble, her voice devoid of the vivacity she had at Blackberry House. "They treat you like a piece of meat, making you strip off to get weighed all the time. Watching you while you eat."

"How are you feeling now?" The question was the best I could come up with as an opener. She gave me an intense look from her amber eyes. *Stupid question.* I saw that she was pinching her arm under the sleeve of her dressing gown. The look in her eyes never changed as she twisted the skin corkscrew fashion. It made me feel sick. Marion's expression had been exactly the same when she wanted to draw my attention to the control she had over her body. *You mustn't think like that. This is Marianne, not Marion.*

"We should never have invited you out for a drink in the first place, Marianne." The words came out without me even thinking about it. The only thing to do was tell the truth. Her eyes narrowed and she let go of the flesh on the inside of her arm. A red mark had blossomed before her sleeve fell back down.

"You couldn't have stopped me finding him," she spat out. "I had to see him. I went there specifically that night. Even after..."

I didn't ask. Her father had told us about her first overdose and her mother said she had done it after she read Cal's book. And the question she had asked at the TV recording was about *The Shell.* That was what had brought her to Broadcasting House that night. She continued to stare at me with those hot eyes, winding dulled copper hair around one finger, first one way, then the other. Finally she began to examine the ends of her hair. When she did that she reminded me of any other teenager. I turned to look out of the window at a square of garden with rose bushes around the edge. A magpie landed in the middle and I had to stop myself from saying 'pardon milord' as Mum had once told me you must if you see *one for sorrow*. Part of another rhyme from her repertoire of bird-verses.

There was no point arguing about whether or not Marianne was a reincarnation of my sister. She hadn't been specific and neither would I. "It's just not to be," was all I could think of to say, turning back to face her. "You have to let go of it. All the things you're thinking. You have a mother who cares about you, whatever you believed before. And your sisters, and your dad. You have to live the life you've been given." *And allow me to live mine.*

While I'd been speaking she'd been chewing the ends of her hair. I pictured the hairball growing in her stomach. Mum had warned Marion and me about it when we were children. I didn't know how to separate this Marianne from my past. But she had a life of her own; it had to count for something, didn't it? She was young enough to put her recent experiences behind her and carve out a future that would be her own.

The tang of her breath hung on the air between us from her open mouth while a silence festered. I saw that my knuckles were white from my clenched fingers and I welcomed the pain as I unfurled them.

"There's a girl in here." Her voice was low. She leaned towards me and I had to withdraw from her bad breath. "She hears voices in her head; I mean actual voices. They interrupt her when she's having conversations with real people and she breaks off from the real people to talk to them, the invisible ones. She wakes up and answers their questions in the middle of the night. The doctors here think I'm like her. They say I'm confused because of – what they think I've got. Not that they know anything." She sat back, fixed me with a challenging stare. I cleared my throat. But she continued speaking before I could come up with a response. "I don't hear those kinds of voices in my head. But. Sometimes. I remember things." Her gaze intensified as her voice hoarsened. "I can't *not* remember. You know what I'm talking about."

A brightly-coloured bird landed on the windowsill. I think it might have been a blue tit but I couldn't be sure. The window was closed and I wondered if Marianne could open it if she wanted. The same primeval sadness overwhelmed me as in the attic when she screamed. Both of us turned our hands over in our laps, examined our fingernails. It seemed to indicate the sisterly connection I had to deny in order to set both of us free. Yet in that moment I did want to keep her. I wanted my sister. The sorrow was sweeter than bitter. I made a great effort to remember why I was there. "You've got to move on. You have to. The past is the past." I turned my face back to the window. The bird had gone but I continued looking just in case it returned.

I heard Marianne get off the bed. She padded barefoot up and down the cubicle, breathing quickly. Her loose gown flapped like a white bird. As she passed me I noted from the corner of my vision how sunlight glinted off the downy hair on her face. Marion grew hair on her face too. Her skin wasn't thick enough to warm her. A scuffed pipe close to the floor crept under the plastic curtain, bringing a belching supply of hot water to the cream-painted radiator. The air thickened as the small space grew even hotter. I pushed sticky strands of hair off my forehead, allowed my glance to fall back on her when she hissed, "It's you who can put your past behind you."

She raised her hands, palms upwards, a gesture like the one she had made on the first night we met. "Your past is just an ordinary one. The things you remember actually happened to you. But I have to keep fighting off memories of things that can't really have happened to me. And yet I know they did. It's inside me. The deep awareness of him... Cal. He's as much a part of my past as he is yours." She pulled at her hair. I decided to be cruel; maybe she had to be hurt even more to be mended again. I looked around quickly to check Jessica wasn't hovering by the door.

"He doesn't want you, Marianne, you need to know that. Didn't you notice that he could hardly look at you when you left? He was wrong to do... we were both wrong. We made a big mistake, and now I'm sorry, but it's over."

I wasn't prepared for the look on her face when I said that, or what happened next. I shouldn't have gone to the hospital. It had only made things worse.

———◆◆◆———

THE PRESENT NO longer seemed real. Recent days – choosing a wedding dress, working on Marion's manuscript and making arrangements for my trip to Ireland, were just a dream. Marianne's existence was an immovable obstacle to contentment. How could I snatch such a thing for myself after messing up her life so badly?

Just as I was about to leave the hospital she'd gone into one of her episodes. Like the one in the attic. Like when I saw

Marion in the garden. Immediately before it she'd turned her furious eyes on me and made a strangled sound in her throat. Then her eyes glazed over. Her jaw went into spasm; she turned rigid on the spot. She stood, her body twisted towards me, completely immobile. I didn't know what to do. My own muscles flooded with adrenalin. At about the same time, Jessica came through the door of the bay and pushed aside the curtain around Marianne's bed.

"Oh no," she muttered. "It seems her medication isn't working after all. You'd better leave. I don't think having visitors is doing her any good."

Chapter 31

6th of August 1989

Sarah

LISA AND I were both pregnant, due at exactly the same time in early February. I was back from Ireland, and Mum had come in to my old room to help me curl my hair on the morning of my wedding. "You always had a wave in your hair, Sarah, that's why it suited you short, even as a child. Caitlin's hair was the same as yours; do you remember her golden curls?"

I nodded. I hadn't forgotten one detail of the brief life of my baby sister. Mum leaned forward so her reflection was next to mine in the mirror. "Now then, this isn't a day for tears. They were the happiest days of my life, when you four were young. You were excellent with Caitlin, even at the age of six."

Get back to the present. "Mum, do you think Cal and Lisa will get married?"

"Oh, I hope so. For now I'm just keeping my fingers crossed that he's mature enough to put other people's needs before his own. He's always been spoilt, our Cal." She met my eyes again in the mirror.

"We're both guilty of indulging him," I said.

"You just did your best, like I did. I do understand, you know." She laid her hand on my shoulder.

"What do you mean?"

Seeing the two ovals of our faces together it struck me how similar we were. I'd never been able to see it before, always looking into her eyes for Caitlin or Marion. But now I saw that I'd been there all the time.

"You tried so hard to look after everyone else. Even me; you never blamed me for neglecting you. And I'm sorry. I just want to say that now." Picking up the curling tongs again she added the final touches to my hair. Silently I handed her the white flower clip to go on the side of my head. With the eyeliner smudged under my eyes I looked like an actress in an old silent movie.

After I had touched up my make-up she fastened the pearls around my neck. "I wore these at my own wedding. If you have a girl you can pass them on to her."

⸻◆◆⸻

WE'D BOUGHT OUR flowers from the Humber market the morning before and Helen and I created our own bouquets, winding them with ribbons from the haberdashers on Hessle Road, setting aside buttonholes for the guests. It was a sisterly activity, highlighting the lack of my real sisters. What age would Caitlin have been by now? Twenty-nine, I worked out. A young woman who looked something like me. I tried to picture Marion without her anorexia, imagined how it would have been to match their outfits up with Helen's. I envied her for still having her sister.

WE WERE MARRIED. Mark and I kissed. We went to sign the register and afterwards we were supposed to turn and walk back down the aisle but Mark stopped halfway. "Hang on a minute there, Sarah." He turned me around, but then took his hands off my shoulders and left me standing there while he returned to the altar.

Someone handed him his fiddle and he began to tune it up. To my astonishment figures with other instruments popped up from the pews, including Mum with her flute. Then Dad got up, fumbling to get his hand into the strap of a bodhran. There was Iris from The Shanbos with her accordion, Frank with his mandolin, bringing the microphone down the steps from the altar so he could sing into it. The musicians arranged themselves into a ramshackle band. And they played my song: *Sarah in the Moonlight*, the one Mark had written just after he met me.

After a couple of verses the song lapsed into an exuberant instrumental, the musicians competing with each other for speed. With a rustling of fabrics and a clattering of high-heels the congregation finally spilled out of the church in a cacophony of music.

THE RECEPTION WAS held at Blackberry House, Lisa and Cal's wedding gift to us. Fairy lights were strung up all over the garden in preparation for the evening; a stage had been set up against my old studio. Turning back from the locked door of what was now Cal's office I saw the garden milling with people. In the five years Cal and I lived together in Blackberry House it had been a place of solitude for both of us. I hoped Lisa would make it into a real family home; the house was perfect for it.

Alice took me up to show off her new rooms, the floors carpeted and the walls freshly painted. I stood on the threshold, reluctant to go in. I repeatedly rubbed the back of my neck. But Alice insisted on dragging me through the rooms to the one at the end that she called her library. I saw them again: Cal and Marianne looking out of that window.

"This is my special princess bed." Back in the first room Alice ran her hand lovingly under the tassels dangling from the canopy above the white-painted bed, every young girl's dream, I imagined. Pink fairy lights pinned to her door spelled out the word ALICE, she switched it on to show me. I fought the dread. "Do you like sleeping up here, Alice?"

"Oh yes, this is the best bedroom ever." She let out a croaking laugh. But at the same time she put up a finger to her mouth, her eyes clouded over. I moved forward a few steps. "What's the matter? You look worried."

She plonked her bottom down on the bed with a rustle of the satiny material of her dress, her hand squeezing the edge of a pink furry blanket draped over the end. "Oh, I'm not worried."

"You're not?"

"No… not worried exactly. She doesn't hurt me; she's not even scary really. I just don't like the way she stares."

My feeling of dread intensified. "Who's not scary?"

Alice gazed up at me, her lips that looked as soft as rose-petals hung open. Her big blue eyes had not yet lost that look of wisdom babies have, as if they've seen things you would never imagine. "Don't stand there." Her voice tightened. She grasped the blanket harder, squeezing and releasing her fingers reflexively. "That's where the funny girl stands."

I looked up to see that I was positioned exactly under the first window, where we had discovered Marianne, standing with wide open eyes the night she had disappeared.

Chapter 32

28th August 1989

Marianne

SHE WAS VERY tired after the journey. She'd had to walk down the long drive of the hospital, catch a bus at the hospital entrance, go from the bus stop to the train station; count out coins that had lain for months in her purse for the driver, all in the pedantic slowness of a dream. The air seemed like syrup, moving her limbs through it took enormous effort.

In the high-ceilinged station the echoing noises hit her eardrums with the sharpness of Ping-Pong balls, cracking the air. There were too many people. More coins; notes to count out for the train ticket, zipping the cloth purse up carefully. Turning slowly on the spot to locate the correct platform. "That one, Miss, over there, you see it?"

She pivoted in the direction indicated, patted her knitted bag, slung across her body. Safe, everything was safe. She had left the suitcase Geraldine brought in for her back at the hospital, not supposed to be leaving until the next day with her parents. This foot, that foot, moving one in front of the other over the chilled stone towards the train. Slide into a seat.

Feel her heart beating under the cold hand on her breastbone. *Take me to Hull.*

She was wearing the clothes she had left Blackberry House in last time. It seemed right; a faded cotton dress, lilac cardigan pinioned by folded arms across her body. A disgusting bulge of a belly swelling beneath them this time. Ugh, day after day they had forced her to eat, watching every mouthful that went in, watching to ensure it stayed down. In the train window reflection she noted a face so bloated it appalled her. She pinched her arms repeatedly. There were many bruises beneath the sleeves of her cardigan. She must not listen to that voice. *Stay here, stay here,* to the rhythm of the train, *I am Marianne. I am.*

For months she had been incarcerated in that place; in white rooms or outside in the hospital garden, in patches of sunlight or in dappled shade from the tall plane trees along the wide path to the entrance. She was allowed to sit there on a bench rubbed raw at its edge by the fingers of patients before her. Wind in the high branches had whistled an aching lament that seemed to get right inside her. Air blew through her clothes. She viewed the slow shuffle of other patients from the corners of her eyes. She waited for Cal, who never came. Cal was always in her mind. Sometimes someone was sitting beside her, an entity both comforting and terrifying. A she-being never visually clear but viewed in increments: the pronounced curve of a wrist-bone poking out from the sleeve of a cheesecloth blouse, a strand of reddish hair similar to Marianne's own, a shrug of a shoulder in denim. In a sudden rush of breeze through the leaves above her head Marianne thought she heard a scornful laugh. For once it was on the outside of her body, not inside like it usually was.

The more food that was forced into Marianne's body, the less real she had become. She had been pushed out of herself, soon there would be no room left for her in the body at all. Some days she had stared for hours at nothing; staff coming to peer at her and issue meaningless words from time to time. Snow White in her glass coffin.

And then the trances would come – the tingle in the fingers and the slight judder followed by rictus in her jaw; the inability to speak or move any part of her body. She was aware of them now, these fits, whereas in the past she had come to, confused, knowing there was some sort of time jolt but with no memory of the episode. Now when the episodes arrested her there was always Cal, sometimes the small boy she had spotted in the mirror in the hallway of her home, sometimes a young man, turning to her with a sheaf of papers in his hand. No other definition than Cal. There was an unfastened lid on this coffin of dreams, but she had not had the courage to open it yet. *But soon, Marianne. He will be so pleased to see you, wondering where you've been.*

Every fucking day Jessica sat with Marianne while she ate, trying to make her 'open up' in group and individual therapy. Marianne was forced to strip off most of her clothes to be weighed. Regular blood tests were done. One day Jessica came into the room, early on, a day on which Marianne had refused to get out of bed. Jessica perched on the edge of the wooden-armed chair covered in orange plastic. She waited until Marianne's eyes had managed to focus on her face and then she spoke. "You know, we need to talk about the baby." *The baby. No. I don't know whose baby you are talking about. Keep your face blank.*

"No? Well, we don't want to push you, but you will have to acknowledge it soon Marianne. I think we should bring it up in family therapy next week."

No, no.

Geraldine had been making such an effort to do the right thing by her for the first time in Marianne's life. *Talk, talk, talk.* "What do you think, Marianne?"

Joseph would be sitting in the circle at other times, sometimes Charissa as well and only once Justine. Marianne was being rehabilitated into her family. Or so the people at the hospital thought.

Exit the train at Hull Station. *Now some feeling comes into the heart.* The feet she walked on took steps across the wide, busy road – the blare of a car horn sent a jolt through her senses. She easily remembered where the bus to Pottersea left from in the centre of town. Every inch of the journey to that longed-for place was a relived memory. She was sitting high up in the bus. It raced past the fields and the small estates of houses, the tightly packed villages and spread-out farms. Emptiness opened all around. She would be able to breathe again, fill her body with air.

"This is your stop, love." She had paid her fare to Blackberry House, Pottersea.

Her legs still felt the motion of the bus as it pulled away. She crossed the road and walked round the house to the back door, expecting to find Sarah in the kitchen. She'd pictured her there preparing food. Maybe Jude would come running to greet her. She was coming alive again, back where she belonged. It had been so long. A flutter, just a tiny flutter of something like moth wings in her stomach.

Something was different about the garden, black soil turned over in clumps. A bright rubber ball lay in the dirt. Nobody answered her knock at the door; peering through the glass she saw the kitchen was empty. This was not how she had imagined her return. Confused, she stepped back. Maybe they had gone for a walk on the beach with the dog, Cal and Sarah. What if Cal had an appointment, an interview or a TV show like the one she had met him at? They wouldn't be back for ages then. But if so, the dog would have been at home, sniffing from the other side of the kitchen door, eager to greet her.

Surely Cal wouldn't mind if she waited inside the house? She needed to sit down, get a glass of water, she was so tired. If only they had left a key. She could have prepared them some food for when they got back.

A small window was propped open above the kitchen sink, too high for her to reach, but she would be able to climb through it, she was sure. A sawn-off section of tree trunk had been pushed against the side of the house, with a flat top like a table, it made a convenient step. Marianne climbed up onto it, holding on to the drain pipe that ran alongside the window. She scraped her shin as she scaled the wall, welcomed the dragging pain as a vivid reminder that she was alive. The window ledge bit into her stomach when she squeezed herself through. She turned her body so that first one foot then the other found the draining board and landed on it. A plastic pot with a small plant in it toppled to the floor. When it had come to a rattling halt the silence echoed around her.

Marianne sat on the edge, sliding carefully down to the floor, her bag banging against her hip.

"Hello… Sarah?"

No reply. The dustpan and brush were kept under the sink; she remembered that, dropping to her knees to retrieve them. She pressed the delicate plant as carefully as she could back into the compost she collected from the floor, replacing the pot on the edge of the draining board. She washed her hands and dried them. Kindling had been lit in her stomach, a fire slowly spread up into her chest. But she was frightened as well. What if…? But he would want to see her, surely. She was back; finally. Oh God, how wonderful and proper. She felt the Marianne she had been in this house coming back to life, blood singing once more all the way to the tips of her fingers. She had been so numb since then.

After folding the towel and replacing it on the pull-out rail she looked round the kitchen. It had a different feel to it – more colour. That pink anorak on the pegs under the stairs stood out, surely not something Sarah would wear. Marianne fingered it, lifted it up: a small child's coat. Why was there a child's coat in Cal and Sarah's kitchen?

An unfamiliar dog bed – not the one Jude had slept in, was under the stairs too, a floppy dog-toy nestled in the centre. Marianne turned slowly, surveyed the rest of the kitchen. In the middle of the table a plastic mug with the letter 'A' hung on the mug tree. A thick sheaf of papers with a photograph tacked to it lay on top of the dresser. She went to look.

When she touched it a weight slammed hard on the top of her head, pushed her into the ground. For a moment she felt cold earth clogging her windpipe, tasted it in her mouth. Her eyes were blind in the silent darkness. *Let me out, help.*

Then breath struggled out, the blackness dissipated. Her hand shook like the wing of a tiny bird as it lifted the picture. *That photograph is of me – but I don't remember having it taken.*

The top page of the manuscript had Cal's contact details typed on, but the name of the author was 'Marion Wilde'. *You look just like my sister, her name was Marion.* Marianne's legs buckled. *There is a bird in my chest, beating its wings to get out. Let it out.* Finish the story; it had gone on too long. Take a breath in, let it out again. Do the same thing over and over. She walked up the wooden stairs, grasped the banister to steady herself. At the top she turned left and went into the living room, examined the new sofa, the different lamps on the two small tables. They were electric ones, although her memory smelled the paraffin fumes from that night in May. In her head she heard the U2 song that had played, felt the buttons of Cal's spine beneath her fingers again as she held onto him. It had been the best night of her life.

She went to one of the windows and looked out at the sea, a shimmering line in the distance. Rabbits bounded across the field over the road. Tears streamed down her face, she put up a long hand to displace them. *I need to see the attic one more time.* The room she had dreamed of so many times during the preceding months. She didn't know where she would go after that. Tip tap tip tap. *The troll under the bridge.* Tip tap tip tap. *Goldilocks climbing the stairs of the three bears' house.* And when she reached the top, what did she see?

Walls where before there had been no walls. She saw a child's clothes all over the floor in the boxed-in section of what had been her own precious attic. They had said she could have this room: *"You could, Marianne, if you wanted to."* A white-canopied bed. ALICE; spelt out in pink lights on the door. *Who is Alice?* Oh. There was the tingling in her fingers, the snap of her jaw followed by rigidity, a paralysis taking her over. Oh no. This time the vision was vivid. She lay on a bed in the breeze of an open window, the scent of apple blossom drifting in from a garden. Cal's face leaned over hers; *"It wasn't meant to be about you, honestly."* But it was. It always had been. She came to standing under the first window, nauseous and scared.

Everything they had tried to do for her at the hospital was pointless; nobody had listened to the truth, and the truth was impossible to bear alone.

Chapter 33

A SHADOW CROSSED the sun, presaging Cal's appearance in the glass of the kitchen door. Marianne's heart struggled to lift. But it felt like a tired bird, the weight of her flesh pinned her to the chair. Cal's hand lowered a key towards the lock in the door but it stopped as his face looked up and saw her. A voice behind him which didn't sound like Sarah's asked, "What are you waiting for?"

Marianne felt detached, only just interested. Nothing more.

"Cal, will you please open the door so we can get in?" The voice was less patient the second time. Still, Cal stared through the glass pane. Marianne kept her eyes on his. She heard a thud, a woman cursing. A child's hoarse voice asked, "Why aren't we going in?" and a dog let out a high-pitched bark. It did not sound like Jude.

Then another shape filled the glass pane in the door, a strong-looking woman with honey blonde hair tied back from her face. She shouldered past Cal, her arms full of a picnic basket and some coats. Managing to free a hand she took the key from him and turned it in the lock. The child slipped through the gap between the woman and Cal, fresh air funnelling in with her, but as soon as she got into the kitchen she stopped, her eyes stretched wide open.

"Mummy. Why is the funny girl in our kitchen now?"

"Lisa, don't..." Cal's words fell too late.

"Oh Lord." She let the coats slide to the floor, groaning to pick them up; placed them on a chair. She was tall, plump, with baby-doll eyes, stirring echoes of familiarity, but Marianne couldn't think from where.

"Marianne." *Oh. Cal.*

"Marion?" the woman breathed. This Lisa. Using that wrong name again. So similar to her own but different enough to be chilling.

I am not Marion.

Marianne's fingers scratched the grooved wood of the table. Laying her hand flat on the surface it felt like an anchor to her palm. She saw Lisa's eyes fix on her torn finger-ends. "Who is she?" Marianne pointed a finger at Alice. She would not look at Lisa, but she could hear her panting breaths. The child seemed frightened, clutching her mother. Cal took a step into the room.

"Marianne..."

"Mari-*anne*... Who is she?"

Those words came from Lisa. A golden Labrador puppy bounded in from the garden, it wriggled straight up to Marianne with a grin on its face. It sniffed at her leg, began to lick the fresh graze on her skin with care. She put her hand down absently to stroke it. The story had changed along with all the characters since she had last been there.

"Cal." That Lisa's voice was sharp, "What's bloody going on?"

Cal ignored all the questions. "I didn't recognise you at first..." His lips continued moving but no more words came out of those strips of pink flesh flapping at the air like a fish on the glass of a tank. "Who *are* they?" Marianne half-stood, but her legs were too weak to hold her up. She dropped back into the chair. The atmosphere was so tense it was almost boring, why bother with all the drama? *Let us just get to the end of the story. I'm tired.*

"How did you get in?" Cal started walking towards her, stopping and then moving forward again. *What's the time, Mr Wolf?* Life was no more than a child's game, a fairy story but with no happy ending to look forward to. She indicated the square window above the sink with her eyes, and they all looked up at it as well, dropping their gaze back down to her in disbelief.

"I expect you're all thinking I'm too fat to get through that."

Marianne pressed at the swelling under her dress, hoping it would go away. Sweat tickled her spine but she pulled the cardigan around her more tightly. Nobody said anything, silence stretched across the room like an elastic band.

"Mummy." The child's voice broke it; not much more than a whisper. "I need the toilet."

Lisa cleared her throat. She put on the kind of voice mothers use for their children. "I tell you what, just this once, I'm going to let you take Bonzo upstairs to your room. You can go to the toilet up there. Stay up there until I call you down, OK?"

But it seemed the child did not want to detach from her mother. "Come with me…" She had her arms tightly round Lisa's waist, refusing to let go. As one form they shuffled across the floor to the bottom of the stairs where Lisa managed to peel her daughter's hands away and fasten them onto the banister. She was rigid, like Marianne when she went into one of her fits. She said to Cal, "I'm taking Alice up to her room. You'd better get this sorted out."

"Her room?" Marianne rose up out of her seat, her hands banging flat on the table. "Her room? They promised that room to me, Cal and Sarah did." Her voice arched towards the high ceiling. It seemed to shake Cal from the inside out. His hands flailed up to his face and down again to his sides. Marianne watched the child's arms coiling back around her mother's waist like a whip, the fingers pinching through the thin fabric of her dress. They were only halfway up the stairs. Lisa was gripping the banister by then with white knuckles.

"Promised it to you... what does she mean?" Lisa directed the question at Cal, taking care to avoid Marianne. *I am invisible.* But he only licked his lips, addressed Marianne. "We didn't think we would ever see you again. Your mother said she would call the police if I tried to contact you."

"Call the police... Oh Lord it was you, the one who..." Lisa finally turned to Marianne. There was twisted compassion and horror on her face, mixed with something else. Fear.

But Marianne kept her gaze on Cal. "And you let my mother threaten you. I've spent months dreaming of coming back here. Months. What are they *doing* here, Cal?" Her arm swept out towards Lisa and Alice. She seemed to drift above the scene in the kitchen. The air in the room wavered like a guitar string after the note had been played.

"Yes, Cal," Lisa put in quietly, "why don't you explain everything?"

Cal made a strangled sound. His hand was on his throat and he couldn't seem to speak. Marianne caught the fear in the eyes of the child still on the stairs. She reigned in her rage. "Perhaps you'd better take her upstairs." The girl reminded her of Justine; she was only a child after all, she would have known nothing of the theft from Marianne of the room she called hers. While Lisa steered her daughter upstairs Cal slunk like a shadow into the cloakroom. The disappointment Marianne felt in him then, the sense of desertion was heavier than the lump they had made by forcing all that food into her stomach. She sat motionless at the table until the action resumed.

Cal reappeared just as Lisa came back, rubbing his hands together as if they were cold. Marianne could tell Lisa was making an effort to stay calm. But she smelt the fear on the older woman. When their eyes met Marianne felt disturbed. She didn't want to think why. But she wanted to know how the new situation had come about. "Why do you live here now? When I was here before it was just Cal and Sarah. How can everything have changed so much?"

"Tell her, Cal, it's not my place to do it…" Lisa sat down at the table, put a hand out to touch Cal, but withdrew it again, curved her fingers protectively inside her palm. She sat with her hands clenched. Cal slid into the seat beside her, they were both opposite Marianne. She watched them exchanging long glances. Lisa pressed the back of a hand to her forehead and Marianne saw Cal give her a worried look. Then he put his tongue between his lips again, brushed them with a thin sheen of moisture. "Lisa and I have known each other a long time. Since we were children."

Marianne studied the two of them, sitting close together but not touching. Something inside her detached itself like that cry that had left her body before. She was usually so controlled. She felt frightened to be coming apart this way.

The hospital had done that to her, taken away her methods of order. *Talk, talk, talk.* She was sick of it.

"So?"

What a long process, so tedious, this eking out of information, and what was the point of it? *Get to the end quickly.*

"She and I…"

"I'm his bloody girlfriend. Alice and I live here with Cal now. I'm sorry if that bothers you, but I don't even know why you're here."

Marianne pulled her bag towards her from the next seat at the table, fumbled in it for a cigarette. Another long silence, this one filled with holes. Into them fell the sounds of Marianne lighting a match, her indrawn breath, the click of Cal's knuckles, Lisa's long sigh. "I didn't know you smoked." Cal's voice sounded as weary as she felt. It was all so impossible, inevitable. She caught a glimpse of the reflection of a girl in the black shiny surface of the oven door. Someone. *Marianne.* A long brittle hand lifted the cigarette between two fingers, placed it in the mouth. Someone else stared out of her own reflected eyes.

"I didn't, before. But they made me eat at that hospital. Forced food into me. They took away all my fucking choice. So I took up smoking. Deal with it." The two others watched with nervous glances as a cloud of smoke engulfed her head and her features temporarily disappeared. She could see them though, through the mist in front of her eyes which pricked and stung. She wondered what she should do about them.

Chapter 34

AT THE TOP of the stairs the attic door banged open. The puppy scrabbled down the kitchen staircase followed by the child. She stopped part of the way down.

"Mummy." Her tone was plaintive but Marianne noticed her eyes flicking slyly from side to side, calculating. "I'm hungry." She progressed down a further two steps. Marianne fixed her with a glare and her eyes widened but her inquisitiveness had won over the fear. Exhaling the last breath of smoke, Marianne stubbed the cigarette out on the table.

"Oh no, Mummy, look at..." But she was sensible enough to halt her words under Marianne's glare. Neither Cal nor Lisa said anything. *You were always so weak, Cal.* A gust of wind blew through the open kitchen door, carrying a breath of the sea. All the people in the room lifted their faces to catch the scent and the dog ran out into the garden, filled with evening sunshine. The child tossed up her head. "Can I play outside?"

"Just for a little while." Lisa stood up, swinging her body around. The bells on her Indian cotton dress tinkled; tiny mirrors caught the light of the sun as she moved. She carried the kettle to the sink, filled it. Plugging it in, she turned to Marianne. "Would you like a cup of tea before you leave?" *Before you leave. So.*

"Yes. Please. I drink tea, Cal, and I eat food now. Can't you see how FAT I am?"

"You're not…"

"Oh don't be ridiculous, what would you know?"

"Do you know how you're getting home?" interrupted Lisa, "Where have you come from?" Her tone trembled on a knife-edge.

A knife edge, ha. (Go away. I am not listening to you. Not yet).

Marianne lifted her chin, neck stiff. "I am not "getting home." I don't intend to go back there."

(Any decision I make is my own, not yours).

"Marianne." Cal was probably more concerned about her mother calling the police than her. "Of course you need to go home. Your mother will be worried about you."

"You know nothing about my mother." *Keep breathing, Marianne. For now.*

"She seemed very…" But he let the words trail off, pointless anyway.

A bounce- bounce- bounce of a ball, probably the bright orange one she had seen in the soil outside, when she had still expected to come in and find Sarah and Cal. There was the skittering of dog paws, the laugh of the child in the transformed Blackberry House landscape. The haven of peace she had envisaged replaced now with a different home, someone else's family.

Lisa had poured mugs of tea and placed them on the table next to a bottle of milk, moving back over to the stove to place a pan of water on it, ripping open a bag of pasta. Marianne saw her stop moving for a moment, press a hand against her abdomen, saw Cal give her a nervous glance. Cal's blunt ended fingers, nails trimmed down to the skin, tapped softly on the table, his lips moved but she couldn't hear what he was saying. Or maybe he wasn't speaking at all.

Deliberately, she drew a mug of black tea towards her, folded both hands around it, pressed hard into the hot porcelain, held tight, watching his face, his coal-eyes burning into hers. A film of sweat sheened his forehead. His lips opened again just as Lisa turned around and Marianne let her hands fly off the cup, blisters already appearing on her reddened palms. Air rushed out through her mouth and she felt her eyelids fluttering. She turned her hands up towards her face, studied them with interest.

"You've burnt yourself. Oh Lord, Cal, do something won't you?"

Lisa moved across the room from the sink, threw a cloth soaked in cold water onto the table and Cal offered it to Marianne, but she laughed. "You think I can't cope with a pathetic pain like that?"

"Marianne." Lisa edged forward. She was holding a tin of tomatoes. "Maybe you need some help. Is there anyone I can call?" She looked exhausted.

"No, I'm fine here, thank you."

The look that passed between Cal and Lisa, it was almost funny how badly they wanted to get rid of her. The girl bounded in. Marianne watched. She looked like her mother had done as a child, all golden hair and blue eyes. Marianne had a clear memory of running out of school across the playground towards their mothers, holding hands with Lisa. *Oh God, how could I remember something like that? I am Marianne.* Repair the shutters again, blank out all the memories. Take sips of the hot tea, burning lips now as well. Light another cigarette.

Alice had finished washing her hands at the sink. She glanced at Marianne and then came to stand next to her. Curiosity crinkled her face. "Nobody smokes in this house."

Marianne took a deep drag, blew a cloud of smoke over the child. It made her cough but she stayed where she was. She met Marianne's eyes steadily with her own blue ones. "Now, look." Lisa wiped her hands.

"Sorry, I didn't mean to make you cough. Alice, is it?"

"Yes." The girl stood in front of Marianne, twisted her hands, the vulnerable points of her elbows poking forwards. She wore a pink t-shirt with a flower on it, faded pink shorts, scuffed trainers. Her legs were long and brown. A frown creased her forehead and then she said, "Why didn't you talk when you were in my room?"

"What do you mean?"

Cal's leg jiggled under the table. His mouth twisted. "Alice…"

"No, don't stop her." Marianne shot him a glance. He looked pathetic. "What do you mean?"

Alice stood on one leg, rubbed the toe of the other foot up and down the back of her calf, leaving a trail of dust on her skin. She wobbled, grasped the back of Marianne's chair to steady herself; replaced both feet firmly on the floor. "Can I touch your arm?"

What a strange child she was. But she reminded Marianne of Justine, also funny and odd. "I suppose so, if you must." Alice stroked a finger down Marianne's arm, her face tilting to one side. Her tongue was just showing between her lips. Marianne wanted to say, 'Wipe your mouth' the way she would to Justine, but she stayed silent, fascinated by the child's concentration.

"You're warm now."

"What do you mean – when wasn't I warm?"

Marianne pulled the sleeves of her cardigan down over her hands, folded her arms tightly. But again, Alice didn't give an answer. At the cooker Lisa's whole body appeared poised to swoop down and gather her up. Cal looked grey in the face. The pasta water continued bubbling.

Alice had moved to the other side of Marianne, plonked her bottom onto a chair with a scrape of wooden legs on the floor tiles. "Have you got any little girls?"

"No, I'm too young for that. I have a sister though, not much older than you. She's called Justine but I call her Jossie. She looks a bit like you." There, she had managed to regain control, make her mouth say normal things. Pretend to be real. *Take a drag on the cigarette Marianne, careful not to breathe it out on the child. That's right. Look at Cal. Everything is coming back to him: I can see it on his face. He knows what is going to happen.*

A smile broke over Alice's face. "I have a little sister too. Well she's my half-sister really from my daddy and his wife Samantha. My little sister's called Charlene."

"That's nice." Marianne had lost interest. She did not have the energy to concentrate. She took another, long drag on the cigarette. Her hands hurt, but it was good to feel pain. Across the table Cal looked quite ill. The kitchen had filled with reddish light. Marianne registered the sound of Lisa's slatted spoon on the side of the pasta pan. She sensed Alice fidgeting, not liking having lost her attention.

"I'm going to have another brother or sister as well!" the child's voiced boomed triumphantly. "Mummy and Cal are going to have a baby, aren't you Mummy?"

Lisa's back stiffened. She was pouring sauce over the pasta. She scraped the sauce out of the pan with a wooden spoon. Cal leaned forward, his hands linked tightly over his waist. Marianne drew harder on the cigarette, her lungs burned with heat and rage. The puppy let out a long sigh, turning around in his basket.

Alice had pushed her chair away from the table. She looked at Marianne, less certain when she spoke again.

"Your eyes look different now."

"My eyes look different now? What on earth do you mean?" The child backed away even further and Marianne demanded, "Tell me."

Alice coughed. "When you were in my bedroom. You just stared and stared straight ahead and you didn't move or talk. Don't you remember?"

The jiggling of Cal's leg rattled the table. His body had a bright halo, angry and red. Lisa moved forward, took Alice by the shoulders. "It's time to eat," she said, "come and get your pasta." She glanced at Marianne. Marianne felt the presence turning over inside her, detaching itself. Her chest was going to burst open.

"No," she said, "don't stop her. You're always stopping her when she tries to tell me something. What do you mean?"

The child shook off her mother's hands. She came back towards Marianne, chin jutting out. "You know, when you were in my room."

"I do not know. When was I in your room? Do you mean when I was here before? But you didn't see me then... you weren't here."

"Yes I *was* here!" Alice's voice grated harder than ever. "You were in my room last night… and some other times as well. And you never talked to me, you just stared and stared."

Marianne's pupils constricted, she felt them, like when they had given her Diazepam at the hospital. She felt the stop of time. A moment when everything was a part of everything else, but in a bleak, desolate way. The moment when a flower's petals curled in for the last time, the machinery of life shut down bit by bit. She was as light as air. If she did not grip the table she would float away.

Lisa stood at the cooker with her wooden spoon held in the air. Transfixed in a half-risen pose Cal managed to break away, his outline cracking. He scuttled towards the cloakroom in the corner. The puppy jumped out of his bed and ran to sniff excitedly under the door at the sound of Cal's retching.

There was a whistling sound as of a wind blowing through a hollow tree-trunk. Marianne was convinced it came from her, although she did not know how she made it. The thing inside her beat its wings. She sprang up from the table, the remains of her cigarette flying out of her hand. Those bird wings were painful in her chest. She must let them out. She hurtled forward, battered herself against the cage of the kitchen walls and surfaces; got caught against the stove. She knocked the empty pan onto the floor where the remains of tomato sauce spread like blood between the tiles. She pushed away from the stove back to the table and then fell heavily forward against the work counter. Panting, she leaned over it for a moment then pushed herself away again, resumed her bid for freedom. But she had lost steam. She came careering to a hard stop against the back door.

"Mummmmy!" The child gave a frantic scream. Through binocular vision Marianne took in the fling of the girl's arms, a simultaneous gesture of warding off and entreaty, stranded in the middle of the kitchen.

She had rammed herself hard against the door. Scrabbling behind her for the handle with both hands, she rattled it with violence. Her voice was a hiss. "Stop it. Stop talking like that, you little bitch! What are you saying? Why are you doing this to me?"

"Alice, come here!" Lisa reached out for her daughter. "Oh Lord, Cal!" But the sound of vomiting continued from the toilet. "Come on, calm down, Marianne."

The one inside is asking "where is Cal?"

"I haven't done anything, Mummy."

"I know, I know. Come on Marianne."

"Yes you have, you have!" Marianne fought for control. Cal *must* have been able to hear. He was the only one who could make it alright. *Turn back the clocks.* "You told lies just like my sister Charissa!"

A drawn-out sound of retching, a high yelping bark from the puppy, Alice's noisy crying. "Alice." Winding her daughter in her arms Lisa crouched down. "Have some dinner. Take it upstairs. The puppy can go with you. Quickly."

Silence stopped time once more. Alice sobbed. Despatched with a bowl of pasta, some biscuits and a dog towards the wooden stairs, she began the climb upwards to that room she called hers.

"What lies does your sister tell, Marianne?"

Lisa's widening pupils darkened her blue eyes. (*She was the only friend I had. Did you know that? Where is Cal?*)

"Lies… Just like that – just like what your daughter said…Awful lies about me."

"Please, come and sit down. Have some pasta, you must be hungry."

Marianne let go of the door handle with one hand, pressed that hand against her diaphragm. *Oh look, your fingers are bleeding.* Red spots on the lilac dress. "I… I can't." Her heart tried to jump out of her chest. "Ghost, Charissa says I am…"

"No, that's just silly… Cal!" (*Never there when you need him.*)

"Come on, Marianne, let's talk about it…"

But Lisa's attention was distracted by the flushing toilet, the rattle of the chain being pulled; the scraping open of the cloakroom door. And Marianne turned *on a knife edge. (Go on!)* She took Lisa by surprise, knocked past her on an unerring trajectory towards the chopping board, too fast to be grabbed by Lisa's flailing fingers. (*Do it!*)

The favourite knife. Of its own accord the blade slashed into a wrist. It switched over to the bleeding hand and sliced the other wrist open. Marianne heard the screaming. Through glazed-over eyes she saw the wide open mouth of the child through the banisters. She felt her head bump as it hit the floor and from her prone position she saw Cal, bursting out of the toilet, a bright shape attaching itself to him, flickering like flames all down one side.

Chapter 35

Marion

Ahhhh.

As the knife hits her flesh there is my moment of triumphant release, exquisite, healing pain. I can smell the apple blossom again and hear the song of a blackbird. It's the one I used to feed breadcrumbs to on my windowsill which was right next to my bed. It sang my requiem the first time I died.

I've managed to escape this body, angry that I've had to snatch a second death. The first one was my carefully orchestrated final work of art. I knew that Cal would use variants of it over and over again in his novels, I would endure through him. This was the course he set when he betrayed me with The Shell. Poor foolish boy; he'll never be able to let me go. I attach myself briefly back on to him, make him feel the way we did at the beginning. Now he'll be haunted by this death, messy and un-poetic as it is. He'll be bathed in my blood.

I was never meant to have come back.

Let me go.

I loosen myself from my brother but I still can't get away. Where is the opening I'm supposed to be able to find? I'm ready, this time, I am. I don't even want to fly; my wings are too weak. I'm just anxious to go. I want to be absorbed into The Everything. But I can't get away. I am being pulled back to her.

Oh, just let me sleep. Let me sleep, for I am sick of care.

Chapter 36

5th October

Sarah

MARK AND I flew over for Cal and Lisa's wedding at Hull Register Office. We stayed with Mum and Dad. Alice had her birthday the following day. She was again a bridesmaid along with her cousin Phoebe. Although Alice was proud of her mum, conscientious in her part, tension showed in her face. It worried me. That evening during the party at the Royal Hotel I pulled her onto my lap, the area not yet obscured by my pregnancy. She squirmed. "I'm too big for that now, Auntie Sarah."

"I know you are. You're eight tomorrow. But will you indulge me? I want to get some hugging practice in before I have my own baby."

"So many babies."

She'd lost all her spark. It made me sad. I still felt guilty; I should have warned Lisa before Marianne turned up in Pottersea.

"I thought you liked babies. What about your sister, Charlene?"

"Charlene is getting a bit annoying. And then there will be Mum's baby and your baby as well! I wish someone would have another older girl, like me."

"You've got Phoebe haven't you?"

"Yes but Phoebe likes *boys*. She's not interested in playing with me anymore. Henry's alright though, he lives next door to me. He's not really like a boy, not the kind Phoebe likes anyway."

The son of my old neighbour Sue; he must have been about Alice's age. "So are you happy living in Pottersea, Alice? Settled in at school and everything?"

"Yes, thank you."

"And you still like your room and that lovely princess bed you have?"

Alice turned to face me, looping her arms around my neck. "You're not going to ask me about that funny girl, are you, Auntie Sarah? Because I already have a lady who asks me a lot of questions about the funny girl and I'm getting rather fed up of it. So please don't ask me, OK? That funny girl is over now."

Alice's 'visions' hadn't made sense. How could Marianne have been a ghost when she was actually alive – or was it the ghost of Marion that Alice had seen?

We still didn't know whether Marianne was alive or dead, the hospital and the Fairchild family had refused to give out any information. But the therapy Alice was having had obviously done some good. Lulled by the music, she tucked her face under my chin, keeping her arms round my neck. I stroked her hair, singing along to the words of the pop song the DJ was playing. Out on the dance floor Lisa swung her magnificent figure in Cal's arms. She looked so much more statuesque in her pregnancy than I did. I just looked shorter and dumpier than ever.

January 22nd 1990

I WAS LUCKY; Connor's was an easy birth. Our friend Iris arrived just in time to shove some piles of newspaper under me where I squatted on the floor; the midwife who had been supposed to accompany us to the hospital came a few minutes later. My baby boy came out with minimal fuss, sliding into the midwife's hands. Afterwards I sat propped up in bed with my darling Connor in my arms. He wasn't taking any notice of anybody, just concentrating on his own special job of drinking my milk. I felt so powerful after what I had just done, like a lioness or a queen. This was finally the new beginning I'd been looking for. The dreams I'd been having about Marianne, the weeping of my dead sister I believed I'd been hearing night after night, she who had hardly ever cried: it must all stop now. I was a mother and my own child was the one that counted.

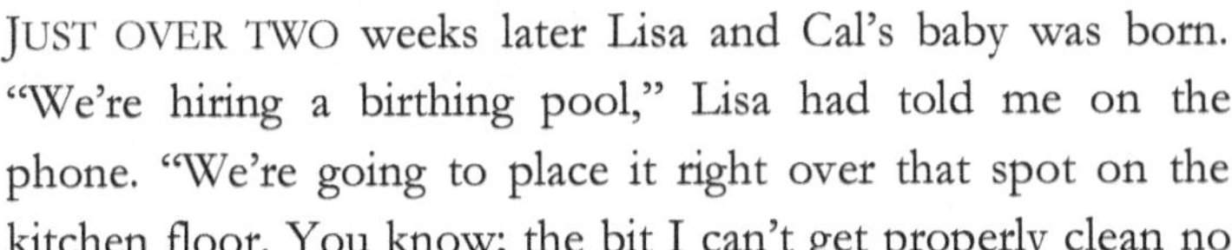

JUST OVER TWO weeks later Lisa and Cal's baby was born. "We're hiring a birthing pool," Lisa had told me on the phone. "We're going to place it right over that spot on the kitchen floor. You know; the bit I can't get properly clean no matter how I try." None of the sprays or powders suggested by her mother who ran a small cleaning firm had done any good. I asked my Irish neighbours for any old wives' remedies for removing blood, but nothing Lisa tried worked. "It's fading over time," Lisa said, "but it still hasn't gone completely."

It was in the early hours of February 10th when Cal got into the pool with Lisa. Aiden Jonah was born into his father's arms. "I can't believe I'm a father, Sarah," Cal said when he called me with the news. "I don't know why *you're* crying." I cried because I kept thinking of Marion. How proud she would have been of her twin brother. At the same time I felt angry with her for having caused a lifelong blight on everything we experienced. I hoped she would be at rest now, a rest that had been disturbed by our connection with Marianne. But that was all over. I had stopped having the bad dreams since my son was born.

Alice came on the phone. "Mummy and Cal let me stay in the kitchen and see my baby brother being born, Auntie Sarah. I was the very second person to hold him, well the very third actually because Cal was the one who catched him when he came out. Then he had some milk off Mum and then Samantha helped me to lift him out of the pool once his rope that attached him to Mum had been cut."

"Samantha?"

It turned out that Alice's stepmother had become a good friend to Lisa, driving out to Pottersea for the birth in case Alice needed looking after. "Something very weird," Lisa told me on the phone the next day as we both sat nursing our babies. I could hear the newborn Aiden's intermittent mewling noises when he became detached from Lisa's nipple. Connor and I were experts at the job of breastfeeding by that time. "Cal was getting really bad pains the day before Aiden was born. It was in the early morning of the ninth. But they had stopped by the afternoon. I wasn't having any twinges at all then, but it was as if Cal had gone into labour before me. Strange, isn't it?"

Chapter 37

Marianne, September 1989

I AM MARIANNE. I *am* Marianne Fairchild. I woke up in hospital yet again. They tell me I was in a coma and that it lasted a whole week. A nurse chatted to me as she took my blood pressure. "There was no real reason for you to be in the coma, apart from the loss of blood. Which we've topped up, don't worry. Oh, and the other thing; you mustn't be concerned about your baby. It's doing fine."

I'd been moved from Hull Royal Infirmary where I was taken – after – to St James' in Leeds, to be closer to my family. I lifted my arms; there were bandages on my wrists. This was the third time I'd apparently tried to take my own life, but I hardly remembered doing the damage that had nearly caused me to die. The nurse had said 'your baby'. I explored with cautious fingers. I could definitely feel a small mound between my hip bones. It was true then. I had the vaguest of recollections that a blood test had confirmed a pregnancy when I was in hospital the last time. My assigned nurse, Jessica, wanted me to acknowledge it. But since I didn't feel real, it didn't make sense that I could be pregnant. But Cal was going to be a father. This baby would be a half-sister or brother to the baby that Alice said Lisa was expecting.

I was exhausted. But it surprised me to find I could eat. Perhaps it had something to do with the baby; I had given it the very worst start in life so far – the least I could do now would be to offer it nourishment. My baby seemed to be a tenacious creature. I was worried I might have damaged it with my anorexia, with my suicide attempts. So I talked it through with a gynaecologist at my booking in appointment the psych staff arranged for me. I was taken down to Maternity a week after I woke up from the coma. They put me in a wheelchair, although I could walk perfectly well. To my relief I was told that because I'd taken those pills only the night after I conceived, they were too early to have done any damage to the embryo. I'd been admitted to hospital the next day and started on a feeding programme; therefore, my baby stood as good a chance as any at being healthy. The most amazing thing of all, I was told by the consultant, was that my body had even got pregnant at all in its emaciated condition. It was rare for someone as anorexic as me to conceive. I hadn't had any periods for two years.

The other thing that worried me regarding the baby was that Cal and Marion were brother and sister. Didn't this mean the baby would be born deformed? But then I remembered that my physical body was made of different genetic material from Marion's, and so that should make everything okay. But I was very confused.

To everyone who knew me, I seemed to be better than I had been for years. I ate three small meals a day. I cooperated with the hospital staff. I communicated with my family. "At this rate," said the psychiatric consultant, "you'll be able to go home next week."

I was barely aware of the events occurring around me. Every week the baby grew and got a bit more real. But I hadn't forgotten anything. I hadn't forgotten my life as Marion or the members of Marion's family. I hadn't forgotten the cruel taunts she put inside my head either. She was both me and not me at the same time. I recognised now the memories I'd always had of peeping out from the hood of a large blue pram; of playing at being writers with my brother, these were real and that I'd had to deny them in order to try and be Marianne. *I am Marianne Fairchild.* Marion's life should have been left behind. Everything to do with it – most notably the years passing which had seen Sarah and Cal grow into their thirties – had left *her* behind. All her own fault. She could not be allowed to stay. Marion had stopped in 1972, aged seventeen. I had no desire to meet my former parents or to resume the close friendship Marion used to have with Lisa. I wasn't even bothered about seeing Sarah again. Cal, as ever, was the one who tore at my heart. I saw clearly now that Cal would only ever be able to relate to me as Marion, the twin he had lost. Me, I was in love with Cal, whereas Marion had said goodbye to her brother a long time ago.

I was allowed home after less than three weeks in the hospital. Everyone could see I was better. I was fifteen weeks pregnant. I could now feel the fish-like movements of my baby. I kept a hand on my tiny bump as I walked up the steps and into the house on Hyde Terrace for the first time in nearly four months. Joseph had picked me up and brought me home: that was easy because he never had much to say at the best of times and he acted the way he always did: kind but slightly detached. Justine greeted me in her usual bullet-like way at the door, charging straight into me. She was getting heavy. I marvelled at my own desire to protect the baby. I still hadn't got used to it, this maternal instinct. But I seemed to have it intrinsically woven into me. Justine's eyes widened. "You look different."

In the hall mirror (I tried to push the little boy and his shadowy sister out of my mind when I looked into it) I saw that my cheeks had filled out. Although objectively I could see I was still thin, I did indeed look much healthier. Geraldine came forward and offered a cool embrace, not her usual thing. "I'm glad you're home." We had undergone family therapy in hospital after the overdose. I allowed a mutual brush of cheeks and then stepped away quickly. "Marianne," she said, "I told Charissa that you two should swap bedrooms, especially with you being – you know – and Charissa not even here half the time."

We sat down at the dining room table with cups of tea: mine contained milk. "Charissa did agree; she can see that it's the only fair thing to do. Perhaps we should put an extra wardrobe on the landing for her clothes." But I was anxious to not have to deal with any more changes just yet. I wanted to keep things steady. I loved my tiny room. It reminded me of looking out from under the hood of a big Silver Cross pram. "Let's not worry about it for now," was my only response.

Geraldine had forgone – that was the way she put it – 'forgone' her scheduled trip to London with Charissa in order to be at home to try and support me. Geraldine's assistant would be staying at the flat with Charissa while they did the rounds of modelling agencies and some photographic work for Geraldine's magazine. Geraldine would have to remain at home 'twiddling her thumbs' for as long as it took. At least she'd learned to cook. Now I was eating I had lost all interest in preparing food, which was a pity for the rest of the family, since Geraldine's idea of a balanced meal was nothing if not bland.

Those months, I didn't do much apart from sit in my compact room reading. I wrote in my notebooks and then tapped away on my typewriter. The baby learned to dance to the tune of its keys. I was working on my first full-length play. But sometimes I would simply soak up the Indian summer sunshine in the back garden, stretched in a deckchair reading. Geraldine had bought Justine a white kitten for her eleventh birthday and it seemed to have taken to me, playing at my feet, pouncing on blades of grass. When Justine got home from school it would go and curl up on her bed.

I loved my baby. I could feel her rippling beneath the skin under my fingers. If I propped a book on my stomach she would kick it off. I took my vitamins and kept up the calorie intake as instructed by the dietician. I attended my weekly weighing sessions at the hospital – a condition of my discharge. I took my low level antidepressants (safe for the baby). Therapy sessions were arranged for me once a week and for the whole family every month. Everything was in place to get me sorted out, for good. But my life felt like a dream. Everybody insisted I was OK and I suppose I was. I just felt detached. Nothing that happened was really real. The baby *was* real but I could never for a minute imagine having her once she was born. There was a catch somewhere; a snag in the fabric of my reality which seemed mismatched to that of everyone else.

In therapy, I decided to bring up the subject of Marion, the past life I remembered. "Marianne, you *are* taking your antidepressants, aren't you?" Katy, my therapist, enquired with a worried look. I only sighed. The psychiatric consultant had informed me that severe anorexia causes disturbances in the brain and that it could be these that accounted for my catatonia and my belief in a past life. So in the end it seemed better not to talk about it. At that time either I was having no catatonic episodes *or* I was no longer aware of them. I caught Charissa looking strangely at me one morning shortly after her return from London, but my sister refused to divulge why. It could simply have been that she was marvelling at the physical shape of my pregnancy.

The question of the room-swap came up again. Even Charissa was all for it. "Marianne, you can't keep a baby in that tiny room with your bed and that enormous ugly old chest of drawers," she insisted. "I'll be able to manage fine in there with my bedside drawers and a clothes rail. I'll have a mirror screwed in between those shelves you had Dad put in and I can keep all my makeup on them. And of course I'll have the extra wardrobe on the landing." But I still wouldn't budge on the matter. Everyone except me seemed to worry about where the baby was going to sleep.

Chapter 38

Leeds, October 1989

GERALDINE CAME UP with a solution to the problem of Marianne's cramped room.

"We'll have to move house."

"You might be right, love," was Joseph's response. He'd always known Geraldine was not happy in their Victorian monstrosity, as she called it. But there was more to it than that. Geraldine had received a letter. She knew from the postmark that Callum Wilde had sent it. Every time she thought of him she was furious and terrified. Seeing him standing there on her doorstep had taken her breath away. The similarity to Marianne was uncanny. Each suicide attempt had been connected with 'Cal', Marianne had muttered about him constantly when she was being revived from her coma. She hadn't mentioned his name since becoming fully conscious, but Geraldine was shrewd enough to know he was in her daughter's mind.

She'd had many a battle with Marianne when she was a toddler. She'd had to fight hard to establish the child's sense of identity. And despite Marianne's anorexia and her recalcitrant nature, Geraldine thought she'd succeeded. But meeting Callum Wilde had got her daughter stirred up and confused again. In her mentally unstable state, she had got it into her head that she was having memories from a 'past life', that in this other life Callum Wilde had been her twin brother. It frightened Geraldine in a way she couldn't put her finger on. There was always, in the back of her mind, that "What have you done with my brother?" Marianne asked her when she was only about two. Not only that, but Marianne was pregnant. He was obviously the father. Geraldine swore he was never going to know about the baby.

In a way, this drama suited Geraldine. It made her better able to adapt to her new role – well it may as well have been new for the amount she had practised it in the past – as a mother.

Geraldine had got Marianne moved from Hull to Leeds as soon as possible. Staff at the hospital had been given clear instructions: "You will not *ever* let that man Callum Wilde speak to my daughter, or let him know *anything* about her condition. Do you understand?" She had fielded Cal's and Lisa's telephone calls to her home, giving them no information at all, even though that wimp of a man had broken down and cried. She was hoping he would come to the conclusion her daughter was dead, though she couldn't bring herself to say it to him. He should have known better than to get involved with such a young girl in the first place. Shortly after Cal's third telephone call she had the number changed. She dreaded to think what would have happened if Marianne had answered the phone. Geraldine was back in a management position, a role she loved. Being confined to the home made a lot more sense when there were such dramatic circumstances involved. And now the idea of moving house had got under her skin.

January 1990

WITHIN THREE MONTHS they had sold their house and moved into a five-bedroomed 'executive' new build on the outskirts of Leeds, right on the edge of some farmland. Joseph really didn't like the house; he preferred old properties, but he was in his element in the surrounding countryside which made it bearable to live there. Geraldine on the other hand adored their new home and did her best to ignore the landscape around it. The scenery reminded her too much of the early days of her marriage when she seemed to be suffering constantly from depression. Marianne was nearly eight months pregnant. Their new house was a short walk from a local railway station. It was a mere ten minute ride into Leeds which made it easy to keep her hospital appointments.

It felt bizarre to Geraldine, accompanying her daughter to an ante-natal appointment. She had never imagined such a thing but there she was, doing it. She sneaked surreptitious glances at her daughter's profile on the train. Marianne's cheeks had filled out and had a rosy glow in them. January had come around but Marianne said the baby made her feel hot and she pulled the Laura Ashley scarf Geraldine had given her for Christmas away from her neck, fanned herself with her train timetable.

The two of them had not exactly become close, but their relationship had come a long way in the past few months. She couldn't imagine what it would be like being a grandmother, but she really did feel this baby would in some way make up for the difficulty she'd had in connecting with her oldest child right from the beginning. To be fair to herself, this had been partly due to the fact that Marianne had denied Geraldine was her mother. But the baby, ah: Marianne couldn't deny that the baby was Geraldine's grandchild. Geraldine was looking forward to it.

She had a niggling worry about Marianne. The girl was taking all the supplements she'd been prescribed, was eating regularly and obediently following all the instructions for a healthy pregnancy. Geraldine had seen Marianne rubbing a hand over her belly and smiling when the baby kicked. She'd even chosen a name for her: Mariana. "What on earth do you want to call her that for?" Geraldine complained. "People will get you both muddled up."

"It's from a Tennyson poem, Mum," Marianne said. "I know it sounds similar but it's not really anything to do with my name." Her last scan had proved that as she'd suspected all along, the baby was a girl. But apart from the name Marianne refused to participate in discussions about the baby. Geraldine's other daughters were understandably excited about her forthcoming arrival. Justine had even learned to knit and made her a very holey pair of bootees. Geraldine had tried to get Marianne interested in colours for the baby's room without success. In the end Joseph painted it yellow, but Marianne hardly glanced in there. Charissa had accompanied Geraldine on shopping trips to buy nappies, all-in-one suits and a maroon-coloured carrycot. All were placed inanimately in the nursery in readiness for their anticipated, very animate occupier. But Marianne only gave a half-smile when she looked at these objects. She couldn't relate them to her baby. Geraldine felt like slapping her sometimes, she seemed so far away. She wondered if she'd ever be able to get through to her daughter.

Marianne never argued with her now; on the other hand she didn't seem affected by her mother at all. Nor, for that matter, did she seem affected by anything else. She showed no emotions, come to think about it – only wandering around with that far-away smile and her hands on her stomach; always her hands stroking the mound containing her baby.

Chapter 39

9th February 1990

Marianne

IT STARTED WITH a pulling ache low down in my belly. I was aware of it only in my sleep at first, and then the pain radiated into my back and the tops of my thighs, waking me from a dream in which I held Mariana. The baby laughed and reached up to touch my face. She knew that her journey had begun: Mariana was coming. It was very early in the morning of February the ninth, 1990.

I just wanted to be alone, pacing around my large ground floor bedroom. The yellow walls were the same as the baby's nursery, attached to my room with a connecting door. I'd quickly settled myself in the space, it felt like home and I associated it with the comforting days of my late pregnancy. For the first time in my life – in Marianne's life – I was in the right place.

The living room of our new house was on the first floor, looking out over fields. It had one large window, bay-shaped, nothing like the living room of Blackberry house with its two framed views of the fields at Pottersea. Standing in the window of this house over a cornfield landscape, I was the red-haired woman in an Edward Hopper painting, looking out at something nobody else could see. The house was built on a slope. From the ground floor, stairs led down to a lower level which was given over to a kitchen and dining area with patio doors leading into a large garden, perfect for a child. Geraldine had spoken about getting a baby swing erected in time for the summer when Mariana would be six months old. I was moved by the extent of Geraldine's offers of help. For years I'd resented my mother and was jealous of Charissa, the perfect daughter. I'd felt I would never match up. But this pregnancy had done something to change the family dynamic. It made me sad that I was only now able to appreciate the family I'd been born into. Too late. I was about to disappoint them. I was about to prove that Geraldine had been right to be detached from me all along.

I'd struggled for the duration of the pregnancy to maintain an identity fixed in the present. As far as I was aware, I hadn't suffered from any episodes, my catatonia stilled for the time being. I had to be grounded for the baby – remain real as long as possible. I didn't know what would happen after the birth. My priority was to get the baby born safely. I couldn't think much beyond that.

I laboured alone, completely focused. In my fantasies of the birth, Cal was with me, preparing to meet his daughter. But it could never happen. I agreed with my mother that I had to be totally cut off from Cal. Geraldine's perspective was that the father of my baby had caused me too much destruction already. Mine was the certain knowledge that to be involved with Cal was to lose myself, Marianne Fairchild. When I was with Cal, I started having thoughts that belonged to Marion

Wilde. Marianne Fairchild should never have met Callum Wilde.

During my pregnancy I had completed my first full-length play: 'Sea Music'. The main character was a girl with multiple personality disorder. I understood how that would feel, though that wasn't what was wrong with me. My problem was that I had met up in my current life with Marion's twin brother. It should never have happened.

I ran a bath in the bathroom opposite my bedroom. Nobody else was awake; I wanted it to stay that way as long as possible. Geraldine and Joseph's room was on the floor above and both Charissa and Justine had rooms right at the top of the house. I lit a candle I'd been saving for this occasion, placed it on the edge of the bath. The crispness of early morning permeated the room. I shivered as I got undressed. With relief I slid under the layer of warm water. Outside a cat yowled and another joined in, crescendo chords ripping out of sync with the tentative notes of bird music that were just starting up. A strong contraction gripped me and I leaned forward until it passed. I was distinctly aware of the baby's feet pushing at the top of my womb.

"You really want to come out, don't you?" I eased out a long breath and managed to manoeuvre myself onto all fours in the water. I would have to get out of the bath and call somebody. But I didn't want the time I had alone with Mariana to be over. At the same time as wanting to hold my baby in my arms, I desperately wished I could keep her inside. But I reminded myself the baby had to come first. "You must have come here for a reason."

I struggled out of the bath, paused to crouch on my elbows and knees on the rug while another contraction swept over me. Eventually I was able to raise my bulk and force myself to straighten up, reaching for my towelling gown and shrugging into it. When I came out of the bathroom, Geraldine was sitting on a stool at the top of the kitchen stairs. "I heard you." She spoke in a matter-of-fact way but her eyes were glittering. I hoped she wasn't going to cry. She said, "Is it time?" I was about to say yes, when another contraction hit and I doubled over. Joseph's footsteps had come down the stairs by this time. "Everything's ready, I'll get the car warmed up." He was carrying a bag I recognised as Charissa's. I straightened up again. "Well, the way you've been I didn't expect you'd got one packed yourself," Geraldine said. "There's a new nighty and dressing gown in it."

"Mum." I clutched Geraldine's arm. I usually avoided addressing her as anything, but suddenly I needed her.

"Let's get you dressed. As quick as you like." Geraldine smiled. "You're lucky; I don't think this baby's going to wait long before she comes out." The morning cold fingered my skin. They helped get me kitted out in a pair of leggings and a t-shirt with a long ragged jumper over the top. I insisted on wearing it, ignoring the Marks and Spencer cashmere one Geraldine was holding out. The old one had belonged to my grandfather and I imagined I could still smell the oily atmosphere of his workshop on it. "Put some thick socks on." I obeyed Geraldine, pushing my feet into a pair of boots with fur inside. But I didn't manage to get them laced up before I was gripped by such a severe contraction it left me shaking.

"We need to hurry." Geraldine sounded urgent. Maybe the thought of me giving birth on her beautiful polished floors made her want to hurry me out of there. In the car I knelt on the back seat on all fours, the only position I could get comfortable in. By the time I was admitted to the labour ward I wasn't really thinking about anything. When Geraldine spoke to me I couldn't comprehend what she was saying. Hair stuck to my forehead, clammy with sweat. A driving force was in my abdomen. I had an urge to let out a roar like a lioness. "It's OK," Geraldine told the midwife who was going to be attending the birth, "don't take it personally, this is the way she always is."

Joseph waited outside in the corridor while Mariana was born. I squatted over a piece of green cotton, clutched tightly onto Geraldine's arms. Geraldine made sure to look the other way. At the point I believed I was going to split apart, Mariana plopped out. She had a shocked expression on her face which quickly changed to one of determination. "Lift her up then." the midwife smiled. A moment ago I'd existed in a world inhabited only by myself and Mariana. Now there were two midwives, Geraldine, a student nurse – and me and my baby. I reached down with shaking arms and picked up my daughter, still attached to the inside of me by her cord. Mariana took a quick look at me and immediately fastened her mouth over my nipple, a miniature hand clutching and pinching at my skin.

"Oh…" This was the most impossible thing – a real and perfect baby.

"Do you want to be the one who cuts the cord?" The midwife asked Geraldine.

"Ugh, no!" But Geraldine seemed entranced by my baby, who had a dark mat of reddish hair and tiny fists which curled open and shut like starfish.

"For Heaven's sake, put some clothes on, Marianne," Geraldine had contained herself for about twenty minutes, "and then your Dad can come in and see his granddaughter!"

"Let's help you up onto the bed." The midwife had just delivered the placenta whilst I still held the baby in my arms. Mariana let go of the nipple to take in a shuddering breath with her newly-working lungs, but it turned into an enormous yawn.

"Now's your chance!" Geraldine was anxious to get hold of her granddaughter. "Give her to me and you can get dressed." Geraldine cradled my sleeping baby while I was washed, dressed and settled between clean sheets on the bed. I lay propped up on pillows, exhausted. I wouldn't be able to hold everything together for long. Joseph and Geraldine cooed over their granddaughter. I watched them for a moment and then squeezed my eyes tightly shut. This was what a family was supposed to be like. I had given my parents something precious, a thing to be proud of at last. I finally felt in the right place at the right time, and yet I was about to tear it all apart and the feeling was too much to bear.

Chapter 40

"PLEASE DON'T MAKE me stay in hospital," I begged. I couldn't bear the thought of my baby's first memories being loaded with those kinds of smells and sounds. "I want to take her home. I have too many bad memories of this place."

"Just one night," said the midwife who was looking after me. She promised I could go home the following day if all was well. "You're a special case, almost a miracle." The staff kept remarking how unusual it was for a baby to be born to, or especially conceived by someone who'd had anorexia as severely as me. She didn't even mention my suicide attempts. I stroked my baby's cheek. Mariana was the miracle.

I was thrilled that my body made food for her. Suddenly eating wasn't something to be feared. The strict diet of my pregnancy had resulted in a healthy infant; the food I consumed now enabled me to keep her alive. "Did you know," said another midwife, "That human milk is known as 'liquid gold' in the special care baby unit?" She reached over and tucked in my sheet. "Your baby's a good feeder; some struggle at first." Mariana seemed to know exactly what she was doing. The look of concentration on her face as she settled her cheek against my breast, her eyes closed, over-whelmed me. Her jaw worked rhythmically, contented noises emitted from her throat.

Joseph arrived on the maternity ward with the brand new carrycot. "Ready?" Before I left I laid Mariana on the bed and changed her nappy, then dressed her in a white stretch suit and cardigan. I manipulated her malleable arms and legs into all the apertures with some difficulty. Next I wrapped her in a white shawl. I tugged a knitted hat onto her head, covering her delicate ears. Her tiny mouth pursed up in a disapproving manner, her dark greenish eyes restlessly roved my face. I stood looking at her for a moment. Then something welled up inside me that I was afraid of letting out. A flood that might never stop. But it was too late. I was crying so hard I would die if I didn't stop soon. It had never occurred to me the thought of losing her would hurt this much. It can't possibly, until you have a baby.

Joseph tutted. He patted me awkwardly on the back and then picked up the baby, settling her carefully into the carrycot which he'd placed across the arms of the chair beside the bed. "Your mother was the same after she had you, you know." He tucked both hands into his armpits, contemplating the baby who stared back at him with interest. "Couldn't stop crying, she couldn't. This one looks exactly the same as you did, you know." The thought that I was truly Geraldine and Joseph's daughter tore me up inside. I'd wasted my whole life so far. I wanted time to go backwards and never to have come face to face with Callum Wilde – or to have read his book. And yet… Even before that I'd never felt I really belonged: not with the Fairchilds; nor in my own life, not in the world at all. Not until now. But this baby who had solidified my existence in the Fairchild family had also ensured I would never be free of Marion Wilde and Cal. Having her growing inside me had kept me weighted down. I'd had to make sure she was born safely. She was my baby, my physical thing, not Marion's. But she *was* Cal's, and I was afraid that was going to be the thing that brought Marion back.

THERE WAS SOMETHING I hadn't told anybody, there was no point because no-one would believe me. The previous night I'd fed Mariana then lain awake watching her by the dim nightlight on my bedside cabinet. I'd got up and hobbled to the bathroom at the end of the ward, a fresh maxi-sized maternity pad hidden in the folds of my new dressing gown. On the way back I'd started to feel that horrible tingling sensation in my muscles that I now knew preceded one of my episodes. I'd almost made it back to my bed. My hand had been on the curtain about to move it aside. I could hear my baby snuffling in the plastic crib behind it.

In the vision I had, Marion – I – was very young, only four years old. Cal stood beside me, we were both giggling because we weren't supposed to be out of bed. We peeped into our parents' bedroom, at the yellow carrycot in which our new baby sister lay... Then I came to in the hospital, with an electric jolt and a gasp. I looked around me with a feeling of shame. Snores reverberated; the curtains surrounding most of the beds were drawn. A baby woke up and whimpered for a moment, whispered back to sleep by its mother. Nobody seemed to have noticed anything amiss. But it was horrible to think that if anyone had seen me they would have been frightened; thinking I was some kind of apparition. I didn't want to be that person anymore. I crept back behind my curtain, pins and needles still in my fingers, my jaw stiff, the familiar sinking feeling in my stomach. Mariana gave a little sneeze in her sleep. A tightly curled fist waved in the air for a moment and then dropped gently down next to her cheek. Easing myself back into bed I put one hand on her, allowing the rise and fall of her breathing to comfort me.

I was frightened for my baby. Afraid that if the fits became regular again I would lose myself in the memories of Marion. I didn't want Marion's choice to become mine. A rhyme came into my head; I couldn't remember where I'd heard it before. I whispered it to the baby, "Chickadee, chickadee, who's been at my cherry tree..." and she seemed to hear me in her sleep, making an "ahhh" sound with a rounded mouth. She began to suckle ferociously at an imaginary nipple. I watched her in the dim light until I fell asleep. She was real, Marianne's baby. *I am Marianne Fairchild.*

"COME ON, CHICKEN," Joseph reverted to his long ago pet name for me. "Let's take this baby home, shall we? Your Mum's gone to the trouble of making a cake for the occasion, I believe. I can't get over the change in her, and it's all down to you and this little one, Marianne."

I followed my father down the length of the ward, him carrying my baby in the carrycot. I had my sister Charissa's bag slung over my shoulder. I walked doubled over with sobs, aware I was drawing attention to myself. One of the nurses was so concerned she tried to prevent me from leaving. Joseph managed to convince her that the best place for me would be at home with my family. "Her mother was just the same after she had her bairns," was his explanation. So they allowed me to go as long as my Dad promised he would ensure I continued taking my pills.

I managed to bring myself under control enough to get out of the hospital and into Joseph's car. There I sat hunched over with my head in my hands. Snot and tears poured through my fingers. Joseph fastened the baby's carrycot into place with the seat belt. "Give me the bag, Marianne." It was a command. He came round to the passenger door and leaned into the car. Still sobbing noisily, I did as I was told. Joseph unzipped the bag and dug inside for a packet of wet-wipes. He pulled one out and handed it to me. "Now pull yourself together and clean yourself up, girl." I'd never heard him sound as stern as that in my entire life as his daughter. Shock stopped me crying. "Now that's better," he continued in the same stern voice. "You're a mother now, girl, and not the first there's ever been, neither! I've been through this three times with your mother. Maybe I was too soft on her and it didn't do her any favours. I'm just giving you the benefit of experience, chicken."

My dad waited while I got myself calmed down. I checked my oblivious daughter, curling one of my fingers very softly over the curve of her cheek. This was what it meant to be a mother. I must not waste time on something as expendable as tears.

Chapter 41

Cornfields Estate, Leeds. July 1990

LIZZY BELL BLEW out a long breath through pursed lips. She'd had a good howl and felt better for it, now she bunched up the rest of the sodden tissues that littered her crowded desk and shoved them into the bin at her feet.

"Better?" Aggie, her colleague, poked her head in the tiny office.

"A bit. It's always a shit thing to have to go through." She'd recently returned from a visit to an outwardly neat home near the centre of Leeds. *Inside the house was a different story — the stench of soiled nappies, or worse, hit you the minute you opened the door. A three-year-old with cigarette burns on his arms called her a fucking bitch and screamed at her to go away. Two older children slithered into what appeared to be a cupboard under the stairs as soon as the uniformed police officers pushed open the front door. The woman of the house, a thin, snot-faced baby in her arms, had a purple bruise on one cheek.*

She met Lizzy's eyes directly, "No…" She backed off, into the kitchen. Lizzy had to swallow down vomit. The kitchen bin overflowed with nappies. There was cat shit in a pile of chip wrappers on the kitchen counter and the cat crouched on top of a wall cupboard, looking down at them. The woman's eyes flashed a warning and Lizzy understood why: a small man with hard eyes stood in the corner by the back door, a knife held out in front of him. The drama was over in a few minutes. Lizzy heard an officer on his radio in the hall and straight away another officer burst in through the back door, wrenching the man's arm up behind his back. The knife clattered to the floor. He was dragged out to a police car wearing handcuffs, bellowing that he would kill the fucking social worker the first chance he got. Under the supervision of a female police officer, Lizzy had to extricate the baby from its mother's arms. The mother screamed and begged them not to take her children away. The three-year-old bit and kicked the hands and legs of his captor and yelled for his mother.

The two children who had hidden in the under-stairs cupboard came out meekly. They were taken to the bedroom shared by all four siblings and assisted in cramming some clothes into a black bin bag by another social worker. Lizzy waited outside with the baby and the now limply crying three-year-old. They sat in the minibus. The two oldest children got into the bus without resistance. They did not look back at their mother. For Lizzy this was the saddest aspect of the whole experience.

Aggie placed a cup of tea on the desk in front of her. Lizzy gave her a grateful look but as soon as she had picked up the cup and taken a sip of tea, the phone on her desk rang. She raised a wry eyebrow at her colleague, who backed out of the office with a palms raised gesture followed by a thumbs-up sign. Lizzy answered the phone. The caller was a young woman. She wanted to make an appointment to speak to Ms Bell about giving up her baby for adoption.

◆❦◆

MS BELL WAS surprised when she pulled her car into the sweeping driveway of the five-bedroomed house on

Cornfields Estate, an executive development less than a year old. She didn't know why – things you would never believe could happen anywhere, but there wasn't much call for her kind of work in this area. It was usually the opposite: interviewing couples desperate for a baby of their own.

Marianne, the name she was known by then, later changing it to Maria, was thin with auburn hair. The most noticeable thing about her was her unusual eyes. They could be described as either green or hazel. But they had an off-putting, haunted expression. She was breastfeeding her baby in the first floor living room of their beautiful home when Lizzy Bell was shown in by a subdued Geraldine Fairchild. The baby – Lizzy consulted her notes – Mariana, looked healthy and clean. A five month old with a suggestion of bright auburn curls already. She was dressed in pale blue dungarees in a soft expensive material, and a white hand-knitted cardigan. On hearing Lizzy and her grandmother coming through the door the baby tore her head away from the breast and whipped it towards Lizzy, offering her a wide, toothless grin. Ms Bell's heart contracted. She felt confused as to why she was here, possibly Marianne's phone call had been some kind of mistake. She hoped that was the case, even if it meant she'd had a wasted journey.

The family room looked out over a crop of corn. Lizzy's professional eye noted that the pale yellow walls and cream sofas were spotless. There was an overflowing box of toys in one corner and a colourful quilt with pictures of animals on spread on the floor in front of the gleaming fireplace. The young mother bent over her baby, pretending to nibble the chubby fingers exploring her lips. The baby plucked her hand away then let out a giggle and offered Marianne the chance to do it again.

Accepting the glass of water brought to her by her mother, Marianne began to talk as Lizzy sipped her tea. She said that she loved her baby beyond reason. That was how she put it. She hadn't meant to get pregnant in the first place, said the girl. You only had to ask her mother what kind of state she'd been in at the time. "I was severely anorexic and very confused." Marianne had a touching honesty. "I can't even understand how I could have got pregnant with my body in such a terrible condition. It's only now that I can see how bad I really was."

"She tried to commit suicide," Geraldine put in, "on more than one occasion."

Marianne had sat the baby up on her lap and was rubbing her back in a circular motion. "You seem to be in good health now." Lizzy spoke in a gentle voice, "and your baby looks perfect. A beautiful little girl."

"She is."

Marianne lifted the baby up so Mariana's cheek squashed against hers and then slid her down so that the baby's chin rested on her shoulder. She continued rubbing her back and eventually Mariana let out a contented burp. "It's just..." Marianne seemed have difficulty finding the words. "She can't stay with me. She's not safe – I'm not safe."

"She can – she is." Geraldine pulled out a tissue and blew her nose. "Marianne's done so well. None of us would have expected her to cope the way she has. She's been through such a tough year, we all have." The older woman's eyes were red from supressed tears. Lizzy suspected many had already been shed.

"Why do you feel you can't look after Mariana safely, Marianne?" There was obviously enough money, the grandmother was supportive. When Marianne didn't answer, Lizzy tried another question, "How many people live here in the house?"

Geraldine answered because Marianne couldn't seem to get her emotions under control. "And you all have enough space?" Lizzy watched Marianne and the baby carefully. There was no evidence of neglect or lack of care. Marianne transferred the baby to the other breast and the little one suckled contentedly, her hand caught up in a fold of Marianne's old-looking lilac cardigan. Lizzy could not even begin to imagine why Marianne was prepared to give her up. Marianne drew in a deep breath.

"We have plenty of space. It's a fantastic house; we've only been living in it a few months. My mother…" Here she paused for a moment to meet eyes with Geraldine. The baby's grandmother slid hers away quickly and reached for another tissue. "My Mum and Dad have been really, really supportive. I've never…" She stopped again. She leaned low over the baby, fighting to hold back tears. "I've never thanked you properly, Mum. So I want to now. I used to find it so hard to be part of this family and now that's the only thing I want…" She let out a racking sob. It startled the baby who broke away from the breast. She looked as if she was about to let out a yell of indignation but instead she fell asleep. A trail of milk dribbled from her mouth. Marianne fastened the cup of her feeding bra and tucked her blouse into the waistband of her flowered skirt. She propped the baby carefully on the sofa beside her, gazing at Mariana for a few moments. Then she wiped the back of her hand across her eyes. In a tiny voice she asked "Have you got a spare tissue, please, Mum?"

Lizzy wrote notes while Marianne blew her nose. Geraldine watched the social worker suspiciously. She leaned across from her sofa to the armchair where Lizzy sat. "This is not going to finalise anything, is it?"

"No, I'm just here to listen to what Marianne has to say. To build up a picture of what's best for your daughter and her baby."

Geraldine gave her a disdainful look. "It's obvious what's best for her!"

"What do you feel that is, Mrs Fairchild?" the social worker spoke neutrally.

"Well to stay here, of course, both of them!"

Marianne wrung her hands together in her lap. "I can't, Mum. There's nothing I'd like more than that either. I love Mariana, it's going to break my heart to be parted from her, but it's for her own sake. You know what happens to me!" Neither of them said anything further. Geraldine's hand contracted on the ball of tissue in her palm. Marianne began chewing at the skin around her fingernail. Lizzy remained quiet, waiting for an explanation.

"It's not your fault, Marianne," Geraldine eventually offered. "And it's not what you say. It's a medical condition. The consultant has said they could try controlling it with medication. You can't give up your baby because of this. What about the rest of us?"

"You could still see her. It'll be better for her if you do — we could ask them to make it one of the conditions of me giving her up."

"It would never be the same. She's our beautiful baby."

Geraldine turned to the social worker, with a look of blank despair. "I was never a good mother to Marianne. I suffered postnatal depression after each one of my girls, but especially after Marianne. She was a year old before I came out of my darkness and by that time she'd already rejected me. We've always had a difficult relationship, until she got pregnant with Mariana. I finally feel I'm making up for my mistakes of the past. And now Marianne wants to take it all away from me. Are you punishing yourself in order to punish me, Marianne?"

"Mum, we've been through this. You know I'd never do that. You've more than made up for the way things were before and I really wish I could stay – I want to keep my baby more than anything. But I'm afraid…I'm scared one day I'll never come back from, you know, or that I'll do something like I did before." Marianne turned her body towards Ms Bell. Slowly she pulled back the sleeves of her lilac cardigan, revealing the still livid scars across each wrist. Lizzy couldn't help letting out a gasp.

"Why are you scared you might do that again, Marianne?" she finally asked.

"It's because of Mariana. Mum – I know you hate it when I say this but. Ms Bell, I have these fits. It's called catatonia. I don't jerk about or anything, I just go really still. Frozen. But it's more than that. I… You're going to think I'm crazy when I tell you this, but it's the truth. Mum, there's no point shaking your head like that."

"Go on, Marianne." Lizzy Bell was transfixed by this girl. The colour of her eyes seemed to change with her emotions.

"This is not my first…" Marianne hesitated. "I mean my life. I was someone else. It's called a previous personality. I've done some research on the subject. I lived before, and I know who the girl was. I became close with her brother and sister. Her brother especially." She fixed Lizzy Bell with a long stare. There *was* something quite unfathomable about Marianne. Beside her on the sofa the sleeping baby stirred, little arms stiffening out to the sides. Marianne put a hand out to comfort her without even looking, making a low murmur in her throat. "He looks just like me," she almost-whispered. She turned to her mother for confirmation.

Geraldine got as far as saying, "That's true but it doesn't mean —" before Marianne stopped her with a, "Shh…"

"What are you saying, Marianne?" Lizzy Bell had never heard a story like this before.

"I'm telling you," said Marianne, still holding Lizzy's gaze, "that I conceived Mariana with the man who was my twin brother in my previous life." She let out a shaking lungful of air. Geraldine had her head in her hands, muttering, "No, no, no," under her breath.

Lizzy's pen hovered above the paper fixed to a clipboard on her lap. She had no idea what to write on it. Anyone listening to the story second-hand would be convinced Marianne was losing her mind. Come to think of it, that was possibly what she was trying to say. "What does this have to do with the fits, Marianne?"

"When I go into one," the girl weighed out her words carefully, "I become Marion. Mar-ri-on. That was the name of the girl I used to be. I have the experiences she had. What I'm saying is, I remember being her, the memories she has are mine."

"I can't take any more of this!" Geraldine exploded, rushing over to the door, gripping the handle. "What I don't understand, Marianne, is what your so-called memories of a past life have to do with you wanting to give your baby away. The baby you carried in your own body – who you're feeding from your own body!"

"Mum…" Marianne's hollow cry woke Mariana up. She wriggled restlessly, moving her head from side-to-side on the cushion, legs and arms pumping. She managed to grab hold of the hem of Marianne's cardigan and tried to stuff it in her mouth. They all watched the baby for a moment, until Geraldine walked over and picked her up, disentangling the scrap of cardigan. She snuggled her face close to Mariana's.

"This is my granddaughter." She made a helpless gesture with her free hand. "The first baby I've really been able to appreciate. Look at me, Marianne. I was prevented from enjoying my daughters by depression. And the same thing is happening to you now. Please let me help you get through this. Don't give my granddaughter away."

Lizzy held her breath, waiting for Marianne's answer.

"Mum." The girl pressed her fist against her mouth, tears streamed down her face. "I don't want to take her away from you. I can leave her with you – I know she'll be safe with you. But then I would never be able to come back. I need to be separated from her, at least until she's safely grown up. It's because of Mariana that I'm having the episodes. She's a physical link to Cal and when I'm linked to Cal I can't escape from Marion. You know what I do when it gets too strong, Mum, and I'm exhausted from trying to fight it all the time." She held her arms out in front of her again, like a sacrifice.

Geraldine buried her face in Mariana's silky wisps of curls. Lizzy had the distinct impression they'd been over this a hundred times before. Eventually Geraldine lifted her head.

She spoke to Lizzy Bell in a broken voice. "If Marianne has her baby adopted, can it be arranged that I continue to have contact with her?"

"It could be one of the terms of the adoption." Lizzy could not believe she might possibly be removing this baby from her family. This looked likely to be one of the most painful cases she'd ever had to deal with, contrary to what people might think. Often she felt relieved to take a child away despite the initial trauma, but in a situation like this…Not that she had ever encountered one before.

"You do realise, Marianne," she said, "that once you've signed all the papers releasing your daughter for adoption there's no going back? Once she's been adopted you can't ever change your mind."

Marianne dipped her head once. She made a small noise in her mother's direction. There was a long pause.

"I won't insist on Mariana staying with me at the expense of losing you, Marianne," Geraldine said. Her eyes were raw but she cleared her throat and straightened her shoulders. "I let you down once, in fact, most of your life. I owe you my support now, however wrong I think you are to send your daughter away."

Some moments passed before Marianne was able to give her mother a wan smile. "I've got something to ask you." She made her fingers into a steeple and rested her chin on them. "Do you remember when I was two years old? I was at some kind of playgroup with you and there was a little boy there. I thought he must be my brother. I remember telling you that my name was Marion Wilde, and that you weren't my mother. Do you remember that, Mum?"

There was a tense, stretched silence. But very slowly, Geraldine nodded.

Lizzy Bell watched Marianne's shoulders drop three inches. The significance of that interchange didn't sink in until later. At that point she just wanted to keep the baby with her family. "Have you considered…" She tried to put it delicately. "I understand you've been in hospital for psychiatric care before, Marianne. Would you consider a spell in hospital for a rest, shall we say, while your mother looks after the baby for you? Then perhaps you might feel better enough to reconsider your decision once they – it's possible they might be able to sort out some more appropriate medication for you."

Marianne stared at the social worker so long Lizzy thought she was seriously considering the proposition. Then Marianne stood up. She went over to her mother and lifted the baby out of her arms. "I'm tired now." She spoke firmly. "But I'd like you to go back to your office, Ms Bell, and start looking for some new parents for my baby girl. I don't want them to have any other children. I want Mariana to be their whole world. I want them to be close enough by so that my mother can visit her granddaughter regularly, and also my dad and sisters. It doesn't even matter whether Mariana understands who they are. They can be called her cousins or something, if you like, as long as they get to stay in her life. And then when Mariana is old enough I want her to be able to contact me, if she chooses; that's up to her. But Mum." She turned back to Geraldine. "You can't let me know where she is or anything about her. Promise me. If you do I'll have to leave and never come back. It's really important you do as I ask. Please promise me that."

Geraldine let out a long sigh. She looked at Lizzy in such a desperate way that Lizzy wanted to cry. She could see that Geraldine had given up hope. There was nothing left the baby's grandmother could do to persuade her daughter she was making the biggest mistake of her life. Geraldine bowed her head. She looked like someone praying.

"I promise, Marianne."

Chapter 42

28th August 2008

Sarah

CAL HAD BEEN staring out of the café window for the longest time. The pavement and road beyond it were crowded with postcard displays and brightly coloured plastic, thronged with holiday-makers shouldering their way in both directions between a gridlock of cars. All going home to tea in their guesthouses and self-catered flats, I imagined, pushing tired children in buggies, carrying bulging beach bags and windbreaks. Beyond the road, masts poked into the sky above the harbour wall. At the end of that was the lighthouse. I followed Cal's gaze even further, up the green curve of cliff with a white path meandering down it. Looking at Cal, I could see he was searching all the time, that he'd examined the faces of every passer-by. If he could, he'd line up everybody from the amusements across the harbour, from the restaurant opposite, he would demand that parents drag their children off the backs of donkeys so he could look into their eyes and ascertain they weren't amber which would turn green in a different light, or vice-versa.

I called to the waitress rearranging cans of Fanta on the brick counter for two last cups of tea. While we were served, someone pulled closed the concertinaed front of the café, muting the outside noise of traffic, seagulls and a child crying. A wasp buzzed near my ear. I jumped up in shock but at a look from Cal sat down again. The wasp only hovered for a moment more before it flew out through the gap just as the front was fastened shut.

Scarborough was where we'd come for our holidays as children. Marion had stood there on a cliff top for the photograph taken on her seventeenth birthday, the one that was used in the inside covers of her two novels: published in 1991 and 1992.

The visit to Scarborough with Cal was bittersweet. My personal reasons were primarily to remember my jolly-holiday-making dad; whose funeral had been the day before. But there was another reason. Lisa had begged me to stay with Cal. It was the anniversary of Marianne's fated visit to Blackberry House, and Lisa was particularly worried about him this year.

"It's always the same day, every year. He has to go looking for 'Marion'. He's convinced she's going to come back again, Sarah. You know, don't you, that last year he got a caution from the police for harassing a young girl he thought looked like her? She wasn't even that similar! But this year, what with your dad having just died… I don't know. He's more obsessed than ever. Please keep an eye on him."

My family had already visited England that year. In early February Lisa had organised a joint 18th birthday party for Aiden and Connor. Blackberry House had been full to bursting then with Mark and me; Lisa and Cal and our older boys; as well as my thirteen-year old twins Fergus and Riley; Cal and Lisa's fourteen-year old daughter Angel; and Alice, returning from the theatre company in London where she had just got her first acting residency.

"We ought to be thinking about getting back, Cal."

I reached over to brush the back of his hand with mine, but he pulled his away. He tucked both hands under his arms, scowling like the brother I remembered from childhood. Dad's death had hit him harder than I would have imagined. In the years since he became a father himself, Cal and Dad had found a point of contact dear to both their hearts. At Dad's funeral, Cal sobbed with the abandon of a small boy. Mum, on the other hand, remained serene and calm.

"He went in the best possible way he could have hoped, Sarah, dozing in his deckchair out on the allotment. His heart just gave out. When I found him he looked peaceful and happy." Dad was seventy-nine years old. I imagined him greeting his lost daughters again. I couldn't decide whether Caitlin would have grown up or stayed the same but Marion would be healthy and finally at peace. It had to be that way. I pictured them all together and focussed on that image.

In the church Cal's daughter Angel, with her spiky dyed-black hair and thick black eyeliner, held onto her grandma. To everyone's surprise she raised her clear voice that she'd recently only used for teenage grunts, in a vocal tribute to the granddad she loved. She had not exactly been singing a solo of *Abide with me*, but the voices around fell away at her tone. I only wished Cal could reach out to the troubled, artistic daughter he had such a difficult relationship with. He'd hardly spoken in the twenty-four hours since the funeral but he was still determined to follow through with his planned visit to

Scarborough on Marianne's anniversary. He said he had a funny feeling.

I was the one who usually got the funny feelings and I hadn't had any this time, so his must have been misplaced. "Come on, Cal." I pushed back my chair. The café was preparing for closing anyway. Cal shrugged me off again. Someone in the kitchen started whistling just as an older man stood up to struggle into his jacket. His wife went forward to open the door but stepped back because a young woman was coming in. Cal's chin had dropped lower onto his chest, that hunk of hair as thick as ever hanging over his forehead, but grey now. He pushed it back impatiently.

"Come on then," I repeated, aware that this was the end of Cal's hopes for another Marianne anniversary. I just wanted to deliver him home to his long-suffering wife. My mind was already at my home in Ireland, on the preparation for my latest exhibition. I'd be dedicating it to the memory of my father and I hoped the whole family would come over. With great weariness, Cal placed his hands on the table and pushed himself out of his chair. I nodded to the waitress and turned to face the door.

The girl who'd just come in was calling out a greeting to the waitress. She had a baby with her. I didn't see her face at first, obscured by a heavy curtain of hair. But the colour of her hair registered sharply.

"Hey, Mariana!" responded the waitress. She came out from behind the counter and knelt in front of the little boy in the buggy. "Hey Gaby-baby, how's my godson-to-be today?"

Too late. I put my hand up to the back of my neck. My mind flashed back to the night they had taken Marion's body away, and then to the image of a white-lit girl in a dark auditorium. I grabbed Cal's arm but I couldn't hold him. He was already in front of her. He was quoting Tennyson's *Mariana* in a rasping voice. She swatted at him angrily when he tried to touch her hair. "Get off me, you old perv!"

"I'm sorry…" Some power beyond me propelled my body across the café floor. I stood in front of them. Cal had quoted those words to Marianne in the garden of Blackberry House nineteen years before. I tried to pull him away, apologised again to this girl I didn't want to look at. If I didn't see her, it couldn't be true. "He doesn't mean anything by it – you remind him of someone. Cal, Love, stop bothering the girl. Come on!"

She whipped her face round, close to mine. She flashed her eyes at me and I saw they were the same shade of amber as his, the same as Marion's. When she moved her head they seemed to change to green. "He wants to be locked up!" she spat out. "What is this – care in the community? You should look after him better."

"I'm really sorry." Cal's body had gone limp and I had no trouble forcing him down onto a seat. "Try not to look at her," I murmured. "You don't want any more trouble." I squeezed my eyes shut for a moment but I could still see her face, familiar as the back of my hand.

Marianne had been gone nineteen years when I saw her again…

If you found the themes in *The Last Time We Saw Marion* interesting, read on for some book club questions that you might want to explore…

*   *   *

1. What effect did Marion Wilde's death have on each of the remaining members of her family?

2. Do you think Cal's action in going behind Marion's back with the publication of his first novel really influenced her decision to die, or would she have behaved the way she did anyway?

3. Why does Sarah feel she has never been a good-enough daughter to Jane?

4. Sarah subjugated her initial chance of happiness with Mark in favour of staying with her brother. Do you think her reasons for this were anything to do with what she felt her mother might have expected of her?

5. How did Caitlin's early death affect Jane's mothering of her other children?

6. Would the idea of reincarnation immediately occur to you if you were met with a person who resembled a loved one at the time they had died as strongly as Marianne did Marion?

7. Would you want to investigate the situation further, as Cal and Sarah did, or would you want to leave well alone?

8. Do you think Cal and Sarah ought to have told their parents about Marianne?

9. How culpable is Marianne, given her age and anorexia, in what happened between her and Cal?

10. Do you think Geraldine manages to redeem herself as Marianne's mother after Marianne takes the overdose?

11. How important are the roles of the fathers within the Wilde and the Fairchild families?

12. What, if anything, makes Cal attractive to women?

13. Would the fact that Lisa and Cal had known each other as children give their adult relationship a strong chance of success? Do you think this is true of relationships in general?

14. Do any of the themes within *The Last Time We Saw Marion* make you feel uncomfortable, and if so, why?

15. How does the novel deal with motherhood?

If you enjoyed *The Last Time We Saw Marion*, be sure to keep a look out next year for her second novel, *Bitter*.

*   *   *

DURING A SPELL in hospital, sensitive Rebecca Grey has a lucid hallucination about a mystical landscape and a boy on a white horse. But the boy rejects her, saying she is not the right one. He leaves her behind in a grey room.

Following her illness, she can't get the dream out of her head.

Her alcoholic mother, Bex, is still buried in the 'Great Grief' of her youth. Rebecca's father, Jack, is bitter that Bex never returned the obsessive love he once had for her and also that she refused to give their daughter his name. He's now remarried and has twin sons.

When Bex and Rebecca inherit the childhood home of Bex's dead first husband, Sebastian Grey, Bex becomes very ill. She is keeping a dark secret. She confesses to Jack that she gave her first daughter away after Sebastian's death.

The night Bex dies, she leads Rebecca to a hidden room in the house which turns out to be the grey room of her dream. Rebecca thinks the boy she has never stopped thinking about is coming back for her. But to her great distress, Sebastian carries her mother away on his horse instead, leaving her alone again in the grey room.

Rebecca is trapped in the dream and it is now up to Jack to come good as a father and help bring her out of it.